CR✛SSFIRE

OTHER BOOKS AND AUDIO BOOKS
BY TRACI HUNTER ABRAMSON:

Undercurrents

Ripple Effect

The Deep End

Freefall

Lockdown

Royal Target

PMD9

A NOVEL

TRACI HUNTER ABRAMSON

Covenant Communications, Inc.

Cover images: *Airport Radar* © George Cairns, *Men Walk into the Light* © Roma-Oslo, *Electric Danger* © Tom Nulens, *Warning: Nuclear Power* © Caracter, *Apache* © Gary Forsyth. Images courtesy of istock-photo.com

Cover design by Mark Sorenson © 2010 by Covenant Communications, Inc.

Published by Covenant Communications, Inc.
American Fork, Utah

Printed in U.S.A.
First Printing: January 2010

17 16 15 14 13 12 11 10   10 9 8 7 6 5 4 3 2 1

ISBN 13: 978-1-59811-944-2

For Mom and Dad

ACKNOWLEDGMENTS

My continued appreciation goes to Rebecca Cummings for her editing talents and her willingness to share them. Thank you to the many people at Covenant who helped usher this book through the publication and marketing process. My special thanks goes to the evaluators, who offered so many helpful suggestions, and to Noelle Perner for helping me use them.

I also want to thank my mom, Dianne Hunter, and my wonderful stepdad, Tom Whalen, for introducing me to the Dominican Republic. Thanks for so many wonderful memories.

Finally, I need to thank my sister, Tiffany Hunter, for being daring enough to break her arm on the flying trapeze. Had you not needed a translator at the hospital, I never would have explored the village in Punta Cana. Thanks to everyone in the Abramson/Hunter/Whalen clan for the exciting adventures. Life with our family is never dull.

1

Lieutenant Seth Johnson wrinkled his nose and fought the urge to sneeze. Any sound right now could be deadly, both for him and for Brent Miller, the other Navy SEAL who was lying a few feet away. Seth tensed as two armed guards approached the hedge that he and Brent were currently burrowed under. Though one of the guards came within inches of his position, he never noticed Seth's dark skin, which was streaked with green, or his camouflaged clothing. Instead, both guards performed a cursory check of the nearby building—a building that was presently housing at least a dozen mercenaries.

Seth's nose twitched again, and he could feel his eyes water. He held his breath for several long seconds until the patrol moved across the wide expanse of lawn to check out the surrounding woods. Silently, he shifted position and pinched his nose to fight the sensation to sneeze.

As a member of the Saint Squad, an elite five-man unit with SEAL Team Eight, he had been trained to be invisible and silent. Putting that training into practice wasn't always easy. This particular sneak-and-peek was a two-man job, and their objective wasn't as clear as Seth would like it to be. U.S. intelligence had recently learned of this growing terrorist cell in the Caribbean, but so far the reconnaissance missions hadn't turned up what they were looking for—or more specifically, who they were looking for.

The top man, Akil Ramir, had been noticeably absent since he was last spotted in the Santiago de Cali airport more than six months earlier. His presence in Colombia had raised concerns among the intelligence agencies throughout the United States and the Caribbean that perhaps he was now dealing arms to the drug cartel.

The Saint Squad already had firsthand experience with Ramir's older brother, Fahid. Three years earlier they had boarded Fahid's yacht and taken him and his family into custody. Seth still had nightmares about the young boy he had seen gunned down right in front of him when he and Brent had been a second too late to save his life.

Akil Ramir was known to be just as heartless as his brother. He had taken credit for a series of car bombs in Paris the year before, bombs that had resulted in nearly a hundred deaths.

Concerns that Akil was now running his brother's operation had made him one of intelligence's top priorities. As a result, he had become a top priority for the Saint Squad.

For the past few weeks, they had been sent all over the region from Colombia to Curacao, and each time they encountered similar scenes: high-tech communications, heavily armed men, and a constant flow of trucks carrying a variety of military equipment.

Brent shifted and gave him an odd look when he noticed Seth holding his nose. Seth gave a helpless shrug, mentally groaning at the absurdity of the situation. Armed men he could handle, but the sniffles were about to be his Achilles' heel. Brent gave a little shake of his head along with a cocky grin. That grin faded when the guards approached once more.

Neither man liked these missions when they were assigned to iden-tify threats but not do anything about them. Still, Seth understood why his superiors wanted them to remain invisible. If Ramir learned that his empire had sprung a leak, the spy feeding them information would be compromised.

Seth didn't know who the CIA had planted inside this terrorist orga-nization, but one thing was certain. Whoever he was, he was in deep enough to know where the terrorists were hiding.

* * *

Vanessa Lauton stood in the shadows of the local cantina, her eyes constantly sweeping the area. Buildings were crowded close together in this part of Suero, a little village in the Dominican Republic. Some were adobe-style structures while others were small shacks that weren't much larger than a refrigerator box. At this late hour, traffic was sparse, and only the cantina and the butcher shop down the street had any lights on.

She glanced at her watch, concerned. Her contact should have been here by now. She estimated that she could wait five more minutes, but anything beyond that would be too risky. Too much effort had gone into establishing her cover, and she couldn't take the chance of blowing it now.

A motor scooter buzzed down the narrow, one-lane street, and Vanessa silently blended into the darkness. She was dressed completely in black, a simple T-shirt tucked into loose-fitting cotton shorts. Her skin was several shades lighter than her clothes, and she succeeded in making herself disappear into the shadows as the driver of the scooter parked and then walked inside the cantina. Vanessa shifted so that she could watch the man, immediately identifying him as someone from out of town. No one who lived here would ever consider leaving a scooter on the street without locking it up.

As though reading her thoughts, a teenage boy slipped out of a small hut down the street. Vanessa was half amused at the boy's predictability as his eyes darted from one side of the street to the other and he stealthily moved toward the scooter. When the front door of the cantina opened once more, he darted back the way he had come as the driver of the scooter came back outside.

Vanessa watched the man drive away, reminding herself who she really was. She had been undercover for so long she sometimes actually thought of herself as Lina Ramir, the oldest child of Fahid Ramir. The real Lina had been apprehended and ultimately convicted on weapons charges three years before along with her father and the rest of her immediate family. When Vanessa's supervisor at the Central Intelligence Agency realized how much Vanessa resembled Lina, he had put the wheels in motion to insert Vanessa into Fahid Ramir's extended family.

Looking back now, Vanessa was amazed that her training with the CIA had been practically tailored for this assignment. Her main specialties were in weapons, aircraft, and explosives—areas that the real Lina would be knowledgeable about. Of course, when she had joined the Agency four years ago, she never would have guessed that her appearance would ultimately become her greatest asset.

In many ways, the plan seemed almost too easy. Lina's uncle, Akil Ramir, had spent the last two decades supposedly working in the oil industry in Venezuela, while Lina had spent her childhood and early adult years living in the United States and in her father's villa in the south of France.

Additionally, the resemblance between the two women was uncanny, especially considering that their heritage was so markedly different. Though the Ramir family had been living in Europe for more than fifty years, most of their family tree originated from the Middle East. In contrast, Vanessa's family was a conglomerate of origins and races. Vanessa's grandparents on her mother's side were dark skinned and had immigrated to the United States from Morocco. Her father, on the other hand, had inherited the fair skin of his English ancestors.

Because her maternal grandparents had lived with her family throughout most of her childhood and into her teenage years, Vanessa was fluent in French, the preferred language of the Ramir family, as well as Arabic. She also had a working knowledge of Spanish due to intensive study to prepare her for this assignment.

No one had been sure where Vanessa would end up living or how she would be received into the extended Ramir family when she had switched places with Lina Ramir. Her superiors just knew that someone needed to get inside to find out exactly what Akil Ramir was up to. Already Vanessa had confirmed at least part of the Agency's concern that Akil was in the process of expanding the terrorist activities his older brother had started.

It had been over a year since the CIA had leaked the information that Lina Ramir was being released from prison. The official report was that Lina had been moved to a minimum security prison for the last few weeks of her jail time. In reality, Vanessa had spent two weeks observing the real Lina, studying her mannerisms and her personality. Then Vanessa had stepped in and taken Lina's place when the prison transfer was made, and Lina had been moved to a secure prison facility where she would be kept out of sight until Vanessa finished her assignment.

Never in her life had Vanessa considered the possibility of spending time in prison, but she had completed the rest of Lina's sentence, using those precious few weeks to finalize her transformation into Lina Ramir. Vanessa knew from the background information on the Ramir family and from her own observations that Lina was strong-willed and ambitious, qualities Vanessa shared. Of course, Vanessa didn't consider money and power more important than human lives the way Lina had when she worked as an integral part of her father's empire.

The ruthlessness and lack of concern for others were traits Vanessa knew she wouldn't be able to adopt completely, but she hoped to find a happy medium between the woman she was and the woman she was pretending to be.

As the government had hoped, when the day came for her to be released, Akil Ramir had sent a driver to pick her up with the invitation for her to join him in Aruba. Vanessa could still remember how nervous she had been; worried that perhaps Akil had been in closer contact with Lina than everyone had anticipated. Akil had sensed those nerves but had misunderstood the cause. Certain that the young woman before him was his long-lost niece, he had offered her every hospitality, including a job within his organization.

No one knew exactly how long Vanessa would stay undercover. In fact, only a handful of people even knew about the switch. Even fewer knew where she was currently located—more precisely, only one person: Devin Granger, a CIA operative out of Puerto Rico, had been her handler from the start.

Granger was the man she was waiting for right now. Officially, Granger was one of several cooks on staff at the Club Med in Punta Cana, a popular tourist area in the Dominican Republic. Unofficially, he continued to meet Vanessa every day or two so that he could collect and pass along the information that Vanessa continued to gather. Though Vanessa wasn't always able to slip away from her current home, Granger was supposed to be at the meeting spot no matter what. Never before had Vanessa been the first to arrive.

Since their meeting three weeks earlier when Vanessa had told him that something big was about to happen, Granger had been even more diligent about meeting every night. Vanessa didn't know exactly what was going on in Ramir's organization, but she knew that tensions were running high and that new training facilities were springing up all over the Caribbean.

Nerves jumped in her stomach as Vanessa waited quietly for several more minutes. Finally, afraid to wait any longer, she crept down the alley from where she had come and headed for her own transportation. She had parked the tiny hatchback two blocks away behind a small adobe house. An elderly man rocked on the little slab of concrete that comprised his front porch, and Vanessa approached him, her eyes questioning.

"No hay problema, señorita," he told her in a quiet voice as he pushed himself out of the chair.

As she did each night, she handed him some local currency and expressed her thanks. She knew that the money wouldn't buy the man's loyalty. That was the reason she had chosen him. If his loyalty could be bought, it couldn't be trusted. This man could be trusted. She was sure of it.

Though she doubted that her superiors at the CIA would approve of her methods, she had staked out the local chapel for The Church of Jesus Christ of Latter-day Saints a few days after her arrival in the Dominican Republic. She had watched the various members of the congregation filter out after their Sunday meetings, her eyes searching for someone who was traveling on foot and heading in the right direction.

Domingo Lomez had been holding the hand of his six-year-old grandson and had been accompanied by his extended family of eleven. Vanessa had waited for the family to pass by before following them the three miles to their home. When she saw the location of the tiny house, she knew she had found the man she was looking for.

Though she hadn't been at liberty to explain why she needed his services, Vanessa had shown him the one piece of identification she had brought with her from the United States: her temple recommend. She had been impressed that Domingo hadn't accepted her offer immediately. After all, he would be paid simply for allowing her to hide her car behind his home each night. Despite his desire to help feed his family, the elderly man had insisted that he needed to pray about it for a day or so.

When Vanessa had returned the next night, hoping and praying that the older man would help her, he had agreed. He had also given her an unsolicited piece of advice that had ultimately saved her life. He had told her to destroy her temple recommend.

His suggestion had been so unexpected that Vanessa had been forced to offer her own prayers before following through. The next day she had returned to her room at the resort she currently called home to find her purse on the floor, the contents strewn about the room. Had she not followed Señor Lomez's advice, whoever had searched her purse would have found the only piece of identification that could have given her away as an imposter.

She had thrown a rather convincing temper tantrum that day about someone going through her things. As a result, her "uncle" had admitted that someone had been concerned that her loyalties might have been compromised after being away from the family for so long. From that moment on, Vanessa had been gaining ground and trust in the organization. Now she just had to find out what the organization was working toward and stop it before it was too late.

2

Commander Kelan Bennett sat in the front seat of the grounded helicopter and studied the mission plan. Something didn't feel right, and he couldn't put his finger on what it was. He and two of his men were currently waiting near an abandoned warehouse a short hop from the extraction point, but a sense of unease had settled over him.

He thought back to the pre-mission briefing and the prayer his squad had offered before leaving their ship. At the time, everything appeared to be in order. They all felt good about their plan for this surveillance mission, and the execution was relatively easy compared to some of their previous assignments. Brent Miller, his second-in-command, and Seth Johnson were two of the best in the SEALs at concealment and surveillance. Yet for some reason his previous sense of comfort had been replaced with apprehension.

The two enlisted men in his squad, Tristan Crowther and Quinn Lambert, had just returned from checking out the surrounding area to make sure they were still really alone out in the middle of this semitropical island. Tristan had taken a position outside of the helicopter, and Quinn had moved back inside to check in.

"There's nothing out there, Kel," Quinn told him.

"Check the intel reports again. I want to know if there's any movement in the area," Kel ordered. "If anything's moving, we'll know there's a problem."

Quinn nodded, switching his combat headset for the heavier headset that plugged into the helicopter's communication system. Quinn set the dial to the right channel and spoke into the mouthpiece using the predetermined code names for the mission. "Night Owl, this is Panther. Request details on any movement in the area. Over."

"Panther, this is Night Owl. Everything is quiet."

Quinn turned to look at Kel, shaking his head as he signed off and replaced his combat headset. "They don't have anything." Quinn's dark eyes narrowed. "What's bothering you?"

"I don't know," Kel admitted as he prepared to send the two men out again for another patrol. "But something's not right."

* * *

Something wasn't right. Dawn was still several hours away, but despite their orders to observe the terrorist training facility for as long as possible, Seth was getting antsy to get out of there. At least the urge to sneeze had finally passed, but he would have preferred that annoyance over this new sense of unease. He shifted slightly so that he could get a better look at the long driveway that led through the grassy field and up to the house.

The road and the surrounding grounds were quiet except for the two-man patrol that was currently fifty yards to his right. The interior of the house was equally calm. The miniature listening device he'd installed when he and Brent had first arrived nearly six hours earlier was still transmitting, but at the moment the only sound he heard was the droning of a television.

Everything was exactly as it was supposed to be except for the unexplained sense of anticipation coursing through him. Shifting once more, Seth angled toward Brent so that he could signal him to move out. If they moved now, they could clear the better part of the yard before the patrol made it to the front of the building once more. To his surprise and relief, Brent signaled him first, apparently having a similar sense of misgiving.

The two men moved in tandem as they left the safety of the bushes and slipped quietly through the night. They cleared the first fifty yards of the open field before the sound of the patrol approaching caused them to drop to the ground and use the darkness as cover. The minutes stretched out as the patrol inspected the front of the house.

Staying low to the ground, Seth and Brent had begun moving forward once more when they heard something out of place. Absolute silence. Whatever animals had been rustling around in the trees were now noticeably hushed. The two SEALs were experienced enough to suspect why the sounds of the night had ceased. There was still life in the surrounding woods—it was life of the two-legged variety.

Brent motioned for Seth to move beside him and then asked through hand signals if he had received any communication from their support team. Seth shook his head as both men considered the possibilities. Their commander would have notified them if there was any movement by the local authorities against this training facility. And if it wasn't a local police or military force that had caused the intense silence, then it was probably a training exercise or some kind of conflict between warring terrorist cells. Either way, Seth and Brent were lying right in the middle of what was likely to be a battlefield within a matter of minutes.

Seth's mind raced as he considered their options. They could move forward and hope that they could penetrate the line of intruders without being seen, or they could stay where they were and hope that the attack would come from a different direction. Their extraction point was over three miles away, not a significant distance for two highly trained military operatives, but far enough that they wouldn't want to have to make a run for it if they were being shot at.

The rumbling of a truck in the distance and the sight of approaching headlights told them they didn't have any more time to decide. Brent signaled to move forward, and Seth nodded, pointing in a direction forty-five degrees to the right of their position. As they angled away from the driveway, the night patrol came rushing to the front of the house to investigate the sound of the approaching vehicle.

A few seconds later, shouts sounded as a set of floodlights illuminated the house and surrounding yard. Brent and Seth were barely beyond the swath of light as the two guards opened fire and a dozen or so armed men came rushing out the front door of the building. The grass wasn't long enough to hide them, and both men knew that if anyone looked their direction, they would be spotted.

Praying that the men were too preoccupied to worry about them, they continued forward, a little faster now. From the woods a burst of light illuminated the area as a projectile was fired toward the house, breaking a window as it entered the building. Movement shifted in the trees as a voice came over a loudspeaker. Brent and Seth looked at each other in surprise. The intruders were the police.

Though he knew it was risky, Seth made the decision to hazard using his communication device to contact their commanding officer, Kel Bennett. "Police on premises. Please advise."

"What?" The voice filled with surprise and fury wasn't Kel's but rather Quinn Lambert's. "Stand by."

Seth bit back on his impatience as he continued crawling forward, knowing that this conflict wasn't going to be settled peacefully. They were only ten yards from the shelter of the trees when someone must have spotted them. The gunfire sparking toward the bunkhouse suddenly shifted, and bullets began whizzing just inches above their heads.

"Go!" Brent ordered. Both men dropped flat onto their stomachs and rolled the last few yards. Breathing heavily, they took cover behind a couple of palm trees as bullets continued to spark around them.

"What's the story, Quinn?" Seth's voice was still low, but now it was filled with urgency. "We're taking fire from the cops."

"Intel still isn't giving us anything. We can't identify who's in charge of this op."

"Advise," Brent interrupted, his voice sharp and to the point.

"We're airborne. ETA to extraction point, five minutes."

"Copy that." Seth said before speaking to Brent once more. "Let's go; they've got to have some vehicles parked down the road."

Brent nodded, his eyes already turning away from the threat as he searched for an escape route. A bullet struck a tree mere inches from Brent's arm. "Give me some cover fire."

Seth didn't hesitate. He squatted down and aimed his weapon high as he shot off three quick bursts. Brent's footsteps were nearly silent, but Seth counted off the seconds that it would take him to clear the trees and make it to the road. If Brent could find them a vehicle, they had a chance of making it out alive without having to go toe-to-toe with the local cops. If not, someone wasn't going to live to see morning.

"I've got it." Brent's voice came over the headset. As soon as Brent gave him the command, Seth started after Brent, relying on him to keep the cops at bay while he zigzagged through the trees. A few shots strayed after him despite Brent's efforts, and Seth was both amazed and grateful that he emerged onto the street still intact.

Seth continued at a dead run to the truck Brent had commandeered. Fifteen seconds later, Seth was in the driver's seat as Brent kept his weapon pointed out the window to keep whoever was following them occupied. With gunfire sounding around them, Seth started to reach under the dash to hot-wire the car only to notice the key already in the ignition. He didn't take time to consider their good fortune; instead, he quickly started the car and slammed his foot on the gas pedal. The truck sprang forward with a squeal of the tires, and they were on their way.

"Are we clear?" Seth asked as the truck gained speed.

A bullet shattered the back window, and both men ducked. "Does that answer your question?"

Seth muttered under his breath as he caught sight of the headlights behind them. He took a sharp corner without slowing down, finally drawing a breath and speaking into his lip microphone. "Quinn, what's your ETA?"

"One minute."

"We're coming in hot," Seth informed him in a clipped tone that disguised the Southern drawl that normally hung in his voice. "Any chance you've figured out who these cops are that are shooting at us?"

"Negative." Quinn's voice was short and hard. "We've contacted the policia in the three nearest towns, but all of them say they aren't involved."

"Maybe these guys aren't really cops," Brent suggested. Several more shots struck the back of the truck, causing him to wince. "I've had enough of this."

Seth nodded in agreement as Brent took aim and shot at the vehicle pursuing them. The sound of bullets striking metal rang through the air followed by the squeal of tires against the pavement as the driver tried to brake as he rounded another corner. A moment later, Seth heard the thud of the car connecting with a tree, followed by the crumpling of metal.

They were nearly to the extraction site when he heard the thrumming sound of the helicopter lowering in the field in front of them. Moments later he and Brent abandoned their vehicle and sprinted to where Kel had landed. As they strapped in and lifted off, flames shot into the distant sky. Seth took a deep breath and uttered a silent prayer of gratitude that they had made it out of the battle safely.

3

Vanessa flipped through the registration system, annoyed to see the resort completely booked for the next two weeks. She knew that for a typical hotel this would be a good thing, but this place was anything but typical. While Punta Cana was heavily populated with resorts and hotels appealing primarily to European and American tourists, La Playa catered to a more selective audience.

Small and exclusive, the resort was visited by guests from all over the world—guests that all had one thing in common: an intense hatred for anything and everything American. Arms dealers, drug dealers, renegade militant leaders. Their professions varied, but their goals were all the same. They all wanted to see the capitalist empire of the United States crumble, and they wanted to see Americans bleed.

When Vanessa had first arrived, she had been considered a guest, being granted one of the resort's beach casitas to live in. Within a few weeks, Akil had trusted her to take over the management of the restaurant. Four months later the hotel manager had mysteriously disappeared and Vanessa had moved up into that role.

Her access to information had increased greatly with the promotion, but there were still obstacles to overcome. Vanessa frowned slightly as she pictured the face of Halim Karel, Akil's top advisor at the resort. Halim seemed determined to keep her in the dark when it came to the inner workings of Akil's growing empire.

She pushed thoughts of Halim aside and continued scanning the guest list for any new names worth passing along to her contact. Peripherally, she became aware of a new set of guests signing in at the front desk right outside of her door. Her mind was so focused on the information in front of her that she didn't notice the raised voices until an argument in the lobby was well underway. She moved closer to her door and listened.

"This is unacceptable," the middle-aged man complained loudly. "I need at least two more rooms for my guards."

"I'm sorry, sir, but we don't have that many rooms available," the clerk, Maria, insisted for what was clearly not the first time.

The man let out a frustrated breath. "Where's the manager?"

Vanessa pushed open her office door and moved to stand beside the desk clerk. "Can I help you?"

"I want to speak with the manager."

"I'm the manager." Vanessa's tone was calm and authoritative. "What seems to be the problem?"

"Your girl here only gave me three rooms. I need at least five."

Giving Maria a knowing look, Vanessa motioned for her to step aside so she could look at the computer screen. "I'm sorry, but you already have a casita and two other rooms even though you only have five people in your party."

"You expect my guards to share quarters?"

"Your casita has two bedrooms, and each of the rooms in the main building has two beds each." Vanessa pointed out. "Even if your guards all sleep at the same time, you have more than enough beds to go around. And, of course, if you felt the need to bring guards, I have to believe that at least one of them will be working at any given time."

"Do you know who I am?" The man leaned forward as he assumed a threatening posture.

Vanessa's eyebrows lifted in amusement. Before she could answer, Halim Karel approached the desk. As always, Halim was impeccably dressed in an Italian suit despite the heat and humidity. Amusement crossed his handsome face as well as he put a hand on the man's shoulder. "Diego, it is good to see you." Halim shifted to shake the man's hand and then nodded to Vanessa. "I'm so pleased you found time to visit us again. It must have been some time since you've been here if you have not met Lina *Ramir*."

Vanessa watched the man's expression change when Halim emphasized the last name. He looked from Halim to Vanessa and then back again. "I wasn't aware that anyone from the Ramir family worked here."

"We are fortunate that Lina was able to join us last year." Halim's eyes were direct, and he held Diego's gaze.

Vanessa picked up the room keys that were sitting on the counter. Motioning to a bellhop, she said simply, "I'm sure that your accommodations will be more than adequate. Perhaps you should take the time to see them for yourself before we discuss this any further."

Diego looked from Halim to Vanessa. His voice was calmer now, edged with a new sense of reservation. "Yes, of course."

Vanessa handed the keys to the bellhop and instructed him, "Show this gentleman and his guests to their rooms."

"Yes, miss." The bellhop took the keys and quickly escorted Diego away from the desk.

As soon as they left, Vanessa nodded to Maria. Her voice was aloof and authoritative. "Let me know if you have any more difficulties with him."

"Yes, ma'am."

Vanessa stepped out from behind the counter and moved to the path leading to the beach. She wasn't surprised that Halim moved to her side. Staring out at the water in front of them, she said, "I could have handled the situation without your help."

"He shouldn't have been speaking to you that way." Halim shifted so that he was facing her, a combination of concern and that familiar spark of interest showing on his face. "I worry that you work too hard."

When he reached over to caress her cheek, Vanessa gave a little shrug and took a step back. "I'm fine."

"It's my job to make sure you stay that way." Halim smiled, his attractive face not showing a trace of his dark side now. "Besides, I enjoy keeping an eye on you."

"I need to get back to work," Vanessa told him, trying to keep the conversation on a professional level. Halim's interest in her didn't seem to be waning, despite the fact that she had never done anything to encourage him.

"Me too. I'll see you at dinner tonight," Halim said, his eyes lingering on her a moment longer. He then moved toward the path that led to the casitas.

As she watched him walk away, she sighed, wishing her life wasn't quite so complicated. Halim was handsome, suave, even interesting, and he didn't have the fanatical look in his eyes that Vanessa saw in many of the guests who came through La Playa. Sometimes she could almost believe he was what he looked like—simply a man who was interested in a woman—but Vanessa knew better. The man was evil.

She didn't know what Halim had done to prove his loyalty at such a young age, but at thirty-five years old he was clearly the man Akil trusted to run the day-to-day operations at La Playa. Those operations ranged from keeping a steady stream of weapons moving through the resort to holding strategy sessions with VIP guests during their stays.

Vanessa shifted her gaze and stared out at the beach for a moment. The view was so perfect, so peaceful. Sometimes she could almost forget that in the surrounding buildings people were plotting to destroy the freedoms and even the very lives of her countrymen.

She tried to push aside the sinking feeling she'd had for some time now—that something was wrong. Akil Ramir hadn't visited the resort in several months, and Vanessa was still hoping to find out where he was. Only twice in the past six months had he shown up at La Playa, each time arriving on his private plane and staying for only two or three days. Unfortunately, every time Akil was present, he made a point of dropping in to see her at odd times. Sometimes he had questions about the resort operations, and other times he acted like a concerned uncle.

Akil's unpredictability and the increased security that always accompanied him inevitably made it impossible for Vanessa to sneak out to meet with her contact when he was there. *If he was there.* The anxious knot in her stomach tightened as she thought about the failed meeting the previous evening. Now even if she did manage to gather the information everyone so desperately wanted, she might not have a way to pass it on.

With a sigh, she turned back toward her office. The only thing she could be sure of was that she had to maintain the appearance that she really was Lina Ramir or she would have a lot more to worry about than why Devin Granger hadn't shown up the night before.

* * *

Seth and Quinn headed toward the communications office on board the *USS Harry S. Truman.* Both men were unusually quiet. The report had arrived an hour before that the vehicle Brent had disabled, the vehicle that had been in active pursuit of Seth and Brent, had been carrying three police officers from Soto. All three police officers were currently in the hospital, one still in critical condition.

A look at the ship's communication log revealed that two calls had taken place between the ship's personnel and the Soto police station the day before. The first call had been initiated by the comm room early in the morning, and the other had been an incoming call just minutes before the police had arrived on scene, where Brent and Seth had come under fire.

Since Brent was still in debriefings, Kel had sent Seth and Quinn to find out exactly what had transpired during those two conversations and to determine who had withheld much needed information from their squad.

Seth pushed open the hatch and folded his enormous frame through the doorway, followed by Quinn. Seth zeroed in on a young ensign and said, "I'm looking for the military liaison officer who was on duty yesterday."

The ensign reached for a clipboard. "That was Lieutenant Kiefer."

"That's who I talked to the first time yesterday," Quinn told Seth before turning back to the ensign. "When is he on duty next?"

"He's right over there." The ensign pointed to the far side of the room.

"Thanks." Seth shifted his focus to the relatively thin, sandy-haired man who was sitting at a communications station. "Lieutenant Kiefer?" Seth began, waiting for the man to look up at him before continuing. "We need your reports on your contact with the Soto police department yesterday."

"There wasn't much to them." He shrugged but made no movement to retrieve the reports.

"Can you tell us what the police told you?" Seth continued, already irritated with the cavalier attitude of the man in front of him.

"I called them early yesterday morning to make sure they didn't have any activity scheduled in the hot spot, but the police chief wasn't available, so I left a message for him to call me back."

"You did *what?*" Quinn's voice was incredulous as he stared at the lieutenant who had been in charge of communication with the local authorities.

The man stood up and turned away from his communication console to face Quinn fully. He was a good three inches taller than Quinn's six feet, and he took an aggressive stance. "Look, I had no idea he wouldn't call back until his men were already heading your way. Besides, I didn't get any information at all from him until right before I went off duty. That must have been about ten minutes before the incident."

"Why didn't you tell us ten minutes beforehand that they were heading our way?" Seth spoke now, trying to bank the anger coursing through him.

"I was off duty. Besides, by the time my replacement received your call, it was too late to do anything about it." The lieutenant gestured with one hand. "It's not like we had a way to contact the police once they were at the compound."

"Did you pass this information along to the person who relieved you?" Seth asked slowly, his voice deceptively calm.

"The petty officer had the report to type up."

Beside him, Quinn's dark eyes blackened. Quinn had personally checked with the communications office when Seth and Brent had requested assistance, and this man had buried the information about the police's presence. Stepping forward, war blazing in his eyes, Quinn spoke in a low voice that vibrated with fury. "If we had known that the cops had come from Soto, their headquarters could have informed them that we had men on scene." He took another step forward, and this time the lieutenant took a step back. "And don't you think these men deserved to know whether they were shooting at police or terrorists?"

"Well, as they say, hindsight is twenty-twenty," Lieutenant Kiefer said edgily. One look at Quinn had him taking another retreating step.

Before Quinn could continue forward, Seth laid a hand on his shoulder and stepped between the two men. "Back off, Quinn."

"Get out of the way, Lieutenant." Quinn's intentions were transparent, and his intense anger had blocked the reality that fighting with this man was going to land him in the brig.

"I said back off," Seth repeated a little more sharply. "That's an order."

Quinn stayed in place, but his posturing shifted ever so slightly, enough that Seth knew he no long intended to attack but was instead hoping that the other man would throw the first punch.

"I suggest you teach your men a little more discipline," Lieutenant Kiefer said arrogantly to Seth. "Picking a fight with an officer is a court-martial offense."

"You're absolutely right, Lieutenant." Seth nodded slowly. "Which is why it's up to me to take care of this problem."

Quick as lightning Seth's fist struck out, connecting with the man's jaw. Lieutenant Kiefer fell backward, slumping down into his chair. Seth took two steps toward him, angling his head to look down on the man. "Don't you *ever* withhold information from my squad again. Is that understood?"

The lieutenant gave a weak nod, but Seth had already turned back to Quinn. "Let's get out of here."

Quinn snapped to attention, gave a sharp salute, and nodded. "Yes, sir!"

4

"What's all this about you striking a fellow officer?" Kel asked, frustration evident in his tone. "Seth, I sent you because I figured you were the only one I could trust *not* to get into a fight."

"Sorry, Commander." Seth said the words, but both men knew that he didn't mean them.

"Sorry you hit the jerk, or sorry there were so many witnesses?"

"Sir, I'll let you draw your own conclusions on that one," Seth said simply.

"Come on, Kel," Quinn interrupted. "The guy should be charged with dereliction of duty after not following through with the police that way."

"Which is exactly why I sent you to investigate," Kel pointed out. "Now if we charge the guy, we're likely to have him counter with charges against Seth."

"Don't let that stop you," Seth insisted, feeling somewhat like a teenager who had been sent to the principal's office. "I'll take my punishment if he takes his."

"If nothing else, I want to make sure he never provides intel for us again." Kel massaged his temples as though a headache was building there. "I hate to break it to you guys, but the whole ship knows we're all Mormon. We're not exactly setting a very good standard by going around picking fights."

"He didn't pick a fight." Quinn spoke up to defend Seth once more. "He finished one."

The corner of Kel's mouth twitched, but he quickly fought it. Then he shook his head. "At least one good thing came from all of this. Amy will arrive tomorrow morning."

"Amy's coming?" Brent's head whipped around at the mention of his wife, who also served as their unit's intelligence officer.

Kel nodded. "I don't know who insisted that we couldn't bring her on board in the first place, but whoever it is probably got chewed out for limiting our resources on that last op." Kel then turned back to Seth. "As for you, you're confined to quarters until I figure out how to handle this mess."

"Yes, sir," Seth said, holding back a sigh. He knew that Kel had to give him some token punishment in case Kiefer tried to press charges against him, but it was annoying to be taken out of the loop of what was going on.

Resigned to his fate, Seth made his way below deck to the quarters he shared with Brent Miller. He knew he shouldn't have hit the other man, but his temper had erupted so quickly he hadn't taken the time to consider the consequences. He was a big man, broad through the shoulders and standing a full six foot seven. Normally he took great pains to keep his temper in check, especially since he knew how lethal it could be when let loose. The news about the injured police officers had been enough to push him too close to the edge.

Lieutenant Kiefer never even realized Seth's fist was coming his way until it was too late. Then again, there was only one other occasion when he could remember someone recognizing his intention and stepping in to stop a fight before it happened. A slight grin softened his features. Vanessa Lauton had been at least a foot shorter and more than a hundred pounds lighter than him, but she had muscled her way between Seth and his would-be opponent on his first day at his new high school.

Seth felt the familiar bittersweet tug in his chest as he thought of Vanessa. It had been nearly six years since he'd seen her, but rarely did he make it more than a day or two without some thought of her surfacing. He tried to fight back the memory, but it flooded through him anyway.

"Let's go!" The burly teen standing in front of Seth punched his fist into his palm and narrowed his eyes. Tough Guy was the star heavyweight of Seth's new high school. He was a few inches shorter than Seth, about six foot four, and probably outweighed him by fifty pounds.

Seth tried a diplomatic approach as a crowd started forming in the school parking lot. "Look, man. I don't want to fight you."

"Then you shouldn't have been talking to my girl." Tough Guy took a step forward.

Seth balanced on the balls of his feet, like a boxer waiting for the bell. "You want to narrow it down for me?"

Tough Guy's first swing was expected and easily avoided. Seth ducked and stepped back as he considered whether to give diplomacy one more chance or if he should just take care of this guy. His years of martial arts training told him to fight only as a last resort. His life of hard knocks taught him that sometimes it was the quickest course of action.

Seth evaded a second punch as his hefty opponent stumbled forward when he missed yet again. This time when he turned, Seth saw the fury in the other boy's eyes. Resigned to the fact that he wasn't going to walk away from this one, his right hand curled into a fist.

To his surprise, at that moment a dark-haired, dark-skinned girl stepped right between them and slapped both hands on the wrestling champ's chest. "Back off, Leonard."

"He started it," Leonard protested.

"How, by breathing?" Sarcasm dripped from her voice.

"Stay out of this, Vanessa." Leonard tried to push her hands away, but she didn't budge. "He was talking to Marcy."

"Oh, grow up," Vanessa scolded. She turned to look at Seth, her eyes narrowing. "Did you want to fight him?"

"Not particularly."

"Good." She nodded and turned back to face Leonard. "Go home, Leonard."

"I should have expected this from you," Leonard sneered. "Standing up for your kind."

"Is that your way of saying that I'm black?" She looked down at her arms as though noticing their color for the first time. "Wow, I am black." She looked up at Leonard again, her eyes dark. "What will my father say when he finds out?"

"Shut up, Vanessa." Leonard pulled free of her grip by stepping back. He pointed a finger at Seth. "Stay away from Marcy."

Seth shrugged as Leonard slammed into his truck, gunned the engine, and let the tires squeal as he pulled out of the parking lot. Slowly the crowd dissipated, and Seth looked down at the girl standing in front of him.

"Well, this was definitely a first," Seth muttered as he dug his keys out of his pocket. "I can't say I've ever had a girl stand up for me before."

"Don't take it personally. I didn't want Leonard to get suspended before the meet tomorrow."

Seth's eyebrows winged up. "School loyalty?"

Vanessa laughed, her features softening. "Family loyalty."

"I'm not following."

"The idiot that just tried to pick a fight with you is my cousin."

"Yeah, I can see the resemblance," Seth said sarcastically. Then he shook his head and let out a short laugh. "And I thought it was tough being the new kid."

"Honey, you don't know the half of it." She put her hands on her hips and nodded at his car. "Since my ride just left without me, any chance you can give me a ride home?"

"You sure you trust me?"

Vanessa stepped back and looked at him as though studying a complicated puzzle. "Yeah. You don't look like the type that wants to start any trouble."

Seth had stared at her, surprised by her perception. He had given her a ride home that day, and the next. Within a week, they had become practically inseparable. She had been both his girlfriend and his best friend during his last two years of high school and throughout college. She was also the reason he hadn't been able to bring himself to date anyone for more than a week or two. No one else had ever measured up.

With a shake of his head, Seth managed to pull himself out of his memories and back to the present as the door opened. He swung his legs over the side of his bunk when Quinn walked in.

"Anything new?" Seth asked.

Quinn nodded. "Yeah, but we're not sure what."

"What do you mean?"

"The admiral wants to meet us in our boardroom ASAP." Quinn motioned for Seth to follow him.

"Are you sure he wants me there too?"

"He especially wants you." Quinn nodded. "Kel said he mentioned you by name."

Seth gave a shrug. "Let's go find out what he wants."

* * *

Vanessa slipped off her sandals and stepped onto the cooling sand. A few palm trees were scattered along the edge of the shore before the beach opened up into a narrow stretch of sand. The sun hung low in the sky, and dinner would begin shortly, but Vanessa needed a few minutes to herself before going back to work.

She often wondered what was harder, pretending to be someone she wasn't or enduring day after day, night after night, surrounded by so many people. It wasn't that she didn't like people particularly. She simply needed her alone time too. In this assignment, with her cover job as resort manager, she rarely had a minute to herself. The few she did find were often spent spying on the guests and Halim.

She sometimes wondered whether she would have gained more trust by now had she developed more than a working relationship with Akil's trusted advisor. Deep down she knew she couldn't take the chance. Even though Halim was often charming and witty, he was also ruthless. Besides, she didn't think she could handle the emotional or moral dilemmas that would follow such a decision.

The fact that Halim was so overprotective also worried Vanessa. As he had that morning, he often stepped in when he felt she wasn't being treated well. He also went to great lengths to keep her out of the loop when it came to his role in Akil Ramir's business. She couldn't be sure whether he didn't trust her or whether he felt that weapons deals and terrorist plots were not suitable activities for a woman.

With another glance at the building where Halim was meeting with some of the new arrivals, Vanessa decided to take this rare opportunity to relax. So far the day had been a wash as far as finding new information. Hoping that her luck was about to change, she reached for a lounge chair on the beach and angled it so that she could face the beach as well as the building where Halim was.

She sat down and shifted her gaze to the water. The Caribbean Sea was calm and peaceful, the crashing of the waves drowning out the sounds of the resort behind her. She watched a boat loaded with tourists cross into her view. The same boat sped by every day, once in the morning as it headed out for Saona Island and then again as it returned in the evening.

As she watched the families on board, she felt a familiar pang of loneliness. At times like these, she wondered why she had never settled down, or at least tried harder to find someone to settle down with. She supposed she already knew the answer to that. She had set her sights too high. Throughout high school she hadn't dated at all—until Seth Johnson had moved to town.

A wave splashed up onto the sand and over her feet, and a pang of guilt speared through her as she thought of how things had ended between them. She'd gone after him to explain, but he had left town before she managed to catch up with him. Vanessa pushed those thoughts aside, instead choosing to remember their early days together.

Seth had been such a breath of fresh air when he moved to town. He hadn't looked at her like the other boys at school did. Most of the people she had gone to school with saw her as one of two things: Leonard's cousin or the dark-skinned girl who had a white daddy. The war between the States may have ended more than a century earlier, but in her hometown in Georgia, memories lasted for generations.

It didn't matter that her father was originally from the North, or that her grandparents were immigrants from Morocco rather than descendants of African slaves. People in the little town had only seen one thing: dark skin.

They hadn't been treated poorly, per se, just differently. Then again, her grandparents had never been terribly comfortable speaking English, and her mother wasn't much better. Since her father had learned French while serving a mission in Switzerland, he was perfectly content to speak French in the home instead of English, a fact which was never understood by their neighbors.

When Seth had moved to town, he hadn't seen her family as a bunch of foreigners who had invaded his territory, but rather had been fascinated by her unique family history. She had only known him a few days when she found out that he too spoke French, thanks to spending much of his childhood in New Orleans. Within a few weeks, he realized that although her grandparents spoke French, they preferred speaking in Arabic. Eager to learn a new language, Seth had insisted on learning a few phrases in Arabic, quickly endearing himself to her grandparents.

She often wondered if her decision to pursue a career in intelligence had stemmed from her early exposure to different languages and cultures, or if it had been the influence of Seth's uncle, Patrick. A retired naval pilot, Patrick had taken over Seth's care when he was young and had raised him as his own son. By the time Vanessa had met Patrick, his health was failing, but his stories always fascinated her. His unwavering patriotism was compelling, and she knew that his influence had been the reason Seth had accepted the Navy ROTC scholarship when he graduated from high school.

She wondered what Seth would think now if he knew she worked for the CIA. She hadn't ever considered such a career while in college. In fact, one of the reasons she had continued her education was because she hadn't yet decided what to do with her life. When a recruiter from the CIA had shown up as she entered her last year of graduate school, her professional goals had clicked into place. If only her personal life would follow suit.

Vanessa let out a sigh, wishing she could go back in time. She didn't know what she would have done differently, but . . .

The sound of a door opening broke into her thoughts. She barely resisted the urge to adjust her dark sunglasses as her eyes shifted toward Halim and the three men who exited the building with him. Halim hesitated a moment when he saw her. He then lowered his voice fractionally even though he was speaking in Arabic, a language he believed Vanessa didn't understand. Lina's family had stopped speaking it after moving to France decades before.

"I assure you, we will have the shipment ready for you," Halim assured the man to his left, who Vanessa recognized as Tod Zimmerman, a regular at La Playa.

"Three weeks," Zimmerman said, anxiety humming through his voice. His eyes were close-set, and they shifted from side to side, reminding Vanessa of a caged animal looking for the chance to break free. "The antiaircraft guns must be in place before the new helicopters are delivered."

"Relax, my friend. We won't need those guns." Halim's mouth curved into a smile. "The Americans don't know anything about our plans."

"How can you be so sure?"

Halim gave Zimmerman a knowing look. "Let's just say I have friends in the right places."

5

"Your team is being tasked with a special assignment." The man who stood in front of the room wasn't in uniform, but instead wore a business suit. The admiral had introduced him as Rick Ellison from the CIA.

"Exactly what kind of assignment?" Kel asked.

"As you are aware, we have an operative inside Akil Ramir's organization," he began. "This operative's contact, the man who has been running this covert op, had to be medivacked to the United States a few days ago."

"What happened?"

"He had a massive stroke."

Kel shook his head in sympathy, but his voice was questioning. "I still don't understand what you want from us. Why don't you send in another one of your own people?"

"Our operative is in deep, so deep that she has been ordered not to divulge any information to anyone besides her contact point. We're hopeful that she'll trust you." He hesitated and nodded at Seth. "Lieutenant Johnson already knows her."

Seth shook his head, confused. "I don't know anyone with the CIA."

"Yes, you do." Rick Ellison said, his eyes serious. "Her name is Vanessa Lauton."

"Vanessa?" Seth stood abruptly, and his chair crashed onto its side.

Rick's eyebrows lifted. "So you do remember her."

"We went to high school together." Slowly Seth shook his head, beyond stunned to hear her name in this context, especially after he had just been thinking about her. His cheeks grew warm as everyone continued to watch him, and he leaned down to right his chair before sitting back down. He blew out a breath and tried to steady the swirl of emotions rushing through him. "I haven't seen her for years."

"Here's a recent photograph." Ellison pulled a glossy photo out of a file marked *Top Secret*. "She traded places with Lina Ramir about a year ago. Her handler was working out of the Dominican Republic when he got sick."

Seth took the photo and sucked in a breath. It was Vanessa, all right. She was older, certainly, but other than that she didn't look much different. Her hair was longer now, cascading halfway down her back, but even in the photo he could see the glint of challenge in her eyes.

How was it possible, he wondered, that Vanessa was now a spy? His heart raced at the prospect of seeing her again, and he thought of the many contrasts he had loved about Vanessa: the warmth of her friendship, her fiery temper, her quick wit. He was also reminded of why he no longer carried her photo. It hurt too much.

Kel's voice broke through his thoughts. "Are you saying you don't know where the contact point is?"

"That's exactly what I'm saying." He nodded. "Our sources indicate that Akil Ramir owns a resort in Punta Cana. We think that's where she's staying. Our man was undercover at the Club Med there. Unfortunately we don't know when or where they were meeting."

"If she's really staying at the resort, we should be able to tail any cars leaving from there and hopefully find her that way," Tristan suggested.

"It may not be that easy. The types of people who stay at this resort are used to keeping an eye out for people following them. It's going to take time, and we don't know how much time we have," Ellison told them. "Vanessa thinks something big is going on, but she hasn't been able to piece together exactly what."

"That's what these sneak-and-peeks have been about," Brent said now as understanding dawned. "Trying to figure out what Ramir's group is up to."

"I considered having some agents set up surveillance around the Punta Cana region, but I don't want to take the chance that my people might get spotted. I'm trusting that your squad can blend in and find Vanessa so that we can insert another contact man for her," Ellison said, his tone serious. His gaze landed on Seth. "You need to understand that Vanessa is not the first operative we have tried to insert into Ramir's organization, but she is the only one who is still alive." Ellison looked from Seth to Kel and added, "No one outside of this room has this information. It is strictly need-to-know."

Seth's stomach clutched as he considered the risks Vanessa was taking, but he spoke with certainty. "We'll find her."

* * *

Vanessa stepped into the dining room and surveyed the guests sitting at the tables scattered around the room. She had deliberately taken her time in her office so that she would be late to dinner. When she scanned the room a second time, she felt a surge of anticipation. Halim was sitting at a corner table with four other men, their body language tense.

When a member of the kitchen staff stopped to greet Vanessa, she granted him one precious minute of her time before picking up a plate at the end of the buffet counter. Her appetite was practically nonexistent, but she forced herself to load up her plate so she would have a reason to stay in the dining room.

Casually, she headed across the room and felt Halim's attention land on her for a moment. She gave him a nod of acknowledgement and then took a seat at the table beside his.

The bullish man to Halim's right leaned forward and lowered his voice as he spoke.

Vanessa couldn't hear what he said, but Halim's words rang out clearly. "Don't worry. She doesn't speak Arabic."

Narain, the wiry man across from Halim, spoke now. "The timing on this is crucial. To have the maximum impact, the Americans can't have time to evacuate."

"What kind of casualties can we expect?" Tod Zimmerman asked, his voice abnormally calm.

"Worst case, in the thousands," Halim said in a businesslike tone. Then evil flashed in his eyes. "Of course, we're hoping for much more than that."

Vanessa forced herself to keep her eyes on her plate, forced herself not to react. All the while, she was hoping, praying that they would say more.

"When do you have to get back?" Halim asked.

"Tomorrow," Zimmerman answered, his voice more nervous now.

"Let's finish this discussion in my office tonight," Halim suggested. "The sooner we lay the rest of this groundwork, the better."

Vanessa stayed in her seat, listening as the men finished up their dinner and moved to leave. She nearly jumped when a hand came down on her shoulder and she heard Halim's voice once more, only now he spoke in French. "Good night, Lina."

"Good night," Vanessa said, hoping her voice sounded casual as she glanced up at him. As she watched him leave the room, she glanced at the clock on the wall. Just a few more hours and she could pass on this latest information. She only hoped that Granger wouldn't be late tonight.

* * *

"She really does look a lot like Lina Ramir," Kel said as he sat down at the worktable with the rest of his squad. Ellison had already finished his briefing and left them to work out a strategy. "I just can't believe she's been able to pull this off for so long."

Seth nodded. He tried to sound casual despite the worry that had settled deep inside him. "I guess it's not that surprising considering her background."

"Exactly what is her background?"

"Her grandparents lived with her when she was growing up. They were both from Morocco and spoke Arabic as often as not. In fact, that's where I picked up a lot of what I know," Seth informed them. "They also spoke French, which was the language her mother preferred. That's also the language she studied in high school."

"Sounds like you know a lot about her," Quinn said carefully, his dark eyebrows lifting.

Seth nodded, a slow smile crossing his face. "She was my best friend in high school and college."

"You act like you were more than just friends," Tristan said, his eyes lighting with curiosity.

Seth spared Tristan a quick glance but didn't comment further on his relationship with Vanessa. Instead he offered a different tidbit of information. "She's also the first person I ever met who was Mormon."

"She's LDS?"

Again he nodded, but now the smile faded. "I had no idea she was working for the CIA. Last time I went to visit her family, I heard she'd gotten married."

"Apparently not." Kel held up the file Ellison had given him. "It says in her file she's single." He set the file aside and then tapped on the map that was spread out on the table. "One way or another, we've got to figure out how to contact her."

Tristan's easy Western drawl cut through the tension. "How about going for a sail?"

Seth looked down at the map, nodding his head slowly. "A sneak-and-peek from the water?"

"With the right equipment, we can get a lay of the land." Tristan nodded. He looked up at Kel and grinned. "You know, my honeymoon got cut short for this assignment. If you want to send me and Riley in for a vacation, just say the word."

Kel looked at him, clearly considering. Even though Tristan's wife, Riley, had worked with them in the past, she wasn't trained in intelligence. Kel looked over at Brent, considered a moment longer, then said, "Brent, call Amy and tell her not to get on that Navy transport."

"What?" Brent's dark eyes narrowed. "I thought you'd want her on this assignment."

"Oh, I do." Kel nodded. "But she's going to meet you in Florida on your way to Punta Cana."

Brent nodded instantly, a smile tugging at his mouth. "That works."

"Hey, I'm the one whose honeymoon was interrupted," Tristan complained.

Kel's eyebrows lifted as he glanced in Tristan's direction. "You were already at the airport ready to come home when we called you. How is that interrupted?"

Tristan's easy grin flashed once more. "I still had six hours before I had to report back in when you picked me up."

Kel shook his head and grinned as he motioned to Quinn. "Start getting our gear together. I want to get settled down there by tomorrow."

"What about Amy and me?" Brent asked.

"I want the two of you to stay at the Club Med in Punta Cana. You should be able to convince everyone that you're there for a vacation," Kel told him. "I want you to figure out what Granger was using for transportation. Maybe we can narrow down where he and Vanessa were meeting."

"Uh, Kel. I don't know about this," Brent said hesitantly. "Amy's never done any work undercover."

"I realize that, but no one is going to doubt that she is your wife," Kel stated bluntly. "We mostly need her to give you a reason to be at the Club Med. Besides, it never hurts to have Amy's take on things." Kel turned back to Seth. "We may not have a lot of time here."

"I know," Seth's voice was low. "We need to get me inside."

"There may only be one way to do that."

Seth nodded in understanding. "I'll grab my gear."

6

"You're doing what?" Halim's tone was condescending and clearly annoyed.

Vanessa's chin lifted slightly. "You heard me. I'm going into town to do some shopping."

Halim glanced around the deserted resort lobby and then looked back at her. "This isn't a good time."

"It's never a good time," Vanessa shot back, trying to squelch the nerves in her stomach.

Time was running out, and her options were dwindling. She had to press for more information. Today she was doing just that by insisting on a shopping spree. "I'm down to three pairs of sandals, and my wardrobe could use a boost. Besides, I haven't taken a day off in months."

"Make a list, and I'll have Roberto go pick up a few things for you next time he goes out for supplies," Halim insisted, referring to one of the pilots who was constantly flying in and out of La Playa.

"I'm *not* having someone else buy me shoes." The absurdity of the idea helped ease the waves of anxiety rolling through her. She stood a little straighter, imagining what the real Lina would do if she were denied such freedoms. "Besides, I'll only be gone for a few hours."

"Lina, you can't go today."

"Why not?" Vanessa let a little whine carry through her voice. "I never get to go out and have any fun."

Halim let out a frustrated sigh and glanced around once more. "We have an important shipment arriving in a few hours. Besides, you know that your uncle is very protective of you. In his line of work, he has to be."

"It's not like you and Uncle Akil include me the way my father did." Vanessa pouted. "Besides, we always have shipments coming through here."

Halim's dark eyes narrowed. He stared at her for a moment and then lowered his voice. "Your uncle doesn't want you linked to this. The Americans are still watching you. We can't take a chance of them suspecting anything."

"The Americans are watching me?" The surety in his voice caused a ripple of fear to run through her. "Why do you think the Americans are watching me?"

"I have my sources."

"Don't tell me you have an American spying for you." Sarcasm coated her voice, and she hoped it would hide the icy fear shooting through her. When Halim simply shrugged a shoulder, Vanessa added, "How do you know this person can be trusted?"

"He has proven his loyalty."

Vanessa let out a sigh. "How much longer until I can go out again?"

"Four weeks."

"Four weeks?" Vanessa's eyes whipped up to meet his. "You expect me to stay on the compound for four weeks?"

"Lina, it's not safe," Halim insisted.

"The Americans aren't going to do anything to me." Vanessa folded her arms. "And my wardrobe isn't going to last much longer. You're going to have to let me have a few hours soon, or I'll be walking around barefoot before the month is out."

Halim studied her for a long moment, then turned and walked away.

* * *

The Club Med wasn't as glamorous as Amy had expected, but it was inviting just the same. She and Brent had already dropped their luggage off in their two-room suite and had changed into their swimming suits. With nothing but a room key and a small tube of sunscreen in the pocket of her shorts, Amy followed Brent through the open lobby area and down the steps onto the pool deck.

She took in the beautiful scenery, the enormous pool, the palm trees swaying in the light breeze, and the beach a short distance away. Looking at a mother playing with her children in the pool it was hard to imagine that such evil could exist right down the road. Logically, Amy knew that her presence here in the Dominican Republic was primarily to help

Brent look like a typical tourist. If only she weren't so nervous that she would make a mistake and compromise their cover.

Walking beside her, Brent took her hand. He leaned closer and whispered in her ear, "Relax."

Amy looked up at him, wondering if she looked nervous or if he could just sense her unease. "I'm trying," she whispered back. She took a deep breath, determined to act the part. Hoping her voice sounded light, she asked, "What did you want to do first?"

"I thought we could take a sail if there's a boat available."

"That sounds like fun." Amy managed a smile as Brent gave her hand an encouraging squeeze.

He looked completely relaxed, even though Amy could feel his tension too. They crossed the pool deck and stepped out onto the beach. Lounge chairs and sunbathers were scattered among the palm trees, and more than a dozen guests were currently engaged in a game of beach volleyball. They skirted along the building that housed the snack bar and headed for a hut farther down the beach where a windsurfing class was taking place.

Amy let Brent lead her toward two men who were standing at the edge of the hut, both wearing only swim trunks and sunglasses. Brent slowed for a moment, listening to the men speaking in French. Despite the fact that Brent was capable of communicating in their language, he spoke in English. "Excuse me. Can you tell us where we can check out a sailboat?"

"Have you had lessons yet?" the shorter man asked, his accent thick enough that it took Amy a moment to decipher his words.

Brent shook his head. "Not here, but I already know how to sail."

The man studied him for a moment and then gave him a nod. "The life vests are over there. You both need to put one on before you go out." He then pointed at the red buoys in the water. "You need to stay inside of the markers at all times."

"No problem." Brent signed the clipboard the man offered him and then motioned to the three tiny sailboats moored in the shallow water. "Does it matter which one we take?"

"Take number five," he said, noting it on the paper Brent had handed back to him.

After stashing their shoes and the towels Brent was carrying into little cubbies in the back of the hut, Brent and Amy donned their life-jackets and crossed the hot sand to the water.

As they stepped into the surf, Amy let herself soak up the atmosphere. An old shipwreck lay on some rocks a short distance away just beyond the buoys. The old vessel reminded her of pirates and days of old. A seagull cried in the distance, and the sweet smell of the salt water washed over her.

"Are you ready?" Brent asked.

"I think so." Amy nodded.

Brent helped her get situated in the tiny boat before unclipping the lines that held it in place. A moment later he was sitting beside her and telling her to duck as the sail swung over her head and they began to pick up speed.

"I'm surprised the sailboats aren't bigger."

"Me too." With his hand still on the rudder, he leaned over and gave her a quick kiss and then winked at her. "But I'm sure we can manage."

Amy smiled and turned her face into the wind. She reminded herself that the mission Brent had been given had little to do with Akil Ramir and his associates; instead, it involved some rather innocent snooping. For the first time since their arrival, she felt herself relax. Brent steered past another sailboat that nearly capsized before the occupant managed to balance the boat in the nick of time. He then cleared a couple in a canoe and headed toward the outer buoys.

"I guess we can eliminate boats as a possible mode of transportation for Granger to get to the contact point," Brent commented.

"I was thinking the same thing," Amy agreed.

They watched a Club Med employee pass by in a speedboat and approach another sailboat that was threatening to move past the outer buoys. "Even if he did manage to sneak out, these boats aren't big enough to be safe at night," Brent said.

"The guards at the gate would probably know if he was taking a cab out of here," Amy noted. "It looked like they were logging everyone in and out as they passed through the gate."

"I don't think an Agency man would want someone keeping track of him like that."

"You think he had a car parked somewhere nearby?"

"Yeah." Brent nodded. "It wouldn't be that hard to sneak out of here on foot."

"So I guess we're going for a walk next."
"With the size of this place, it's going to be a long walk."

7

Seth drove the tiny rental car along the market district of yet another village near the beach region of Punta Cana. He searched for any place that might make a logical rendezvous point for Vanessa and her handler, still not exactly sure what he was looking for.

The heat and humidity flooded through the open windows, and Seth wished for the fortieth time that the little car had come with a working air conditioner. It was bad enough that he had to slouch down in the seat to keep his head from touching the ceiling.

He glanced down at his watch, wishing he had more time. Kel had given him three hours to check out a few of the towns near La Playa while the rest of the squad gathered their supplies for this assignment. Already one of those hours had been wasted when he'd encountered a road blocked by an overturned produce truck. Now he hoped to make up for lost time.

Even though he knew that spotting Vanessa was unlikely at best, he found himself searching for any sign of her as he drove through the narrow, crowded streets. He still couldn't quite picture Vanessa as a spy. Then again, he was having a hard time facing the reality that if their mission was successful, he would be seeing her before the week was out.

Memories of the past, memories he was forever fighting against, were surfacing with painful clarity. He didn't want to remember the way Vanessa had shown him around town that first day he had given her a ride home or the way their friendship had grown into something more.

When Seth turned a corner and saw an LDS chapel off to the left, he could only shake his head as yet another memory flooded through him. He didn't fight this image, the image of Vanessa's father and the way he had sat him down the night he had come by to pick Vanessa up for their first official date.

A little smile crossed his face as he remembered her dad's words when he had explained in no uncertain terms how he expected his daughter to be treated. He had then gone on to explain that they were members of The Church of Jesus Christ of Latter-day Saints and told him a little about their beliefs.

The Mormon culture had been completely foreign to Seth at the time, and he still marveled at the way the Lauton family had taken the time to get to know him and had ultimately included him in so many of their family and church activities. Then again, the concept of family was foreign to Seth as well.

Seth's own family was a disjointed mess, one he barely understood. If his mother knew who his father was, she had never admitted it. Of course, his mother hadn't exactly been an ideal parent. By the time Seth was eight, she had decided that raising a kid on her own was too much for her and had sent Seth to live with his uncle Patrick. Though he had been hurt and confused at the time, Seth could now admit that his mother's decision to send him away was probably the best thing she could have done for him.

Recently retired, his uncle had opened his modest apartment to Seth and given him his first taste of what home was all about. Rather than leaving Seth alone at night so he could go out the way Seth's mother had, Patrick would walk with him to the park or take him to the library. He had signed him up for karate and football, always trying to help Seth overcome the neglect and poverty he had endured during his early childhood. He had also told Seth stories about his life in the Navy, sparking an interest that had ultimately helped him find his direction in life.

The experience of seeing his uncle weak and broken in his hospital bed as he lost his battle with cancer had been extremely painful. Patrick had insisted on being at Seth's graduation from high school, an event that occurred only weeks before his death. Without Vanessa's support, and the support of her family, he wasn't sure he would have made it through that difficult time. He also doubted he would have taken advantage of the ROTC scholarship he had been offered for college that next fall.

He wondered what the Lautons would think now if they found out that he had converted to the Mormon Church. More specifically, he wondered what his life would have been like had he accepted the gospel a few years earlier.

The familiar old hurt washed over him as he wished for what could have been. He couldn't be sure why he never seriously considered joining the Church when he was a teenager. Even though he had always admired Vanessa's family and their lifestyle, the idea that he could have that for himself had never occurred to him. He had felt that religion wasn't for him. Somehow those feelings had changed when he started working in a profession that forced him to face his own mortality on a regular basis.

Seth forced his thoughts back to the present as he passed by the church and turned down yet another narrow road. As he looked at the rows of dark alleys and tiny houses, he realized that it might very well take a miracle to find Vanessa.

* * *

"It's got to be around this area," Brent commented as he led Amy past the tennis courts.

"How can you be so sure?"

Brent waited to answer her until a group of teenagers passed by them. As soon as they were out of earshot, he walked to the last tennis court and looked around. "This is the only common area that borders the strip of jungle near the road. Not to mention that Granger wouldn't raise any suspicions coming here since the tennis courts are open all day long."

She considered for a moment. "Yeah, but if they were meeting at night, he wouldn't have a reason to come this way. He wouldn't want to raise suspicions."

"I don't think it would have been too hard for him to slip past everyone. This place isn't too far off of the main trails, and it's well hidden by the trees."

Amy nodded as she considered his logic. She stopped by a drinking fountain labeled "potable water" and took a sip. As she stood, she noticed the path continuing past yet another tennis court. "What about down here?"

"It's worth taking a look," Brent agreed, stopping to take a quick drink himself. They moved down the sidewalk, past a tennis court, and emerged next to the archery station for kids.

He stopped and watched as an instructor assisted a boy of about ten with his stance before letting him try to shoot the bull's-eye of one of the targets lined up in a fenced area. The high chain-link fence was covered by black mesh for privacy, but it was barely visible through the vines and foliage growing up it.

Noticing the sign for the main archery station, Brent veered left down yet another sidewalk and slowed once more when they reached the currently vacant adults' archery range. "Did you want to give it a try?"

One of Amy's shoulders lifted. "Sure, why not?"

They each selected a protective brace from a bin and moved to adjoining stations.

Amy sat down to fasten her brace and glanced over at her husband. "You know I haven't done this since I was in high school."

"You just have to remember one thing," Brent said as his grin flashed and he leaned toward her.

"What?"

Brent pointed toward the targets. "Aim that way."

"Very funny," Amy said wryly as she stood up and retrieved her bow. Positioning her body the way she had been taught years before, she lifted the arrow and placed it against the string of the bow. She drew back the string, focused on the bull's-eye, let out a little breath, and released. And watched the arrow skip right over the target.

She let out a sigh of frustration before trying once more. This time she aimed a bit lower, but when she released, the arrow ricocheted off of the side of her target and landed in the side of her husband's target, where he had already placed his first two arrows in the inner ring surrounding the bull's-eye.

Brent spared her a glance and struggled against a grin. "Interesting shot."

"Oh, be quiet." Amy stuck her tongue out at him, struggling not to laugh herself. "I'll figure it out."

"Just remember, point that direction."

Amy chuckled as she lifted her last arrow and reminded herself to adjust her stance and relax. This time when she released, the arrow connected with the target—kind of. She didn't hit the actual target, but the arrow embedded into the bale of hay it was attached to. "At least I'm getting closer," she told Brent as he motioned for her to follow him into the target area to retrieve their arrows.

"A couple more rounds and you'll be hitting the target every time," Brent encouraged, his voice laced with humor.

"By then, you'll be hitting the bull's-eye every time."

He pulled his three arrows out of the target and grinned at her. "Planning on it."

Amy retrieved her first two arrows, one from her target and the other from Brent's. She then went behind the targets and scanned the ground for the first arrow she had shot. She made it all the way to the fence and still didn't see it. Turning around, she looked behind her once more, wondering if perhaps she had walked past it. Still nothing.

Turning back to Brent, she called out, "I can't find it."

Brent headed her direction, searching the ground as he walked. "I thought it skipped right over the target. It should be right where you're standing."

"That's what I thought, but I don't see it anywhere." Amy ran a hand over the privacy-covering on the chain-link fence. "Maybe it's stuck in the fence."

"It's got to be here somewhere," Brent agreed. "I'll look over here again."

He turned to search the area behind Amy's target once more while Amy searched the fence. She leaned down and pulled back a thick section of vine where she thought the arrow had landed. Behind it was an opening in the fence. The chain-link section had been cut up about three feet high and was pulled wide enough that someone could squeeze through. Sure enough, her arrow lay in the dirt just beyond. "Hey, Brent!" Amy called over her shoulder. "I found it."

"Good. Let's try again," Brent said starting back toward where they had left their bows.

"No, Brent. You don't understand." Amy waited for him to turn back to face her and then waved for him to join her. He stared at her for a moment, but when she continued to wait for him by the fence he closed the distance between them and squatted down beside her. She looked up at him with a triumphant little smile and said, "I guess I hit the bull's-eye after all."

8

Seth moved silently through the night, carefully picking his way past palm trees and through the thick underbrush. Kel was moving beside him fifty yards to his left, and he expected that Brent would appear momentarily. Seth glanced at his watch, noting that it was ten minutes until two. Two o'clock in the morning was the time for Brent to check in. Their meeting place was a short distance away from the hole in the fence Brent and Amy had found, and Kel and Seth were currently searching for the vehicle Granger had been using as they moved from the road toward the back fence of the Club Med.

As he worked his way forward, Seth tried not to let his thoughts wander to Vanessa. But as usual, it was useless. The fact that she had been out of contact for more than a week had created a sense of urgency not only in Seth, but in the rest of his team as well. They had seen enough over the past few weeks to know that whatever was going to happen was likely to happen soon. Seth could only pray they would find Vanessa before it was too late.

He edged forward, estimating that he and Kel still had another quarter mile to go before they met up with Brent. Their search would have been easier during the day, but they couldn't take a chance of being spotted. Instead, Kel and Seth each wore night-vision goggles to assist their already heightened senses.

Seth started to step over what appeared to be a shallow rut in the ground, then stopped mid-stride when he noticed the unusual pattern in the dirt. Squatting down, he ran his fingers lightly over the depression, and a slight smile of satisfaction crossed his face. Standing, he signaled Kel as he began looking for a second tire track. When he found none, he narrowed down the possibilities, realizing that it wasn't a car they were looking for, but rather a motorcycle.

Trained to remain silent, Seth didn't speak to Kel when he approached, but instead pointed to the track in the dirt. Together, they tried to identify the origins of the vehicle they were searching for despite the fact that most of the ground was covered with thick palm fronds and other underbrush that effectively hid the tracks.

Methodically, they searched through the tangle of vines and fallen palm fronds. The search only took another five minutes before Kel lifted a stack of palm fronds and uncovered a small motorcycle. He and Seth uncovered the bike completely as Brent came into view.

Kel nodded at the motorcycle. "Did you find anything else at the resort?" he asked Brent, his voice low.

Brent nodded, pulling several slips of paper from his pocket. "Granger's gas receipts were neatly organized in his wallet."

"His wallet was still in his room?"

"Yeah, it was in the safe there." Brent shrugged. "I guess since he's technically still an employee here, the managers left his belongings in his room." He held the receipts out to Kel. "Anyway, you should be able to figure out how far he was going based on these now that we know what he was driving."

"What should we do with the bike?"

"Leave it here for now in case Brent needs transportation while he's here," Kel suggested. He turned to Brent, and a touch of humor sparked in his eyes. "You might consider finding the key so you don't need to hot-wire it."

"I'm way ahead of you." Brent grinned and pulled the key free from his pocket. "But do you want me to stay at the resort now that we found what we were looking for?"

"For the time being." Kel nodded. "I'll send you a coded e-mail in a few hours once we figure out our search range. Then we may have you and Amy take a few day trips."

"We'll look into it in the morning." Brent put a hand on Seth's shoulder and gave it an encouraging squeeze before heading back the way he had come.

"Come on," Kel motioned to Seth, his voice still low. "Let's get to work."

With a nod, Seth followed him back into the darkness.

* * *

Vanessa fiddled with the strap of her leather sandal where a small rip had started. She thought of the scissors that were in the drawer in the kitchen and wished she could take the easy way out, but she couldn't take the chance. She had to make her sandal look like it had broken from simple wear and tear.

It was silly, really, that she had stooped to using her wardrobe as a way to escape her gilded cage, but she was running out of options. She was also running out of time. One way or another, she had to find a way to get a message out. The question of who she needed to get the message to was still a concern she hadn't completely resolved, and now that she knew there was a leak, her options were extremely limited.

Most nights she was still able to make it to the contact point, but her hopes that Granger would show up were fading fast. She was afraid to find out what had happened—especially considering the possibility that one of Ramir's men had discovered how much Granger knew. Could the leak that Halim spoke of have found out that Granger was the source, and if so, was her cover still intact?

Vanessa pushed that thought aside. She was only one person, she reminded herself. From what she had learned so far, the terrorist attack that was being planned would affect thousands.

Over the past few nights, her prayers had been focused on her options and her need for guidance. She had finally decided to try to get a message out to her former boss, the same man who had recommended Vanessa for this assignment in the first place. But first she had to find a way to get away from the resort during business hours so she could get to a computer that couldn't be traced.

When a knock came at her door, Vanessa dropped her shoe to the floor and slipped it on, pleased that it looked ratty and in need of being replaced. Her eyes widened when she pulled the door open to find Halim standing on the other side holding three huge shopping bags.

"This should last you until it's safe to go out shopping again," Halim said as he walked into her living room and set the bags down on the coffee table.

"What's all this?"

"You said you needed new shoes."

"These are all shoes?" Vanessa asked incredulously. Her pure female instinct was to be thrilled, but the fact that Halim had eliminated her best chance of getting out of the resort during the daytime sent a shiver of panic through her. Every time she figured out a way to leave the resort, Halim countered with a reason she had to stay. She was beginning to feel like a hostage in the very real sense of the word.

"I wasn't sure what you wanted, but I'm sure you can find something you like." Halim motioned to the ragged sandals she was currently wearing. "After all, we can't have you wearing those when your uncle arrives."

Vanessa let her surprise show even as she tried to hide her trepidation. If Akil Ramir was making plans to come to Punta Cana, she might have less time than she thought to get a message out. "Uncle Akil is coming? No one said anything to me."

"His plans haven't been finalized yet," Halim said quickly as though he realized he had said more than he should have.

Vanessa let her frustration surface. "Why is it that you always seem to be protecting my uncle from me? He is my family, after all." She paced to the window and stared out for a moment before turning back to face him. "You know, before the Americans messed everything up, my father trusted me in every aspect of his business. Perhaps it's time you and Uncle Akil stop trying to shield me from everything."

"That's between you and your uncle," Halim said simply. He hesitated a moment and then closed the distance between them. She stared up at him and fought the instinct to step back as he ran a finger down her cheek. "As for me, I don't want to see you hurt."

Vanessa swallowed nervously. "I appreciate your concern, but you needn't worry."

He stared at her a moment before dropping his hand back to his side. He stepped away, his eyes unreadable as he motioned to the shopping bags. "Enjoy your new shoes."

Vanessa gave a brief nod followed by a sigh. "Can you at least tell me how long it will be before I can go into town again?"

Halim hesitated briefly before giving her an answer. "Only a few more weeks."

Vanessa watched him open the door and then disappear outside. As soon as she was alone, she lowered herself onto a chair. Halim's feelings for her were becoming more obvious, and she wasn't sure how she should feel about the notion that this man seemed to care for her even though her main purpose in being here was to destroy his plans. She took a deep breath and then pulled the closest shopping bag into her lap. Shaking her head, she stared at the pair of sandals on top and wondered how she could possibly get a message out.

* * *

Quinn blended into the dark night, impatience shimmering through him. Ellison had been correct when he said the people at La Playa were accustomed to watching for people following them. As he had taken up his position near the resort entrance, he had already bypassed several warning systems that had been installed to alert the residents to intruders.

If he had really wanted to, he could have penetrated the resort itself, but at this point it wasn't worth the risk of discovery. For now, his location a few hundred yards from the main entrance would serve his purpose well.

He didn't want to think about how many hours he had already been lying in the dark. That would only lend credence to the very real possibility that he might be in this position well into the next day. It wasn't the first time he'd been in this situation, he reminded himself, and it would undoubtedly not be the last. Still, he knew that the SEALs' best chance of finding Vanessa Lauton was to stake out the resort where she was believed to be staying and hope they could see her leave for the contact point.

The gas receipts Brent had come up with had narrowed the search drastically. With the given gas mileage and frequency with which Granger had filled up his tank, the SEALs thought they had identified the town where the contact point was located. Now they had to find out where in the town—and when.

Quinn's job was to find the when. The rest of his team would work on the where. Even now, Kel was staked out down the road in an old pickup truck waiting for Quinn to signal him when Vanessa headed his way. If Vanessa appeared at all, that is.

Brent was standing by with Granger's motorcycle on the outskirts of Suero, while Tristan and Seth were both on foot keeping an eye on different areas in town so they could move quickly in case Vanessa was spotted.

A car pulled out from a narrow drive a few hundred yards from the main entrance. Quinn narrowed his eyes as he looked through the binoculars, spotting the single figure inside the vehicle. With a rare smile, he gave the signal.

9

Something was wrong. Vanessa's steps slowed as she approached the edge of the alleyway. She glanced back over her shoulder, seeing Domingo sitting on his front porch. A rodent scampered along the edge of a garbage can, and she could hear birds calling from the trees nearby. She couldn't smell anything but overripe garbage and the lingering scent of diesel fuel.

Everything looked and smelled the way it always did, but it didn't *feel* the same. She took two more steps forward as the uneasiness grew. Over a week had passed since she had last seen Devin Granger, but she came each night, praying for a clue. She stopped once more and listened to the night. For months she had been coming here, but never before had she felt this impending sense of danger. Could someone have followed her? Had Granger somehow jeopardized her cover?

She wanted to continue forward. After all, this might be her last chance to get out before Akil Ramir arrived. Once he left, it might be too late. It might already be too late. Panic coursed through her as she debated whether to push forward or listen to the warning bells sounding in her mind.

Just as Vanessa started to turn, a flash of movement caught her attention. She whirled toward it, but before she could turn fully the huge man emerging from the shadows grabbed her, covering her mouth with his hand before she could scream for help.

"Shh. I'm here to help."

Even as he spoke, her training kicked in. She jammed her elbow back, barely missing a particularly sensitive spot of his anatomy. Still, the impact caused his hold to loosen slightly and evoked a muffled groan. She prepared to strike again, but instead stumbled forward when she was suddenly released.

"Vanessa, knock it off." The deep voice was clipped, nearly disguising the familiar Southern drawl. "I said I'm here to help."

Her heart pounding, her adrenaline still pumping, she turned and looked up into the man's face. Her eyes narrowed, and recognition dawned. "Seth?" she asked, realizing now that he had called her Vanessa, not Lina. "Seth!"

Seth's eyes widened as Vanessa launched herself at him again, only this time she wrapped her arms around his waist. She was too stunned to notice Seth's hesitation before his hands came around her to hug her back. She held on for several long seconds before asking the obvious. "What are you doing here?"

"I'm your new contact." Seth stepped back so he could see her more clearly. "Granger had a stroke a week ago."

"What?" Confusion crossed her face. "Why did they send you?"

"No one knew where your contact spot was, and the Agency said that you were told not to divulge information to anyone but Granger." Seth's shoulder lifted. "They sent my squad in to find you and make contact because they figured you would trust me."

"Your squad?"

"The Saint Squad. It's a five-man unit with SEAL Team Eight."

"You're a SEAL?"

Seth nodded.

Vanessa gaped at him, her mouth dropping open for a moment before she remembered why she was standing in a dark alley in the middle of the night. "I definitely want to hear all about this, but I don't have much time." Vanessa motioned down the alley and headed back to where she had hidden her car. "I'm not sure, but I think there's at least one leak within the CIA, maybe more," Vanessa told him. She stopped and faced him. "In fact, I can't be sure that your contact at the Agency didn't send you in so that he could find me."

"Rick Ellison knows your cover story. If he was working with Akil Ramir, he could have simply told him who you really are."

Vanessa nodded, recognizing the truth to his statement. "Even if we can trust him, I can't be sure who else I can trust."

"You can trust me."

Vanessa stared up at him, their eyes meeting. "I know."

Seth was silent for a moment as he looked down at her. Then he shook his head slightly and asked, "Do you have any new information since you last saw your contact?"

Vanessa recognized the subtle shield Seth was putting up between them and wondered if he could ever manage to trust her again. Trying to focus on the present, she took a deep breath. "Akil Ramir is due to arrive any day at La Playa," she began. "Once he gets here, I probably won't be able to get out, but something big is definitely being planned."

"How big?"

"9/11 big," Vanessa told him. "A few days ago I heard Halim talking about how he expected the casualties to be in the thousands. One of the guests also mentioned some antiaircraft guns he had ordered and how he needs them to arrive before he gets his shipment of helicopters."

"Helicopters?"

She nodded. "We're not talking about the little news choppers either. I think someone out there is either selling or stealing Z-10s."

"Why would they want Chinese attack helicopters?" Seth asked. "And how would they be able to get their hands on them?"

"I'm not sure. I haven't been able to figure out why all of these training camps keep popping up either. They're training for something, but I don't know what."

"We have to figure this out and soon."

Vanessa rolled her eyes. "Tell me something I don't already know."

"We need to set up a secondary contact point in case you can't get out," Seth said, ignoring her sarcasm. "Do you ever go out sailing?"

She shook her head. "Halim has me on a pretty tight leash right now."

"Is this Halim guy always at the resort?"

"Halim Karel. He's the top advisor for Akil at La Playa." Vanessa nodded. "He rarely leaves, which makes me think that at least one of the leaks in our intelligence has to be someone stationed here." She paused for a moment and looked around the alley before bringing her eyes back to Seth. "He said he has people in the right places," she continued. "I haven't been able to break into his e-mail accounts, but I can trace where his e-mails are coming from. None of them come from the U.S."

"I'll talk to my commander and see if we can track down the problem," Seth told her. "In the meantime, do you have any ideas for someplace we can use as a second meeting spot?"

"If I can't get here, I won't be able to get anywhere," Vanessa insisted. "When Akil is at the resort, there's no way I'll be able to get past security."

"If you can't get out, I'll have to come to you."

"Seth, there's no way you could get into the resort. There are armed guards everywhere, plus all sorts of alarm systems."

"Vanessa, I'm a SEAL," Seth reminded her. "This is what I've been trained to do." He retrieved a folded paper from his pocket and handed it to her. "This is a map of the resort. I need you to identify everything for me so I know what I'm up against."

"You're serious." Vanessa's eyes widened.

Seth nodded. "Let's start with where you live."

Slowly she nodded and pointed to the map. Then, hesitating a moment, she looked up at him. "Seth, I'm really glad you're here. I hope you can help me figure out what's going on before it's too late."

Seth stared at her a moment, a flash of something in his eyes that she couldn't identify. Then he spoke softly. "Don't worry, Vanessa. I've got your back."

She let his words seep in, and she could almost feel the weight on her shoulders lift. "I'm counting on it."

* * *

"Kel, you can't be serious." Brent's voice was charged with anxiety, an emotion that was extremely rare for him. He paced across the lounge of the boat that had been rented for the team to use as its home base. Turning back to face Kel, he shook his head and added, "It's too risky."

Kel understood his concern, but he had also made up his mind. They had to find the leak in the CIA. Until then, they wouldn't know who they could trust, and they couldn't risk losing the information Vanessa Lauton was feeding them. "I know you don't like this, but Amy is the only one who can get away with it."

"She's not an undercover operative. She hasn't been trained for this."

"Exactly," Kel agreed, throwing Brent off balance. "But she has been trained by the CIA as an intelligence officer, and that is exactly what we need her to be." Before Brent could voice any more objections, he continued. "If Vanessa is right, the leak has to be in the field office here in the Dominican Republic. By putting Amy in as an employee there, we'll have the eyes and ears we need to figure out who that leak is."

"What about her safety?"

"Brent, be logical for a minute. We're shorthanded here, especially now that we know we can't rely on intel," Kel insisted. "Besides, it's July, the prime time for government and military rotations. No one is going to suspect that an intelligence officer showing up for a new assignment is a plant. Not to mention that this source, whoever he is, doesn't know we're onto him."

Brent let out a frustrated sigh. "Will you at least let me go in as her backup? The field office is over an hour away. We can't leave her unprotected."

Kel let out a sigh of his own. Slowly he nodded. "I'll let you go and do your own digging, but you have to trust your wife to do her job."

As if on cue, Amy walked into the room holding a stack of papers. "I have the bios on the CIA personnel in Santo Domingo. The good news is that we only have five people there."

Resigned, Brent motioned to the coffee table. "Show me what you've got."

"Okay." Amy spread out the five profiles, each of which included a photo. "We have the chief of station and his deputy, one secretary, and two operatives."

"What about other support personnel?"

"The deputy doubles as the finance officer, but I doubt she's our leak." Amy tapped a finger on the picture of a woman who looked to be in her mid-forties. "She only transferred to this station in May and she came from headquarters. I couldn't find any way that Halim Karel could have come into contact with her."

"What about the others?"

"The chief and his secretary have both been here for two years. One of the operatives, Al Medrino, transferred in last summer from Rome, and the other one came from headquarters, but he got here only three weeks ago."

"Then our focus is on these three." Brent slid the three bios closer and pushed the other two aside. He studied them for a moment before looking up at his wife. "Once you figure out their work schedule, I can go check out their houses to see if I can find anything that way."

"Just don't get caught."

"I won't get caught if you promise to be careful," Brent countered.

Amy cocked her head to one side. "I'm always careful. You're the one who's always jumping out of moving vehicles and calling it training."

Kel stepped between them and put a hand on each of their shoulders. He shook his head, but humor and sarcasm tinged his voice. "You know, sometimes life gets really complicated having a married couple on my team."

"Hey, you're the one who hired her." Brent grinned.

"You weren't married to her then," Kel reminded him. "In fact, you probably owe me for bringing her on board."

Ignoring the banter, Amy fought back a grin of her own and tapped on her watch. "I hate to break this up, but I've got to go."

"Be careful," Brent insisted. "I'll be right behind you."

"Don't worry," Amy told him. "We'll figure this out."

Kel nodded. "Just don't take too long."

10

Seth leaned against the starboard side rail of the forty-two-foot fishing boat that he would be living on for the foreseeable future. He wasn't sure how Rick Ellison had managed to rent the boat without raising any suspicions, but he was grateful to have this extra resource at their disposal.

Behind him, Tristan Crowther appeared completely at ease as he stood at the helm. "We're coming up on La Playa," Tristan told him as he adjusted their heading and they neared the resort where Vanessa was currently staying.

Seth itched for a pair of binoculars to check out the beach and the neat little houses that made up the resort. Unfortunately, he knew that he had to trust Kel and Quinn, who were currently below deck using a variety of surveillance equipment to scope out the area.

The purpose of this reconnaissance mission was to determine the safest way to penetrate Ramir's defenses at the resort if it became necessary. Armed with the information Vanessa had given him the night before, Seth was confident his team could insert him if they needed to, but they wanted more than just an easy way in. They also needed to set up a warning signal for when Akil Ramir arrived in Punta Cana.

Seth knew that the rest of his squad was curious about his past, especially the part Vanessa played in it. He should be amused, he supposed, that Tristan had been the one brazen enough to ask about Vanessa. Tristan was almost as private about his personal life as Seth was. Of course, that had changed the year before when he had met his wife. Seth knew he could trust every man in his unit with his life, but when it came to Seth's personal life, he considered his a closed book.

Since seeing Vanessa last, Seth hadn't dated anyone seriously, and never once had he been able to mention Vanessa's name or the fact that his best friend from high school had been Mormon. Even when Seth had converted to the Mormon Church a few years earlier, he hadn't been able to open that door to his past and confide in his friends that he had known someone in the Church. Seth kept his eyes on the beach, his futile wish for a glimpse of Vanessa going unfulfilled.

As soon as they passed the resort, Kel came topside.

"Did you see anything?" Tristan asked.

"Lots of armed guards."

"We already knew about that," Seth commented, still keeping his eyes on the resort.

"We also think we located the storage facility where they're housing the guns they're shipping through there," Kel told them. "It's about a mile north of the resort, and it has a small airstrip right next to it."

"How are they getting planes in here without being detected?" Tristan asked. "There are tourists all over the place."

"Yeah, but this resort is isolated enough that if they came in at night, no one would hear them coming," Seth pointed out.

"And with the airstrip right next to the beach, they could come in under the radar, although I doubt the Dominican Republic has the kind of defenses we're used to dealing with," Kel added.

"So now what?" Seth asked.

"I'll send Quinn and Tristan in tonight to set up a sensor at the airstrip so we know when they have planes coming in," Kel told him. "And tonight you'll find out everything you can from Vanessa Lauton. We know that she's been feeding names of suspected terrorists to the CIA through Granger, but they don't know about the attack helicopters. We need to put people in position to help us figure out what we're fighting against."

"I thought we weren't going to involve anyone else in intelligence."

"We aren't, but we can pull in the rest of SEAL Team Eight to back us up."

"As long as Vanessa's identity remains need-to-know," Seth said in a commanding tone. "I don't want anyone else to know she's our source."

Kel's eyebrows shot up in response to Seth's tone, but his voice was mild when he spoke. "Don't worry, Seth. We'll keep her safe."

* * *

For the past few days Vanessa had been trying to bring her new reality into focus. The news that Devin Granger had suffered a stroke had been a big surprise, especially since he was barely fifty years old. And finding out that her new contact was the man she had been in love with for half of her life had completely altered her reality.

As she updated the reservations for the week, Vanessa let her mind wander back to the last time she had seen Seth. They had attended different colleges that were located over an hour apart. Still, they had remained close throughout their college years and had continued to date. She had just moved into a new apartment as she prepared to start her graduate work when her family had decided to surprise Seth and attend his graduation.

He had been so touched that her parents and grandparents had made such an effort. Her father had taken them all out to dinner afterward, bringing home the fact that Seth didn't have any family of his own to attend his graduation. After dinner, Seth had pulled her dad aside and made Vanessa wonder if perhaps he was finally planning to take their relationship to a new level.

Throughout college, she and Seth had talked about getting married after they graduated from college. Vanessa had accepted it as inevitable, both that they would get married and that her love for Seth would prevent her from being able to marry in the temple. Despite Seth's exposure to the gospel during their courtship, he had always insisted that religion wasn't for him.

As she watched Seth with her father, Vanessa had felt more fully than ever the gravity of the choice she would have to make. One possibility was to settle for a marriage outside the temple. The other option was to walk away from Seth and hope that someday she would find someone to marry within the Church.

After a moment, Seth had sat down beside her at the table, but Vanessa had focused on her parents. Seeing what they had, and seeing all of the blessings that had come into their lives because they had chosen a temple marriage had finally forced her to see what she had been avoiding for the past six years with Seth. She didn't want to settle for anything less than what her parents had. And her heart had been broken ever since. Now, with all of the years that had passed, she wondered if perhaps it was time to rethink what was really important to her.

Letting out a sigh, she knew it was probably too late to repair the damage to her relationship with Seth. She also knew that she couldn't consider her personal needs right now. She had a job to do, and she couldn't afford to let herself get distracted.

As she shifted the paper on her desk to look at the next reservation, her hand froze. The name glared up at her as if highlighted. Everyone at La Playa knew of Morenta. And everyone feared him. He had long been the most influential member of the drug cartel in Colombia, but he rarely left his villa there. If he was coming to La Playa and Akil Ramir was expected soon, Vanessa was afraid to imagine what horror they had planned for the United States.

* * *

Amy stepped into the suite of offices used by the Central Intelligence Agency's local field office. She was immediately spotted by the pretty young woman behind the large desk in front of her. "Can I help you?"

From the personnel file she had read, Amy recognized the woman as Gina Morgan, the chief's secretary. Offering a smile, she introduced herself. "I'm Amy Miller."

"Oh, the new employee." She stood up and motioned down the hall. "Come on, and I'll introduce you to the chief of station." She glanced back and added, "By the way, I'm Gina."

"Nice to meet you," Amy said as she followed Gina to the office at the end of the hall.

Gina rapped on the door twice before pushing it open and poking her head inside. "I have your new employee here to meet you."

"Thank you, Gina." The chief of station stood up and offered his hand, a look of surprise crossing his tanned face as he realized that Amy was six feet tall, an inch or so taller than he was. "Amy, I'm Carl Dowdy."

"Nice to meet you." Amy shook his hand and then sat in the chair he indicated.

"I have to admit I was surprised when I received the cable telling me that I was getting another employee." Carl's dark eyes looked at her with curiosity as he tapped a finger on his desk. "Last year the director of operations was threatening to take away one of my operatives."

"That's what I heard," Amy told him. "I guess they decided to shut down the office in Puerto Rico instead, since that's where I thought I was going until last week."

"It seems like we're always the last to hear the news out here." He shrugged. "Anyway, we don't really have an office set up for you yet, but you can use Al's desk for the time being. He's on vacation until next week."

"Really, where did he go?" Amy asked, skipping over whose desk she was using and zeroing in on the whereabouts of her coworker.

"He's on home leave visiting his family," he told her. "Florida, I think."

A knock on the door interrupted the conversation, and Gina poked her head into the room. "Excuse me, Carl, but you have a call from Washington."

Carl nodded as he reached for the phone. "Can you introduce Amy around and show her Al's desk?"

"Sure." She motioned for Amy to follow her.

As soon as Amy exited Carl's office, Gina closed the door behind them and started down a short hallway. "So how long have you been working for the Agency?"

"Three years," Amy told her. "How about you?"

"About the same," she said. "I took a job at headquarters and then was lucky enough to get this assignment." She paused long enough to knock on a door before pushing it open. "Hey, Cindy, this is Amy Miller. She just transferred in."

"Welcome." Cindy smiled and stood up. "After Gina finishes showing you around, come on back to my office. I have a project I can have you start on."

Amy nodded as Gina ushered her out of the office, calling out, "She'll be back."

As soon as the door closed, she added, "Be careful. Since the day she arrived, she always has a new project to hand off. I think she spends her spare time dreaming of things to have us do so we won't be idle."

"I gather she has you working on something too?"

"Always." Gina nodded. "Today it's tracking down a money transfer she thought looked suspicious. Yesterday I got to alphabetize the list of people Customs currently has on their watch list. It's never ending."

"Sounds like I won't get bored in this job," Amy commented.

"Not a chance," she agreed.

11

Seth waited ten minutes, his concern growing with each passing second. Vanessa had managed to sneak out every night over the past week, and he had been impressed with how punctual she was. He had also grown increasingly worried that his feelings for her hadn't dimmed in the slightest over the past six years since he had seen her last.

In many ways she hadn't changed much over the years. She was still independent, and her need to prove that she could stand on her own two feet was still an essential part of her personality. Her vulnerability was still there as well, and she was still trying to hide it like she had in high school. He didn't know why that had always attracted him, the way she could stand up to the biggest bully one minute and then the moment they were alone confide in him with her deepest fears as well as her hopes and her dreams.

Of course, back then her hopes and dreams had never included becoming a spy. He wanted to ask her what had possessed her to get into the world of espionage, but their time together so far had been extremely limited. Each night, Vanessa arrived on time, stayed just long enough to pass along any new information, and then she was gone. Now, for the first time since his arrival, he was waiting and she was late.

Logically he knew that Vanessa might not be able to slip out each night to meet him, but since finding out exactly how risky it was for her to sneak out at all, he had become more and more paranoid that something would happen to her. When he heard footsteps, his concern heightened.

He wasn't hearing quiet, barely audible footsteps like he had the night before. Rather, he heard what sounded like two people making their way down the alley, their voices muffled. Seth drew his weapon and ducked into a dark doorway.

"No one's here," one man said in Spanish.

"Of course not," the other responded. "I told you it was your imagination."

"I'm telling you, she was here." The footsteps drew closer, close enough to cause Seth to grip the handle of his gun tighter.

"And I think you're seeing things," came the response. "Come on. Let's get out of here. It smells."

Seth listened to the retreating footsteps and played the conversation over again in his head. If these men were from La Playa, Vanessa's cover could be in greater jeopardy than he'd thought. Perhaps she had come tonight but hadn't been able to lose the men tailing her. Whatever the reason, Seth wasn't going to wait another day to make sure she was safe.

* * *

Vanessa ducked under the leaves of a palm tree and then took a sharp left to avoid the motion sensor in front of her. This weaving obstacle course to get past the many layers of security at La Playa had become second nature to her over the past year, but tonight she had encountered something new. A flat tire. She couldn't believe she had managed to get all the way off of the compound only to find that the car she kept hidden couldn't take her the rest of the way.

She had changed the tire, but by the time she was done it was too late for her to make the rendezvous point and get back without being missed. She had managed to get most of the grease off of her hands using a towel she kept in the car for just such an emergency, but she was anxious to get back to her casita and shower off the rest of the dirt and grease the experience had left on her.

Stepping into the darkness behind a nearby building, she waited for the sound of footsteps to indicate that the night patrol on this side of the resort was passing by. She had to wait for nearly fifteen minutes before she heard the patrol approaching the far side of the building. She circled opposite of them, finally reaching the path that led to her casita.

As always, she ducked behind a thick palm tree next to the side entrance of her casita and listened for a moment before opening the door and slipping inside. She closed the door behind her and started for the kitchen. It was then that she noticed that the curtains had been closed. Every night when she left, she made sure several lights were on to give the appearance that she was still at home. She also left the curtains open so that it wouldn't look like she was trying to hide anything, but rather that she was simply in the back part of her house.

Quietly, she stepped back to the entryway and reached into the pottery urn filled with decorative silk flowers—and her pistol. With both hands on the gun, she kept her arms straight so that the gun barrel was pointed at the ground as she began searching her house.

Not sensing any movement in the living area, she moved forward, keeping her back against the wall. As soon as she determined that there wasn't anyone in the living room or kitchen, she started for the bedroom. Holding the gun in her right hand, she reached out to push the door with her left. Her heart skipped a beat when the door opened without any effort on her part.

The gun came up at the same time someone grabbed her wrist to force her hand back down and wrestle the gun away from her.

Vanessa's eyes stayed on her gun, panic flashing through her before she lifted her eyes to identify the intruder. Then she heard the familiar voice.

"Stop, it's just me." Seth held her hand and the gun firmly as he waited for her to register the fact that he was standing in the doorway to her bedroom. He then turned the gun so that the handle was facing Vanessa and handed it back to her.

"Do you have any idea how lucky you are I didn't shoot you?" Vanessa took the gun from him and moved back down the hall to put it away. She looked over her shoulder as he followed her into the living room. "How did you get in here? And how did you get past security?"

"You're full of questions tonight," Seth mumbled. Then, shaking his head, he looked down into her eyes. "I told you I would come to you if you didn't show up. I wanted to make sure you were okay, especially when I saw two guys come into the alley tonight looking for you."

"What?" Vanessa's eyes whipped up to meet his. "Who?"

"Sorry, but I haven't been here long enough to know all of the players," Seth reminded her. His voice grew serious as he added, "They were speaking in Spanish, and both of them sounded like they were in their early twenties."

"I have no idea who that could have been." Vanessa's stomach tightened as she considered the possible implications of someone knowing the meeting place.

"We can't meet there anymore," Seth insisted. "I'll come to you from now on."

"That's too risky for you."

Seth's eyebrows winged up, half in amusement, half in challenge. "What do you suggest then?"

"There's an old boathouse on the beach that isn't used anymore. The patrols check it each night around midnight, but then they don't go back over there until after two," Vanessa said. "If you can get all the way to my house without being spotted, getting there should be a piece of cake."

"Okay, I'll meet you there every night at one," Seth agreed. "So what happened to you tonight?"

"I had a flat tire." Vanessa moved to the kitchen sink and squirted some liquid soap on her hands before turning on the water. Looking up at him, she added, "I still don't understand how you managed to get past all the security."

"Very carefully." Seth smirked at her, reminding her of the man she had dated so many years before. "Have there been any new developments today?"

"Yeah, a big one." Vanessa shut off the faucet and grabbed a hand towel. Leaning back against the kitchen counter, she dried her hands and looked up at him. She still couldn't quite believe he was here. Her heart ached a little as she thought of what could have been, but she pushed the past aside to focus on the present. "Morenta is due to arrive next week."

"The drug lord?"

She nodded. "I've only met him once, and believe me, his reputation of being ruthless is well deserved. He is one scary man."

"I've heard plenty of stories, including the one about how he killed two of his rival drug lords in one day when they tried to hone in on his territory." Seth shook his head. "You said you met him once before. When was that?"

"Almost a year ago," Vanessa told him. "I was still managing the restaurant here at the time, so I couldn't pass on the information that he was here until after he had left."

"Do you have any idea why he was here?"

"I figured he was here to buy weapons, just like most people who come to this place. Now I'm not so sure. He showed up less than a week after his nephew was arrested in the U.S. for smuggling." Vanessa tossed the hand towel aside and shook her head. "Akil is supposed to be coming soon, and I doubt it's a coincidence that they're both showing up about the same time."

"What are you thinking?"

Her chest ached as she considered the possibilities. "I think the drug cartel may be giving financial backing to Akil Ramir. If that's the case, we have a bigger problem on our hands than I thought."

"Think for a minute." Seth slid onto a stool next to the counter. "What are they trying to accomplish?"

"Everyone here hates Americans. It's hard to know what they want except to see the United States suffer."

"But suffer how?" Seth posed the question before suggesting some possibilities. "Do they want to kill Americans, cripple us economically? Are they trying to keep us out of their business, or do they want a full-scale war with the U.S.?"

"I don't know." Vanessa shook her head, having wondered the same thing countless times. "If the drug cartel is involved, I have to think that weakening our borders would be a major objective, especially with the new surveillance grids that are being set up along the Mexican border."

"What surveillance grids?"

Vanessa looked at him a little sheepishly. "I know I can trust you, but you have to understand that what I'm telling you is top secret." She took a breath and forced herself to continue. "In response to all of the problems with illegal immigrants coming over the Mexican border, a team of scientists came up with a new solution, a series of motion detectors along the border between the southwestern U.S. and Mexico. They're supposed to sense both ground movements and also be equipped with a radar system that will pick up low-flying aircraft. The last I heard, the first stage of this new electronic surveillance system was supposed to become active around now."

"Do you think Akil found out about the new security system?"

"I don't know. None of this makes any sense." Vanessa shook her head. "The increased security of our borders is going to have a huge impact on the drug trade, but I don't know how Morenta or Akil could know about the surveillance grids. I also don't know how any of this would play in with these training camps and the helicopters I heard them talking about."

"I'll do some digging on my end," Seth told her. He started to reach for her hand as he had so many times in the past and then suddenly dropped it back to his side. "I'll meet you tomorrow."

"Seth, wait." Vanessa reached out and put a hand on his arm. She hesitated a moment and then forced herself to say the words. "We need to talk about what happened before."

His jaw clenched for a moment. "I'll meet you tomorrow," Seth repeated and silently moved to the door. With a last glance at her, he pulled the door open and disappeared into the night.

12

Brent watched Carl Dowdy pull out of his driveway at precisely seven-thirty. Patiently, Brent watched from his hiding place across the street until Dowdy's wife loaded her kids into the car to leave for school. He counted the family members as they got into the vehicle to make sure they had all indeed left their residence. As soon as they pulled away, Brent made his way down the block and circled back so that he could enter Dowdy's house through the small backyard.

If his information was correct, he only had twenty minutes before the wife would return, followed shortly by the cleaning lady.

Picking the lock took only a few seconds, but bypassing the alarm took several precious minutes. Brent quickly scouted out the main level and immediately focused on the small office. He pulled what looked like an oversized flash drive from his pocket and plugged it into the computer. The device immediately lit up to indicate that it was doing its job of copying the entire hard drive.

While the computer files were copying, Brent turned his focus to the desk drawers. Finding nothing of particular interest, he pulled open the top drawer of the filing cabinet. A glance through the financial records revealed nothing unusual, but a tattered file labeled "vacations" caught his eye. Brent pulled it open, his eyes narrowing as he spied an upcoming airline itinerary.

Brent pulled a mini-camera from his pocket and methodically photographed several of the pages in the file. After a quick search of the rest of the office, he retrieved the flash drive from the computer and quickly headed upstairs hoping for more clues.

* * *

"Everyone's financial records are clean," Kel stated as he took a seat on the couch in Brent and Amy's temporary apartment in Santo Domingo. He had made the drive to their location so that he could meet with Brent and collect the intelligence Brent and Amy had gathered over the past two days. "Even Dowdy didn't show any unusual deposits or unusual purchases."

"But that doesn't mean he doesn't have an offshore account somewhere," Brent said. "The fact that he has a trip planned to Colombia worries me. That country is still off-limits for intelligence personnel. The only ones who go in there are on assignment. Besides, if Dowdy was traveling for the Agency, he shouldn't have had the itinerary at home."

"I'll check with Ellison and see if he knows anything about it," Kel agreed. "What about the others?"

"Everyone else looks clean," Brent told him. "Al Medrino is still on vacation, so it was easy to check out his place. The apartment barely looked lived in. Not a lot of furniture, only a couple of changes of clothes, and no personal photographs or anything else that would identify who lives there."

Kel leaned forward and rested his elbows on his knees. "Maybe he's our guy and he's left for good."

"Could be," Brent conceded. "Did Quinn figure out where he is right now?"

"He flew out of here to Miami, but he never cleared Customs," Kel told him. "We aren't sure if he called in some special privileges to get past Customs since he's Agency, or if he turned around and left the country on a different flight."

"I hate spying on spies," Brent muttered.

Kel nodded in agreement. "What about the secretary?"

"She's the complete opposite of Medrino. Talk about clutter." Brent shook his head. "She has photographs all over the place, a couple of days' worth of dishes in the sink, and clothes all over her bedroom floor."

"Any chance you found a diary?"

"Nope, and nothing exciting on her computer either," Brent told him. "The only thing that was a bit odd was that she didn't have a password on her computer."

"Yeah, but if she lives alone, she probably doesn't figure she needs one," Kel noted.

"Maybe, but most people who work in intelligence aren't so cavalier about security. In fact, a lot are downright paranoid."

"It sounds like she doesn't fit the norm there," Kel agreed. "For the time being, we'll keep Amy in place. Hopefully she'll pick up on something that will point us in the right direction. You can work from here and keep looking for any connections between the CIA staff here and Ramir's organization."

"In other words, you want me to keep tailing Amy's new coworkers."

"Exactly."

* * *

Vanessa stepped onto the cooling sand, the breeze lifting the ends of her hair off of her back. For once the weather was perfect, not too humid, with a light breeze coming off of the water. Normally Vanessa used days like this to help bring her life into focus and remind herself that there were still good people in the world, people who needed her to make these sacrifices to keep them safe. She could live without their thanks or knowledge of the work she did, but today she felt like she was losing herself and couldn't quite escape her assumed identity. The information that Morenta would be arriving in a matter of days scared her more than she would ever admit, even to herself.

Vanessa fought against the memory of his last visit, the memory of the woman he had killed in a cold, calculated rage because her husband had not cooperated quickly enough. She hadn't seen it happen, but she had heard the man argue with Morenta, and she had heard Morenta's eerily calm voice followed by a single gunshot. Then she had seen the body, the life drained out of the young woman, a woman who had barely begun to live.

The helplessness had been overwhelming as had been the fear. Those emotions washed over her now. Alongside them was the concern that her presence wouldn't make a difference despite the many sacrifices she had made over the past year.

She had known coming into this assignment that it would be difficult to be cut off from her family for so long, even though everyone but her parents thought she was living in Virginia with her make-believe husband. She had never dreamed that she would be put in a situation where she would have Seth in her life again, especially in such a limited way. Seeing him over the past few days had reawakened memories and feelings she had locked away long ago, feelings she wasn't sure she was prepared to deal with right now.

She stepped closer to the water and let the surf wash over her bare feet. She let her mind wander, remembering the summer vacation she and Seth had taken to South Carolina with her family. Together they had walked on the beach near Charleston, sharing their dreams of the future. At the time she had still been undecided of what she wanted to do, or even what she wanted to declare as her major in college. Seth, on the other hand, was bound and determined to become a Navy pilot.

When she had seen him last, he was within weeks of reporting for his first assignment. Where he went after that, she didn't know, but obviously he had altered the direction of his career at some point if he had ended up as a SEAL.

Now that she thought about it, she wouldn't be surprised if Seth had been recruited into the SEAL program. His background would have made him the perfect candidate in so many ways. Not only was he athletic and one of the fastest runners in the state of Georgia throughout high school and college, but by the time he graduated high school he was already fluent in French and was becoming so in Arabic. He also had that heartfelt patriotism that penetrated every aspect of who he was.

Down the beach, she spotted an armed patrol headed her way. During the first few months she was at La Playa, her stomach had jumped with nerves each time a patrol approached. Now those nerves had deadened, leaving her stomach with a constant gnawing fear, not so much of discovery, but of failure.

She stared out at the sun hanging low in the sky, mentally reviewing the facts she had ascertained in recent weeks. The comments she had overheard in the dining room all pointed to something big, some single strike that could potentially kill thousands of American citizens. Antiaircraft guns, helicopters, and many other potentially deadly tools of war continued to flow through La Playa, and somehow the intelligence community had sprung a leak. Then there were the training camps that had been created around the region.

Vanessa didn't know what these camps were being used for. She had simply become resourceful in revealing their locations. Perhaps if she knew what they were doing at these training camps, she would be able to put this complicated puzzle together. As her mind turned to Seth once more, she considered the fact that she might not be the only one uncovering new intelligence. Maybe once all of the facts were on the table, so to speak, the picture would begin to take shape a bit more clearly.

* * *

Darkness was already falling when Seth made his way to the crew quarters of the fishing boat to prepare for his meeting with Vanessa. In the compartment beside him, Quinn and Tristan were currently monitoring the sensors they had placed several days earlier at the airstrip near La Playa. No one was happy that they had already tracked several planes flying in since they had placed the sensors, averaging two a night.

Seth considered the information that Vanessa had passed to them during the two weeks, almost afraid to find out what she might uncover next. He drew out his sidearm and began to clean it. When the door opened, he looked up to see Kel walk in, frustration vibrating from him.

"What's wrong?"

"I just got off of the phone with Ellison." Kel shook his head.

"And?"

"It looks like we're in the middle of a territorial war between the CIA and the Navy," Kel told him. "Even though our orders are to stay here as long as necessary to protect Vanessa, a new CIA operative is due to arrive tomorrow to take over as Vanessa's contact."

"What?" Seth demanded. "How can intel possibly want to mess with changing things up at this point?"

Kel let out a frustrated sigh. "I don't agree with it either, Seth, but like it or not, we aren't in charge this time."

"What did Ellison say about the potential leak?"

"He did some extra checking for me on the staff here," Kel told him. "Apparently, the trip the chief of station has planned to Colombia was cleared through the CIA. Ellison couldn't tell me why he's going, but it sounded like it was Agency business."

"What about the others?"

"Nothing really suspicious except that no one is sure where Al

Medrino is on his leave." Kel shrugged. "I can't tell if they really don't know where he is or if they aren't telling."

"I still don't understand why they would want to pull us out, especially since the contact point appears to have been jeopardized."

"That's another thing." Kel grimaced. "We think the two men you heard in the alley are local thugs who were hoping for a quick score. The locals have reported several muggings and assaults in the area. There's always a possibility that those guys had seen Vanessa on a different night and had chosen her for their next target."

"But we can't be sure," Seth insisted. "Whoever the leak is might have learned that someone was sneaking out, and had men waiting there so they could identify Vanessa."

"Look, Seth, Ellison wants to leave us in, but his boss is convinced that the leak doesn't exist. He said if there is a leak, he's sure it isn't within the CIA," Kel told him. "Apparently he kept going on about how they do routine polygraphs on all of their employees and how so much of their intelligence is given only on a need-to-know basis."

"I have two words for him," Seth said simply. "Aldridge Ames."

Kel gave a wry grin at the mention of the CIA employee who had been convicted more than a decade earlier for leaking sensitive information that had ultimately severely crippled the CIA before he had been identified. "Seems to me I may have already mentioned those particular words to him. Unfortunately, that incident didn't have much of an impact on Ellison's boss. The good news is that Ellison neglected to tell his boss that he placed Amy in the field office here. Maybe she or Brent will find something."

"Still, we can't leave Vanessa in there." Seth's voice took on a sense of urgency. "Once the new contact person knows who she is, her cover is at risk."

"What do you suggest?"

"I think it's time to pull her out of there completely."

"The CIA isn't ready to lose her as a source," Kel reminded him. Before Seth could argue, he held up a hand. "But we could leak the word that Fahid Ramir is sick. If she had a reason to leave for a few days, we might be able to buy the extra time we need to make sure her cover is still intact."

"The CIA will never go for that, especially if they don't think there's a leak."

"I wasn't planning on telling them." Kel's eyebrows lifted. "My orders are to protect our source. That's what I intend to do."

Seth nodded slowly. "It's better than nothing."

13

Vanessa swung open her door, only to find Halim standing on the other side, his hand lifted to knock. She put a hand to her chest as her racing heart settled back into its normal rhythm. "You startled me."

"I have something for you." Halim's eyes met hers, and once again she could see the spark of interest there.

"Not more shoes," Vanessa said, hoping to keep the conversation light.

"No." Halim granted her a small smile. "This is something that will last longer."

She gave him a quizzical look as he drew a plain white box from his pocket and extended it to her.

"What is it?" Vanessa kept her eyes on his for a moment before curiosity won and she pulled off the lid. Her breath caught in her chest when she saw diamonds winking at her atop black velvet. She fingered the elegant bracelet before looking back at Halim, her expression guarded.

"Don't you like it?"

"It's beautiful, Halim," Vanessa began, struggling to find the right words. She wondered what the real Lina would do and realized it didn't matter. She couldn't allow Halim's feelings to distract her from her mission. "I'm sorry, but I can't accept such a generous gift."

"Of course you can," he insisted. "This is a token of my affection. It says nothing of your feelings for me." He lifted the bracelet from the box and carefully clasped it around her wrist. "But I will continue to hope that someday you will feel for me as I do for you."

"Halim . . ." Vanessa started, feeling somewhat like a dog that had just been collared and tagged.

He held her hand up and drew it to his lips. "I will see you tomorrow."

Vanessa watched him disappear back into the night before looking back down to the sparkles on her wrist. *Such beauty,* she thought, *and so many complications.*

* * *

Seth waited impatiently beside two palm trees a few yards from the boathouse. He was prepared to convince Vanessa to come with him tonight, but he was also prepared for the possibility that her cover might have already been jeopardized. He was dressed completely in black, a handgun tucked into the waist of his cargo pants and concealed beneath his loose T-shirt. His spare weapon was strapped to his calf.

Because there was always a risk of being spotted, he was without the combat vest he typically wore. And instead of his typical lightweight headset, he wore a more compact communications device disguised as a Bluetooth cell phone attachment. He would have preferred his usual gear, but at least this way he could stay in communication with the rest of his squad.

Even though Seth didn't dare make a sound, the mini-transmitter was switched on so that the rest of the squad would hear everything Seth heard. Or nearly everything.

The sound of footsteps was muffled, but he could hear Vanessa moving toward him. Still, he stepped farther into the darkness until he saw her emerge through the dense foliage. She quietly scanned the area before moving through the open doorway to the boathouse.

Seth waited a full minute to ensure she hadn't been followed before crossing a small clearing and entering the boathouse. Vanessa was standing in a splash of moonlight just inside the door. Seth's eyes met hers, and for a moment he simply stared. He didn't know how it was possible that he could still love her even after all of the hurt she had caused him and all of the time that had passed, yet somehow time had not erased what they had once shared.

He didn't dwell on how things had ended between them, however. Instead he thought only of getting her to safety. He stepped toward her. "There's been a change of plans. We're pulling you out tonight."

Her eyes reflected both relief and panic. "But we don't know enough yet."

Seth opened his mouth to explain, but then he spotted the bracelet on her wrist. He reached out and fingered the tennis bracelet, the diamonds sparkling in the moonlight that spilled in through the doorway. "Where did you get this?"

"Halim gave it to me." Vanessa looked a little embarrassed as she glanced down at it and gave a little shrug.

"You shouldn't be wearing something like that out here. If the moonlight reflects off one of those diamonds, someone might see you."

"I know, but I couldn't get it off one-handed. Halim insisted I put it on after he brought it to me, but the clasp is too tight for me to undo by myself."

Seth leaned down to examine the bracelet more closely. A sinking feeling settled in his stomach as his eyes darted to hers. Then he heard the movement and he knew it was too late. Though his instinct was to reach for a weapon, Seth surprised Vanessa by pulling her closer.

Leaning down, he covered her mouth with his, kissing her as though no time had passed since they had dated so long ago. He heard her little gasp of surprise and then felt her arms encircle his waist as she leaned into the kiss.

One part of his brain remained alert and aware of his surroundings, yet somehow he was also able to be absorbed in the moment. For so many years he had dreamt of doing this, of holding Vanessa in his arms again. He tried to remind himself that Vanessa had refused him once, but now, for one insane moment, he wondered if she would change her mind if she knew . . .

Then the voice cut through the darkness.

"What do we have here?" Akil Ramir stood in the doorway. He rubbed his dark mustache, his expression both calm and curious. Behind him, Halim stood silently, his eyes hard, his fingers clasped tightly around the handle of his pistol.

"Uncle Akil." Vanessa spoke automatically in French, her voice clearly surprised as she pulled out of Seth's embrace, stepping in front of him so that she was between Seth and Akil. "I didn't know you had arrived."

"That much is obvious."

"Lina, aren't you going to introduce me?" Seth said in French, moving to Vanessa's side.

When she looked up at him, speechless, he continued as though amused by how flustered she was. "I am Seth Billaud, Lina's fiancé."

Halim's expression twisted into a scowl. Beside him, Akil's eyebrows lifted as he studied Seth. "How is it that I did not know of your engagement?"

"We only settled it tonight," Seth continued, reaching for Vanessa's hand and giving it a squeeze. "I spoke to her father only yesterday to ask his permission. Unfortunately, Fahid has become ill and wishes to see Lina. He asked me to escort her to the United States."

"Why didn't you announce yourself when you arrived?" Halim asked now.

"Forgive me, but after working for Fahid for many years, I am not accustomed to announcing my presence," Seth said smoothly. "In my line of work, I rarely walk through the front door."

"Exactly what did you do for my brother?"

Seth let a smile cross his face. "I guess you could say I was one of his managers."

"Check it out," Akil ordered Halim. "See if he really visited my brother recently."

Halim nodded and retrieved a cell phone from his pocket before stepping out into the night.

Seth forced himself to appear relaxed as he prayed that his team would be able to intercept Halim's call. Feeling the tension still emanating from Vanessa, he gave her hand another squeeze and then linked his fingers through hers. "It is fortunate for us that you are here to share our happy news."

Akil studied Seth for a moment before turning his gaze on Vanessa. "Why did you never mention Seth to me before?"

Vanessa stiffened slightly, but Seth was pleased to see that she had that look in her eyes that said she was willing to fight. "Exactly when was I supposed to talk to you about such things? You keep me here in this gilded cage, and I never see you."

"You of all people know how demanding my work is."

"How would I know that? Halim tells me nothing of what you are doing, or even when you are coming." Vanessa stood a little taller. "My father trusted me in everything he did. You trust me with nothing."

"I have trusted you to manage this resort," Akil said, his own voice becoming somewhat defensive. "Besides, how can I trust a woman who sneaks around with a man I've never met?"

"Seth was one of my father's most trusted advisors," Vanessa improvised. "But he was fortunate not to be on the yacht the night we were all arrested."

"I see." Akil kept his eyes on Seth as Halim entered the boathouse once more. Slowly, he turned to face Halim and asked, "Well?"

"He speaks the truth," Halim said with some surprise. "Your brother has become quite ill, but he had a visitor yesterday." He motioned to Seth. "A big man named Seth Billaud."

Seth hid the relief pulsing through him. Hoping he appeared relaxed, he motioned to the door and looked at Akil once more. "Forgive me, but we really must be going. I promised to bring Lina to see her father as soon as possible."

"That will have to wait."

"What?" Vanessa asked before Seth had the opportunity to respond. "My father is ill. I need to see him."

"Your father understands that some things are more important than a visit with his daughter."

"Like what?"

"We are relocating," Akil said simply. "The Americans are watching us here."

"How?"

To Seth's surprise, Akil answered her despite his presence. "They must have someone working here." Akil motioned to the door. "We are leaving right now."

"Now?" Vanessa's eyes widened. "I haven't even packed."

Fear settled in the pit of Seth's stomach as he considered that he might have to leave Vanessa behind despite the fact that he had no idea where Akil was taking her. "Fahid is not going to be happy if I return without Lina."

"You're coming with us."

"Excuse me?" Seth managed.

"The Americans are watching too closely. I'm not taking the chance that you will be apprehended."

"They don't have anything on me."

"Perhaps not, but my brother wants to keep Lina safe," Akil stated. "I am tasking you with that responsibility."

"Then why must she remain with you?" Seth somehow managed to keep his voice calm. "I can protect her better on my own turf."

"With me is the only place I can be sure that she will be safe over the next few weeks." Akil's voice was clipped. "Enough of this. We are leaving."

Seth fought against his instincts to lash out when Akil motioned to Halim, who then moved forward and removed the communications device from his ear. Seth was confident that he could take both of these men, especially since Halim was the only one with a weapon drawn. He couldn't risk it though, not with the possibility that Vanessa might not survive the encounter. Equally important was the fact that whatever terrorist activity Akil was planning might go forward with or without his involvement.

"You won't need this," Halim said quietly, now holding the Bluetooth ear attachment in his hand. Halim glanced over at Vanessa briefly, his eyes flat, and then motioned to both of them with the gun he held.

"Take his weapons too," Akil told Halim even as his eyes met Seth's. "After all, he won't need those while we are traveling."

Seth considered for a moment before reaching for the handgun he had hidden in his waistband. He pulled it free and handed it to Halim.

"And the other one," Akil insisted.

Seth's eyebrows lifted, and he calmly reached down to his leg, where his second handgun was holstered. "You are as perceptive as your brother."

"I would hope that I am more perceptive than my brother. After all, I'm not in prison." Akil tilted his head and motioned to the door. "Shall we?"

"Are you going to at least tell us where we're going?" Vanessa asked Akil.

"You will find out soon enough." With that, Akil stepped outside and escorted Seth and Vanessa to the airfield.

Seth looked out into the night, hoping, praying that his team had heard enough to know that he and Vanessa were going to be on the next plane that left La Playa. With the sensors they had placed at the airfield, he knew they could at least track when they left. If all went well, they might also be able to narrow down their heading.

His confidence that his team could track them faltered when he looked up and saw three planes in the airfield. Two were idling at the far end of the runway, and the other was in the process of taking off.

As though she sensed his concern, Vanessa gave his hand a squeeze. She looked up at him, unspoken questions shining in her eyes.

Seth leaned closer and spoke softly. "You know I won't ever let anything happen to you."

Tears glistened in Vanessa's eyes, but she quickly blinked them away. Moments later, they were airborne.

14

"What?" Brent asked incredulously. He sat down on the couch in the apartment he was currently sharing with his wife in Santo Domingo and adjusted the communications headset he wore so that he could talk to Kel without worrying that someone else was listening in. When he had received Kel's call, the last thing he had expected to hear was that Seth was on an airplane with Akil Ramir. "I don't understand why Seth didn't take him out if he had the chance."

"I don't get it either," Kel admitted. "Maybe having the Lauton girl there complicated things."

"Either that or he was worried that Ramir's plans were going to move forward whether he was alive or not." Brent rubbed a hand over his face as he considered the possibilities.

"Have you and Amy had any luck narrowing down who our mole is?"

"We haven't found anything substantial," Brent told him. "I'll do some more digging into Medrino's background today. Something is definitely suspicious there, but he isn't due back for a few more days."

"Do what you can. Maybe we can use the mole to our advantage in figuring out exactly what Ramir is up to."

Brent nodded to the empty room before signing off. He then went into the kitchen, where Amy was pouring herself a bowl of cereal. She looked up at him and asked, "Anything new from Kel?"

"Yeah." Brent let out a sigh and dropped onto the chair across the kitchen table from her. "Akil Ramir showed up last night at the contact point. He's now on a plane somewhere with Seth and Vanessa."

"What?"

"That's what I said too." Brent leaned back and stretched out his legs. "Apparently Seth passed himself off as one of Fahid Ramir's advisors, and so far Akil seems to be buying the story."

"Yeah, but how long do you think he can keep up appearances? He wasn't prepped for this."

"Actually, he was," Brent admitted. "Sort of."

"What do you mean?"

"We knew that we might have to get him inside Ramir's organization, but we thought we were going to have to take someone out in order to insert him."

"You were going to kill someone so that Seth could take his place?"

"Forcibly remove someone," Brent corrected and then shrugged. "At least, that's what we had hoped to do."

"Yeah, but he still wouldn't have been prepared to pretend he used to work for Fahid."

Brent shook his head. "Seth was on the mission when we apprehended Fahid Ramir and his family," he reminded her. "And that wasn't the first time we tried." He reached across the table and squeezed her hand. "Seth has a good handle on the Ramir family, but I don't know how long he'll be able to keep up appearances. We need to find that leak, and we need to figure out where Seth is now."

* * *

Vanessa had no idea where she was. She also wasn't sure whether to be relieved or terrified that Akil and Halim appeared to accept Seth's story that he used to work for Fahid Ramir. During the year she had been at La Playa, she had seen more than one individual arrive blindfolded or drugged to ensure they could not identify their location. The fact that Seth remained completely alert during their flight indicated one of two things. Akil bought his story, or he planned to kill Seth. Chills ran through her as she considered the possibilities. She glanced at him sitting beside her. Surprisingly, he looked relaxed, and she couldn't help but wonder if he had been placed undercover before. She had been trained not to react to the unexpected, but Seth could have taught the class.

Seth shifted to look at her. "We're about to land."

Vanessa nodded and glanced out the window. Dawn was breaking, but she couldn't see anything but ocean. She swallowed hard as she considered the fact that she and Seth were now on their own without any backup. "Do you think my father will understand why I didn't come?"

Seth nodded, apparently understanding that she wasn't referring to Fahid Ramir but rather his squad. "He has been in the business a long time. He will figure out why we had to change our plans."

"I hope so," Vanessa said as she felt the plane begin its descent. Fifteen minutes later they touched down, and the nerves in her stomach multiplied.

As soon as she stepped off the plane with Seth, she turned to Akil and asked, "Where are we?"

"Welcome to my home away from home." Akil moved away from the plane and motioned behind them.

Vanessa turned, and her jaw dropped open. A huge building was situated several hundred yards away, where the dense jungle gave way to a sandy white beach. The structure was the size of a ten-story hotel, the first two floors sprawling across the strip of land in front of the beach. The dense jungle on the other side of the building had been cut back at least a hundred yards so that anyone approaching would be visible to the occupants.

In the center, the building continued upward with balconies visible on the top four floors, several of them manned by men with automatic weapons. A Z-10 attack helicopter sat idle on the helicopter pad situated to the left of the building. Vanessa turned to see that three more fighter helicopters were on the far side of the runway along with various other aircraft. "Are you using this as a house or a hotel?"

"A little of both. I like to think of it as my personal fortress."

"I see you've done some remodeling since you moved in," Seth said as he stepped beside Akil.

Vanessa looked at Seth trying to hide her surprise. How could Seth possibly know this place? Then she realized that she too should be familiar with their new accommodations. She quickly tried to remember all of the briefings she had undergone before beginning this assignment, the numerous locations that were known to belong to the Ramirs.

Afraid she might say something wrong, she said nothing as Seth motioned to the armed men on the balconies. "Are you expecting company?"

Akil's eyebrows lifted. "It pays to be prepared."

"I agree." Seth reached for Vanessa's hand. "Still, I'm surprised you find it necessary to have a bodyguard for Lina here at the fortress."

The fortress, Vanessa repeated in her mind, trying to remember the details of the site. She recalled that Fahid Ramir had used the fortress as his base of operations in Central and South America. She pushed aside her annoyance that the agents who had briefed her for this assignment had barely mentioned it to her and that they apparently hadn't considered the possibility that Akil would take over this location.

"I'm sure my niece will feel more at home if you're here with her," Akil said without emotion. He then turned and spoke in Arabic to one of the men who had come out to meet them. "Have them shown to their rooms."

Vanessa watched Seth for a moment, wondering if he would let on that he too spoke Arabic. If he was really a trusted advisor of Fahid Ramir, would he speak Arabic? She was impressed to see that he didn't show any sign of whether he understood Akil or not, but rather waited for the man to motion for them to follow him.

Seth moved forward slowly as another man began speaking to Akil in Arabic.

"We just got word that the last shipment of weapons from Natero was incomplete. Apparently he wants more money before he sends the remaining items."

"Tell him you'll bring him the money in person when you pick up the shipment."

The man looked at him, both wary and surprised. "You're going to pay?"

Vanessa glanced back in time to see Akil's eyebrows lift in amusement. "Of course not. After you load up the weapons, you can kill Natero and return my money to me. Take a few extra men if you need to." Akil shook his head now and his voice became indignant. "No one renegotiates terms with me. Make sure Natero's successor understands that."

"Yes, sir."

Vanessa felt Seth take her hand, pulling her forward even as she tried to comprehend the conversation she had just heard. Akil had actually ordered a man's death because he'd tried to renegotiate a business deal. Struggling to stay calm, Vanessa let herself be escorted across the tarmac to the vehicle waiting to drive them the short distance to Akil's fortress. She forced herself to remember her training, to watch for the various security measures that were in place and begin to devise ways to pick her way through them. An intricate set of motion sensors was barely visible, and guards were posted along the airstrip and the long driveway that led to the house.

When they passed through the huge double doors in the center of the building, Vanessa expected to see something similar to a hotel lobby. Instead, she found that the entrance resembled that of an office building. Straight in front of them were two elevators and wide hallways that led to what appeared to be offices on either side of them.

A man appeared in front of them and nodded a greeting. "I am Fernando. I am here to see to your needs." Motioning to one elevator, he ushered them inside and then pushed the button for the ninth floor.

Vanessa presumed that Akil had taken the penthouse on the tenth floor for himself. She hoped that he had put her on the floor below him due to the fact that she was family—as opposed to the fact that he'd be able to keep a better eye on her there.

As soon as they stepped out of the elevator, Vanessa gave herself a moment to look around. Instead of being in a hallway like she had expected, she was standing in the middle of a huge living room.

"Miss Ramir, you will be in your old room." Fernando motioned to the open double doors to the left. He then motioned to a hallway that led from the main living area. "Mr. Billaud, you will be staying down the hall."

"What about clothes for us?" Vanessa asked now. "My uncle didn't give us the opportunity to pack before we left."

"Everything you need is in your rooms," the man said. "Breakfast will be served in an hour."

Seth's eyebrows lifted. "How did you know I was coming?"

"The pilot radioed us after you left Punta Cana to inform us of what was needed." He moved back to the elevator. "I hope you are comfortable."

Vanessa managed a smile. "Thank you."

As soon as they were alone, Seth rested his hands on her shoulders. He leaned down, and for a brief moment she thought he was going to kiss her again. Instead, he leaned his head close to her ear and whispered softly, "Bugs."

Vanessa nodded, shaken by how much she needed him here and at the same time how hard it was to have him close. "I'm going to go freshen up."

"Me too," Seth agreed. "I'll see you in a few minutes."

With a nod, Vanessa disappeared into her new bedroom.

15

Kel walked into the SEALs' temporary control room on board the fishing boat and dropped a file on a small table. "Here's what we've got so far on tracking those planes," he told the rest of the team. "The first plane never came onto the *Truman's* radar, so they think it's somewhere nearby."

"Yeah, but it left before Vanessa and Seth could have gotten on it."

"I know," Kel agreed. "Unfortunately, the other two dropped below the radar long before they landed. We have general regions of where we think they ended up, but no one can be sure they didn't change direction before they approached land."

Quinn and Tristan moved to study the reports with Kel. The crew of the *USS Harry S. Truman* had managed to track one plane to within about a hundred nautical miles of Nicaraguan airspace. The other had turned southward toward South America before it too had flown under the radar and disappeared from their view. Unfortunately they couldn't be certain which plane Vanessa and Seth had been on, or where their final destination was.

"Ramir has half a dozen places where he could be hiding in this region." Kel shook his head. "My best guess would be his place in Aruba or the fortress in Nicaragua."

Tristan tapped a finger on one of the reports. "With this plane heading toward Nicaragua, I'm afraid we may already know the answer."

Quinn shifted beside him. "What I want to know is how Akil knew Seth and Vanessa were at the boathouse."

"Maybe he had Vanessa followed," Tristan suggested.

"I don't know." Kel shook his head. He felt like he had an itch in the middle of his back, right in the place he couldn't reach. They were missing something, but he couldn't put his finger on what it was. "Replay the tape again."

"I'm surprised you don't already have it memorized," Quinn muttered as he hit the PLAY button yet again.

Halim gave it to me . . . the clasp is too tight . . .

"Stop it right there." Kel motioned to Quinn as the talking on the tape stopped, leaving nothing but the silence of the night. "Why didn't Seth respond?"

"He must have heard something."

"He didn't hear something. He was *listening* for something," Kel corrected. "Whatever piece of jewelry he was talking to Vanessa about must have had a tracking device in it."

Quinn sat up a little straighter. "If we can figure out the frequency . . ."

"We might be able to hone in on the signal," Kel finished for him. "Run a check on all of the communications frequencies from last night. Let's see if we can narrow it down."

"I'm on it," Quinn agreed.

"Tristan, call Amy," Kel said now. "If we can ferret out this mole, maybe we can figure out where Akil is staying."

"And where he's keeping Seth and Vanessa," Tristan added.

* * *

Seth examined the room he had been offered, uncovering three listening devices in his first sweep, two in the bedroom and one in the bathroom. The fact that Ramir would have the bathroom bugged proved that he was either very thorough or completely paranoid. Seth wasn't sure he wanted to know which one.

The bedroom was enormous, with an oversized bed occupying the center of it. A set of French doors opened to a balcony that ran the length of the suite; thankfully, it was furnished with two wicker chairs and a table rather than an armed guard. The armoire and dresser both contained an assortment of clothing that appeared to be his size.

To his relief, he found no hidden cameras in his bedroom, although he spotted two in the living area. He opened the door to the balcony and stepped outside, his eyes immediately sweeping the area for cameras and listening devices. He found only a single listening device located on the underside of the railing.

Casually, Seth leaned against the railing and reached down to disable the device. He hoped Akil's security people would assume that the elements had shorted it out, due to its location. He shifted his attention to what lay beyond the building, staring out over the expanse of lawn. First he studied the terrain leading to the jungle, and then he looked to where the grass gave way to the sandy beach.

A guard crossed into his view, circling toward the airfield from the west side of the house. Seth watched for a few more minutes, studying the movement of the personnel at the airfield.

He and the rest of the Saint Squad had been briefed on this hideout three years before when they had originally planned to infiltrate the fortress and take Fahid Ramir into custody. They had spent weeks memorizing surveillance photos and the floor plans that intel had managed to gain access to. Ultimately, the squad had determined that arriving by stealth would be extremely unlikely, and their mission had changed. Instead, they had chosen to apprehend Fahid and his family aboard his yacht in the Mediterranean.

The fact that his squad knew this place existed gave Seth hope that they would be able to narrow down where he and Vanessa had been taken; however, knowing that Lina Ramir definitely would have stayed at the fortress in the past left a feeling of dread in the pit of his stomach. Somehow he had to get Vanessa alone so he could brief her on what she needed to know before it was too late.

Turning his attention to the beach once more, he took a deep breath and decided it was time for him to play the part of Lina Ramir's fiancé. He only hoped his heart could handle it.

* * *

"Everything's in place," Tristan told Kel as he stepped on deck of the fishing vessel where Kel and Quinn were discussing their next move. "Fahid Ramir has been moved to a new facility, and the switchboard at the prison has been informed that he was ill and is in a prison hospital and is expected to stay there for several weeks."

"You were able to make the adjustments without informing the CIA?"

"Yeah." Tristan nodded. "I called Amy's friend over at the FBI, and he took care of it for us."

"Good." Kel looked out at the water toward La Playa. "Any luck with the transmitter that was on Vanessa?"

"Nothing." Tristan shook his head. "It looks like it was a short-range tracker. We didn't pick anything up on our sensors, and we were only five miles away."

"There is another way we might be able to flush out this mole in the CIA."

"How?" Tristan asked.

"I think we should set up a raid on La Playa using the local field office as intel support."

"You think that our mole will try to contact Halim?"

"Yeah." Kel nodded. "And with any luck, we'll be able to trace the call to where Akil is with our people."

"Do we want to take the chance of tipping Akil off that we're on to him?"

"After that firefight Seth and Brent got caught in in the middle of Curacao, he has to know that someone is on to him," Kel pointed out. "Besides, he said that the Americans were watching him. That has to be why he didn't stay at La Playa like Vanessa thought he was going to."

Quinn spoke now. "It would be nice to see what they're storing in those weapons bunkers."

Kel nodded and turned to Tristan. "Call Ellison and see if he can help us put this plan in motion."

"Do you think he'll help us?" Tristan asked.

"His boss may not have a clue what's going on, but Ellison still believes that Vanessa is right about there being a mole in the Agency somewhere." Kel nodded. "Tell him to try for tomorrow. I don't want to leave Seth and Vanessa without backup for long."

"You know, if they were on that second plane, we already know where they are."

"That's what I'm worried about."

* * *

"Let's go take a walk on the beach," Seth suggested.

"Do you think my uncle will mind if we go wandering by ourselves?"

"I don't know why he would. After all, this was your home long before he took over your father's business."

Vanessa nodded, her stomach clenching at the realization that had Seth not been with her, she very well might have given herself away. She hoped her voice sounded casual when she said, "A walk on the beach sounds great."

Seth led the way to the elevator. He didn't seem surprised when the doors opened and Fernando was inside.

"I'm glad you're here," Seth told him. He stepped inside the elevator with Vanessa and pushed the button for the main floor. "Can you tell me if anyone is at the shooting range right now? We want to go walk on the beach, but I don't want to go over there if anyone is practicing."

Surprise crossed Fernando's face as he shook his head. "Akil moved the range when he renovated."

"Really? Where is it now?"

"On the other side of the airfield."

Seth nodded as though he approved of the change. When the elevator doors slid open, he took Vanessa's hand and led her into the lobby. Then he turned and addressed Fernando once more. "If anyone needs us, we'll be on the beach. I'll make sure we stay in sight."

Fernando hesitated a moment as though debating whether to let them go. He then nodded his assent. "Very well, sir."

Vanessa walked with Seth down the path that led to the beach. She was a bundle of nerves, and she wondered if Seth could feel the way her hand kept trembling. She desperately wanted to stop and look around. She wanted to know if the guards on the upper balconies had their weapons trained on them. She needed to know if Akil Ramir had picked up on the fact that she had never been here before, and she especially worried about whether or not he believed Seth's story.

Seth must have picked up on her fears because he gave her hand a squeeze and began talking calmly to her. "A walk out in the fresh air will do us both some good," he began. "Then we can come back and get something to eat and you can take a nap. You didn't get nearly enough sleep last night."

"You're right," Vanessa agreed, trying to relax. "You must be tired too."

"I'm okay for now," Seth insisted. He stepped out onto the sand and headed straight for the water's edge. Not until the waves were washing up over their feet did he turn and start walking down the beach. "We should be able to talk here."

"I have so many questions I don't know where to start," Vanessa began. "Like how do you know about this place?"

"I'm sure you already know that Fahid used this place as his base of operations for his arms deals with his customers in Central and South America," Seth told her. When Vanessa nodded, he continued. "A couple of years ago my squad was responsible for the capture of Fahid Ramir. We had considered coming here to Nicaragua to capture him, but when we found out he was going to be on his private yacht in the Med, we went after him there instead."

"But how do you know so many details about the fortress? You said that Akil remodeled after he took over for Fahid, and you know where the shooting range used to be."

"I memorized the floor plans when I was prepping to come here." Seth's eyes narrowed. "Why do I get the feeling that I know more about the fortress than you do?"

"Because you're very perceptive." Vanessa shook her head in frustration. "The briefings I was given on the Ramir family focused on locations that belonged to Akil. They only mentioned the fortress in passing as one of the properties Fahid Ramir owned."

"Unbelievable," Seth muttered. Then he looked at her and seemed to sense her unease. He managed a casual shrug as he added, "The good news is that my squad knows this place too."

"So would Lina," Vanessa said, nerves evident in her voice.

"Intel indicated that she came here regularly before she and her family were arrested." Seth nodded. "The room you're in right now is Lina's old room. That means I'm probably in her brother Anado's room."

"What else can you tell me?" Vanessa asked softly.

"You lucked out when you asked if Akil was using this place as a hotel or a home," Seth told her. "Fahid did both. There were times that he had numerous people staying here to plot and plan. Sometimes it was terrorists, sometimes drug cartel members. This was a one-stop shop to get weapons and hire mercenaries."

"I can't believe I almost blew it. I should have known this was where we were." Vanessa let out a shaky breath. "I'm sure Lina knew some of the staff here. I don't know how long I can go before someone realizes I'm not who I say I am."

"Don't focus on that now. So far Akil seems to be buying our story," Seth assured her. "No one is going to suspect you're an impostor, but you probably need to keep some distance between you and the staff just in case."

"How?"

Seth gave her a wry smile. "I guess you'll have to focus all of your attention on your new fiancé."

Vanessa managed a smile now. "I might be able to do that."

Seth stared down at her, a myriad of emotions in his eyes. Then he shook his head slightly and said, "How have you managed to live this lie for so long?"

"I guess you could say I've been trained." Vanessa lifted one shoulder. "Haven't you ever worked undercover?"

"Not like this." Seth shook his head. "I've gone through the training, but my kind of undercover is usually the type that involves hiding in bushes, not lying about who I am." He studied her for a moment and then asked, "Isn't it hard knowing that you're deceiving people? I mean, you're the most honest person I've ever known."

"It isn't always easy. I guess it's kind of like a soldier who has to kill in war. I have to think the Lord understands the incredible evil we're facing," Vanessa said softly, understanding in her eyes as she stared up at him. "Besides, I try to use the truth as much as possible. People can tell if you're lying, so you learn to leave holes in the truth when you need to. So far it's worked." She glanced up at the balcony where one of the guards was watching them. "I hope it keeps working."

Seth followed her gaze before looking back at her. "You know, we are going to have to make it look like we're really engaged."

"I know." Vanessa's voice dropped to a whisper. She looked up at him and lifted her hand to touch his cheek. "I really am sorry about what happened before."

"It's in the past," Seth said, but not very convincingly. He stared for a moment before leaning down to kiss her.

Vanessa reminded herself that he was just playing a part, but the moment his lips touched hers she could feel her world tilt. The past and present fused, and the loneliness faded for that brief moment as Seth consumed her thoughts. *I missed you,* she thought to herself. Or maybe she whispered it between kisses.

When Seth pulled away, his dark eyes met hers once more. He stared at her for a long moment before he finally spoke. "I should tell you what else I know about this place," he said as Vanessa struggled to regain her composure. "I hope that my squad was able to track us, but we may have to get out of here on our own when the time comes."

Vanessa slowly nodded. "Just don't leave me behind, okay?"

Something sparked in his eyes as he lowered his voice and kissed her once more. "I'm not leaving you."

16

Vanessa woke up disoriented and confused, sunlight streaming in through the thin white curtains in her room. She sat up and looked around, running a hand over the silk sheets she had slept on. Slowly the facts sorted out in her head—of chief importance the reality that she was in Nicaragua with Seth and dozens of men who were currently putting some terrorist plot into motion.

With Seth's help, she had made a brief tour of her current home, beginning with breakfast in one of the dining rooms on the second floor. Seth had then casually suggested that they take a look around and see what other changes her uncle had made since taking over the fortress. So far none of the hired help seemed to know that she wasn't the real Lina Ramir.

Vanessa already knew from her extensive briefings at CIA headquarters that Lina was not the type to mingle with the hired help. She realized what a great advantage Lina's elitism gave her now since Vanessa couldn't be sure who might have worked here when Fahid was still the man living in the penthouse.

Swinging her legs over the side of the bed, Vanessa took a good look at her surroundings. The room had several strategically placed listening devices, but like Seth, she hadn't found any surveillance cameras in her bedroom. She wondered briefly how Lina Ramir might have felt about her room being bugged, or if she had even known that it was.

She imagined that the real Lina would have been quite indignant about the whole thing and would have demanded the listening devices be removed; however, it was doubtful that she had the technical training that Vanessa did to be able to spot the bugs. Vanessa wondered for a moment if the cameras and listening devices were the reason Akil didn't find it necessary for her and Seth to have a chaperone.

The idea of a chaperone was incredibly old fashioned, but she couldn't be sure how removed the Ramir family really was from their Muslim origins. Clearly they had deviated greatly since none of the women she had come in contact with at La Playa wore the traditional garb, but she had seen the lingering chauvinism in the way women were typically kept out of the business dealings. That was one thing she hoped to rectify.

The shock of finding herself in a new place without any backup was beginning to wear off, and her determination to uncover Akil's plans was resurfacing. She hoped that the real Lina would refuse to be left in the dark. Now that she was living in the same place as Akil, she was intent on working her way into his confidence.

She quickly changed out of the clothes she had slept in, opting for a light cotton skirt and button-up shirt. When she swung her bedroom door open, she was a bit surprised to see Seth sitting in the living area flipping through a magazine. Her heart ached as she thought of the way he had kissed her on the beach earlier.

He had held her as though she was still the center of his world, as though their last moments together had never happened. Vanessa bit back a sigh. She couldn't believe that over the past six years he hadn't found someone else. After all, just because her heart had never really healed since she had seen him last didn't mean that his love for her had survived both their time apart and the hurt she had caused him. She stared at him for a moment, reminding herself that no matter how she felt about Seth, one thing hadn't changed. He still couldn't take her to the temple.

Seth looked up at her, his dark eyes studying her in his quiet, thoughtful way. "Did you manage to get some sleep?"

"I did, thanks." Vanessa nodded. "What about you?"

"I took a nap a while ago." Seth stood up and stretched his arms above his head. When his hands didn't run into the ceiling halfway through the gesture, he looked up and grinned. "You know, I could get used to these high ceilings."

"I guess we'll have to make that a priority when we decide where we're going to live," Vanessa told him, deliberately not looking at the surveillance cameras.

"We can decide that after we see your father," Seth said simply.

"Do you think he'll be okay until we can visit him?"

"He's tough and he's smart." Seth nodded. "If we can't go visit him in the next couple of days, he'll figure out where we are and why."

"I hope so," Vanessa said, hoping that she understood Seth correctly. Would his squad really be able to figure out where they were within a couple of days? And if so, what would they do with the information? The fortress's security made breaching La Playa look like a walk in the park. There was always a patrol visible no matter when she looked out her window, and the surveillance cameras were everywhere, both in the building and on the grounds.

Her heart sank a little as she reminded herself that this was real life. Unlike the action movies she'd always enjoyed watching as a teenager, she couldn't expect all of her problems to be solved in the next few hours.

Seth put a hand on her arm and motioned to the elevator. "Why don't we go get some dinner, and then we can take another walk on the beach. It's beautiful here at sunset."

"I'd like that."

* * *

Tristan read through the encrypted message three times hoping to find some indication that the information it contained could be wrong. Finally he shook his head as he considered the latest news. Naval intelligence had uncovered the location of the plane that had been heading south out of La Playa.

A comparison of satellite photos from the night before and that morning had revealed a plane on an airstrip near Cali, Colombia, that was known to be controlled by Morenta, a man considered by many to be the most ruthless drug lord in Colombia. The route was consistent with the flight path of the plane that had been heading toward South America.

Kel entered their temporary command center and asked, "What have you got?"

"You aren't going to like it." Tristan swiveled in his chair to face Kel. "Our best guess is that Seth and Vanessa are either at Ramir's fortress in Nicaragua, or they are the newest guests at Morenta's villa near Cali."

"You've got to be kidding me." Kel shook his head. "I'd rather try to break into the White House on Pennsylvania Avenue than either of those locations."

The corner of Tristan's mouth lifted. "That's only because you know how the Secret Service runs their security."

"And they're a lot more likely to give you warning before they shoot you down," Kel agreed.

"What's your best guess?"

"The fortress," he said. "I think Akil went home to get ready for the strike."

"Makes sense," Tristan agreed. "I doubt he would want to be a houseguest anywhere else when everything is going down."

"Which means we might not have as much time as we thought." Kel shook his head. "The question is, how can we be sure where Ramir is?"

Tristan shrugged as the door opened and Quinn walked in. "It looks like Christmas came early this year."

"What have you got?" Kel asked.

"The satellite photos for Morenta's villa." Quinn dropped a file on the work table and flipped it open. "Look at this."

Tristan and Kel both moved closer. The photo had been enlarged and enhanced, the focus on a dozen people on the runway next to the plane that had landed that morning. Kel studied the photo for several seconds before a smile spread across his face. He looked up at Quinn. "There aren't any women in this photo."

"Exactly." Quinn nodded. "They have satellite feed starting before the plane landed and it goes for nearly thirty minutes. None of the photos show any women."

"Which means Vanessa is at the fortress," Tristan said. "Maybe it's time to hitch a ride on a sub and head for Nicaragua."

"Let's see how the raid on La Playa turns out first," Kel told him. "We'll plan on shipping out right after we finish up here tomorrow." Kel motioned to the computer. "Ask Navy intel to get us the latest satellite photos for the fortress and the surrounding area. Maybe they've gotten more lax with their security since Akil took over the business."

"You don't really believe that, do you?"

"No, but I'm hoping." Kel ran a hand over his face. "I'm trying hard not to remember why we didn't go after Fahid Ramir there a few years ago."

Tristan could only nod in agreement. "They call it a fortress for a reason."

"Let's hope Seth is in a position to help break down their security from the inside."

* * *

Complete darkness surrounded Seth as he reached the penthouse balcony. The clouds looming overhead were a blessing so far, and he hoped the rain would hold off until he was back in his own room. Climbing up the outside of a building from the ninth to the tenth floor wasn't much of a challenge for a trained Navy SEAL. Making that same climb in the pouring rain was another story, especially with armed guards both above and below him.

Seth couldn't believe his fortune when he realized the balcony door was open with only a screen door in place to keep the mosquitoes at bay. He didn't dare step onto Akil's balcony, and instead settled onto the outside ledge. He knew it was a bit risky being there. Even with his dark skin and dark clothes, he couldn't be sure he would be able to blend into the background if Akil came out onto the balcony. Seth could only hope that he would hear Akil coming if he decided to get a breath of fresh air.

Vanessa was currently on the balcony below him so that it appeared to anyone watching the surveillance cameras in the living area that she and Seth were both outside enjoying the night air. While they were walking on the beach, Seth had informed her of the listening device he had disabled on the balcony. So far no one had tried to access their room to investigate why it had stopped working, and he hoped the malfunction would remain low on their priority list.

Seth had also told Vanessa of his plan to climb up to the penthouse. She hadn't been thrilled with the risks he was willing to take, but they both knew that they had to do what they could to gather information.

Seth stayed on his perch outside of the penthouse for nearly an hour before he heard any movement in the room. Then he heard two familiar voices, Akil's and Halim's.

"What are we going to do about Seth?" Halim asked.

"Lina will keep him occupied." Akil's voice was filled with confidence and authority. "She may not be happy she's being kept out of the loop, but she knows her duty."

"I don't like her spending so much time with him."

"They're engaged." A touch of sympathy sounded in Akil's voice. "I know this is hard for you to accept, but my brother approved the match."

"I still don't trust him. How can we be sure he's really who he says he is?"

"He must be telling the truth. How else could he know this place?"

"He could be a spy, someone who has done his research."

"That's what I love about you. You are even more paranoid than I." Akil let out a short laugh. "If he was a spy, Lina wouldn't be vouching for him, and he certainly wouldn't have known what the fortress looked like before we renovated." Akil's voice took on an edge as he added, "Now, enough about this. Is the shipment ready?"

"The freighter leaves port tomorrow."

"When will it arrive?"

"Wednesday, Thursday at the latest," Halim informed him.

"Good. Start shutting down our training camps and get our personnel in place," Akil ordered. "I don't want any last-minute problems."

"Nothing is going to go wrong." Halim's voice took on a new sense of confidence. "The Americans still know nothing."

"I gather our sources are still feeding us what we want?"

"Absolutely."

17

Brent adjusted his headset and waited. Kel, Tristan, and Quinn had arrived at his and Amy's apartment before dawn. After talking to Ellison, Kel had decided to let Interpol and the locals handle the raid on La Playa while he and his squad relocated to Santo Domingo in hopes of identifying the leak.

The raid itself wasn't planned until ten o'clock that night, but the call requesting support from the field office was due to be made at eight in the morning. Depending on how quickly they could identify the source of their leak, Kel hoped to have his team back at La Playa to get a firsthand look at the types of weapons they were shipping through there.

For now, everyone was stationed in various locations around Santo Domingo. Quinn had drawn the short straw and was cooped up in the apartment, along with some eavesdropping equipment.

Amy had gone into the field office earlier than usual. Her mission was to wait until after the daily security sweep before planting several listening devices near the telephones. She would then remain in the office and signal Kel if she saw anything suspicious.

Kel had assigned himself to follow Carl Dowdy, the chief of station, while Tristan waited outside the field office to tail anyone else who might leave from there. Brent had taken a position across the street from Medrino's apartment to see if he had finally come back into town. According to Amy's information, he was due back at the office today, but so far no one had seen any sign of him. If Brent's instincts were right, Medrino was the mole and he was already long gone.

Several minutes passed by, along with a few pedestrians, until the monotony of the stakeout was broken up by Quinn's voice over the headset. "Amy has the bugs in place. So far the only people in the office are Amy, the secretary, and the deputy director."

"Copy that," Kel responded.

"Still no activity here," Brent said as he stifled a yawn. It was barely seven-thirty in the morning, and Amy hadn't been able to figure out when Medrino normally worked—assuming he was coming back to work at all.

When a taxicab pulled up in front of the apartment complex, Brent sat up a little straighter. He simply stared when Al Medrino stepped out of the cab, retrieved two suitcases from the trunk, and then disappeared inside.

"Looks like I might be wrong about Medrino being the mole. He just got home."

"Stay on him," Kel responded.

Brent signaled his assent as his eyes swept from the apartment to the parking garage entrance where Medrino kept his car. Sure enough, twenty minutes after Medrino had disappeared into the apartment building, his car pulled out of the garage.

Keeping him in sight, Brent eased his car out into the early morning traffic to follow him. When they approached the field office, Brent became even more convinced that he was wrong about Medrino after all.

"Medrino's parking at the field office," Brent informed the rest of his team. "Tristan, do you have a visual?"

"Affirmative," Tristan said.

"I'll take the back door," Brent said, indicating that he would park on the other side of the building to set up surveillance.

Quinn's voice came over the line. "Ellison just called. The message about the raid will be sent in five minutes."

"Let's hope our mole jumps on it," Kel muttered.

* * *

Amy tried to look relaxed as she loitered near Gina's desk. Carl Dowdy was expected to arrive any minute, and Amy was hoping he would walk into the office before the call came asking for support. She still wasn't sure what to think of Al Medrino, who had arrived at the office a short while ago. He had been their best suspect until he'd shown up for work that morning.

Now Amy wondered if perhaps the leak might be Carl Dowdy.

Looking for a reason to stay near Gina's desk, she struck up a conversation with the young secretary. "Do you have anything exciting planned for the weekend?"

She shook her head. "Not really. My boyfriend is out of town for work this weekend."

"Really? What does he do?"

"He's a pilot." Gina's face lit up. "I did get to see him last weekend. He gave me this."

Amy watched her touch her necklace, a single black pearl set in a delicate gold setting. "Wow, that's beautiful."

"Thanks," Gina said, beaming. She lowered her voice as though sharing a government secret and added, "The way he's been dropping hints about getting married, I thought for sure it was a ring."

"Maybe he doesn't want to rush things," Amy ventured cautiously.

"That's what I think too." She nodded. "Besides, he knows I would want to pick out my own ring." Gina paused long enough to open her desk and pull something out of a drawer. She then dropped a thick file on her desk with a thud.

"What's that?"

"Oh, it's my wedding file." Gina opened it up to a copy of *Bride* magazine with several sticky notes affixed to the cover. "Do you think green and purple could work together as wedding colors?" Before Amy could struggle with an answer, Gina pressed on. "I know it's a bit different, but I don't want to be ordinary."

"I guess that could work . . ." Amy said helplessly. "Does your boyfriend like those colors?"

"Oh, he always says those kinds of details are up to me. Besides, I don't get to see him that often, so I've made most of the plans for us. At least he calls me every night. I mean, I guess it could be worse."

Amy managed a smile. "He sounds great."

Gina started to respond but was interrupted by the telephone ringing. Amy watched her answer it and listened while she took the message for Carl, who still hadn't arrived. As expected, it was the call Amy had been waiting for.

To Amy's surprise, the news that the field office was going to be involved in a raid in a matter of hours didn't seem to rattle Gina in the least. Instead, she took down the information, hung up the phone, and then turned back to Amy. "Can I ask you something?"

"Sure." Amy nodded, expecting her to turn the conversation to work. To her surprise, Gina took the conversation in the opposite direction.

Gina flipped open the magazine and pointed to a frilly dress. "What do you think of this dress?"

"Um, it's nice," Amy managed, trying to gather her thoughts. She couldn't help but wonder how Gina had ended up working in intelligence when news of a major event didn't even seem to faze her. A little curious now, she asked, "So how long have you been dating your boyfriend?"

Gina smiled, her cheeks flushing a bit. "Long enough, I think."

Carl walked into the office, offering greetings as he passed Cindy's office and then proceeded to greet Gina and Amy.

"You got a call a few minutes ago. I guess Interpol is planning a raid tonight and wanted some information."

"What?" Carl's eyes widened and he snatched the message slip that Gina held out to him. He scanned it quickly and immediately disappeared into his office and closed the door.

Hoping to linger a bit longer, Amy asked Gina, "Does this kind of thing happen often?"

"Not that I know of." She gave a careless shrug before launching back into a monologue about her boyfriend and wedding plans.

Amy knew she should be grateful that the tedious conversation about this man was keeping her near Carl Dowdy's office, but all she could think of was how grateful she was that this assignment was temporary.

Gina's monologue was interrupted when Carl came out of his office and told Gina to have everyone come to his office.

Amy gave an inward sigh of relief.

18

Seth sat down in a wicker chair on the balcony and steepled his hands together. For the past several years he had started each morning with a prayer, usually with the rest of his squad. In their line of work, it seemed natural to ask for the Lord's guidance each day as they went about their duties, whether it was a training exercise or an actual mission.

Ironically, he had been the one to suggest that the squad pray each morning as a unit, despite the fact that he had always shied away from organized religion in the past. He couldn't say exactly what had prompted him to make the suggestion any more than he could explain why he used to avoid church even though he had always believed in God. When the Saint Squad had been created, the team commander had decided to put all of the Mormon boys together but had been one short. Seth had been the odd man out until he had been baptized a few years later.

Seth thought about the men who had become his family over the past five years. This was the first time since their unit was created that he had ended up on a mission without one of his teammates watching his back. He figured that this gave him even more reason to offer up his prayers this morning.

With the bugs in his room and the surveillance cameras in the living room, Seth figured the best he could do for the time being was to offer a silent prayer here on the balcony. He closed his eyes, bowing his head down until his forehead touched his fingers. Words ran through his mind, words of appreciation that he and Vanessa had managed to survive this charade so far, and pleading requests that they would stay safe.

He heard the balcony door open, but he didn't move as he closed his silent prayer. He then looked up to see Vanessa watching him.

Vanessa stared at him curiously for a moment before closing the door behind her. "Good morning."

"Morning." Seth watched her sit beside him. "Did you sleep okay?"

"I guess so." Vanessa brushed over his question and leaned closer. "You know, we may not have much time. I think we need to figure out a reason for me to spend some time with Akil so I can try to get a better handle on what he's up to."

"I don't know if that's such a good idea," Seth said cautiously.

"Seth, this is what I've been trained for," Vanessa insisted. "I need to do this, or we may not find the information we need."

Seth let out a sigh. He didn't like the idea of Vanessa being alone with Akil, but she was right. They weren't going to find out what Akil was planning if someone didn't win his confidence. "All right, but you have to promise to be careful."

"Trust me," Vanessa said softly. "I'm always careful."

* * *

Vanessa held the diamond bracelet in her hand as she stepped off of the elevator on the second floor. She still wasn't sure what to think about what she'd seen that morning when she walked onto the balcony. If she didn't know better, she would have sworn that Seth was praying. She shook this thought away, focusing instead on her current goal.

She immediately spotted Akil in the dining room where he was finishing his breakfast. After Seth had made her aware of the tracking device that was implanted in the bracelet Halim had given her, Vanessa had decided to use Halim's ploy to her advantage. She only hoped that she could pull it off.

Akil looked up and saw her enter, nodding a greeting. "Good morning, Lina. Where is Seth this morning?"

"He's working out in the weight room upstairs," Vanessa told him. "He knew that I wanted to speak with you privately."

Akil's eyebrows lifted. "Really?"

"Did you know about this?" Vanessa held out the bracelet Halim had given her, the tracking device in the clasp now exposed.

"Of course," Akil said unapologetically. "That is how we knew you and Seth were together at La Playa."

Vanessa let her voice become indignant and she slammed both hands down on the table. "How could you let Halim treat me this way?"

"My dear, it is difficult for a man to desire a woman and know that her heart is elsewhere." Akil's voice was deceptively understanding.

The tone of his voice made her wonder who had really wanted her followed. "Was the bracelet really from Halim, or was it from you?"

"I had to make sure that you weren't sneaking out to meet someone who wasn't worthy of you."

"But Halim suggested it."

Akil reached out and put a hand on hers. His eyes darkened as he squeezed her hand. Hard. "Don't forget your place." He kept his eyes on hers, and Vanessa felt chills run down her spine. "And remember, Halim has been my trusted advisor for many years."

When Akil released her hand, Vanessa took a deep breath and gathered her courage. "Perhaps it's time you start trusting those in your own family."

"If I didn't trust you, you wouldn't be here." Akil pushed his plate back and stood up. "Your father may have allowed you to be involved in his affairs, but he would never involve you with the people I am working with now."

"You're talking about Morenta," Vanessa said, surprising herself.

"His money will help us accomplish what your father started out to do," Akil admitted. "But I won't risk your safety and have you involved. Morenta has been known to kidnap or even kill the family members of his business partners when he feels they aren't cooperating with him."

Vanessa's eyes narrowed. "You think he might hurt me?"

"That's exactly what I think." Akil nodded. "I owe it to your father to protect you from him."

"Why exactly are you involved with Morenta? We don't need him," she said, her voice becoming a bit petulant.

"We do, but only for a little while longer," Akil said with a patronizing tone as he patted her hand, gently this time. "Get something to eat, take a walk on the beach. I don't want you to worry about these things."

Vanessa clenched her teeth. She took a breath and let out a frustrated sigh. "When can I go see my father?"

"You'll have to wait a little while longer."

* * *

Seth's arms pumped as he continued running at full speed on the tread-mill in the well-equipped weight room on the fourth floor. The stress of the last thirty-six hours was weighing on him, and he wondered how Vanessa had managed to live these lies for more than a year. He could barely stand it, and it hadn't even been two days.

Through the wall of windows across from him, he could see the beach and the constant surf. This place would have been a paradise if not for the armed guards everywhere—not to mention the misguided moral compass of the current tenants. He watched a midsized jet flying in over the ocean. When he realized it was going to land at the airstrip, he slowed his pace to a jog and then to a walk. Grabbing a towel off of a nearby shelf, he wiped the sweat off of his face and moved closer to the window.

Three vehicles were waiting near the runway, apparently to bring the new arrivals to the house. Seth took a deep breath as his pulse began to steady. He stared as the airplane door was opened and the first passengers began to deplane. He counted nine people before his eyes narrowed as yet another man appeared in the doorway.

Even from this distance, Seth recognized the man. Morenta, the man responsible for countless murders and nearly half of the drug traffic coming through Mexico; the man who had been on the government's most wanted list for as long as Seth could remember. More than once Seth's SEAL team had prepared to apprehend him, but every time they came close, Morenta would return to his stronghold in Colombia, where the U.S. military had no right to go.

The elevator doors opened, and Seth turned to see Vanessa walk in. Relief pulsed through him as he considered that he didn't want her anywhere near Morenta and the men who had arrived with him.

"My uncle knew all about it," Vanessa said, annoyance in her voice and challenge in her eyes.

"Really?" Seth's eyebrows lifted, and he fought the smile that tried to surface. Seeing Vanessa shaken and vulnerable the day before had been harder than he ever could have imagined. The woman facing him now, the one who looked like she was ready to take on the world despite the odds, was the Vanessa he remembered. The Vanessa who no matter how hard he tried to forget had stayed firmly rooted in his memories.

Oblivious to Seth's rambling thoughts, she lifted her hands in frustration and then let them slap back down to her side. "I don't know who came up with the idea, but somehow Halim must have figured out that I was seeing you."

"It wasn't like we were really hiding it." Seth played along. "After all, your father approved of us a long time ago."

"Yeah, but my father trusted both of us. I hate not knowing what's going on," Vanessa told him.

"One thing I do know. Morenta just arrived," Seth told her. By the look on Vanessa's face, he suspected that she already knew of his impending arrival. Seth draped the towel he held around his neck and added, "I'm surprised to see your uncle doing business with him. Morenta isn't known for playing well with others."

"Uncle Akil knows that. He told me this morning that he doesn't want me anywhere near him."

"Your uncle is very wise in that regard. I'm sure he doesn't want to risk your safety," Seth told her. "Morenta has a tendency of hurting those close to his associates when things don't go his way."

"It sounds like I might be safer going to visit my father after all."

"Unless Morenta is involved with plans for a strike on American soil," Seth surmised.

Vanessa stared up at him, clearly having deduced the same thing. "Like I said, I hate not knowing what's going on."

* * *

"I don't understand." Kel shook his head in frustration as he settled down on the couch in Amy and Brent's temporary apartment. "If the mole had been someone in the field office, the guards at La Playa should have been ready for the raid. According to the police, there wasn't any indication that they'd been tipped off."

"I didn't pick up on any unusual calls coming from our suspects either," Quinn said, tapping on the communication reports he had printed out. He had stayed in constant contact with Interpol from the time the raid began shortly after dark until an hour ago when Interpol had faxed over a preliminary listing of what they had found.

"This doesn't make any sense." Brent shook his head as he looked over the weapons inventory list. "They still had quite a bit of firepower at La Playa as well as a cargo plane on their runway. I really think they at least would have cleaned the high-tech stuff out of there if they had known the cops were coming."

"I agree." Kel nodded. "So now what? Amy, did you see anything unusual?"

"Not really." Amy shook her head. "Everyone was pretty stressed trying to put together the intel reports for the raid all day. Almost everyone," she corrected as she thought of the secretary. "Gina wasn't really involved, but she doesn't seem to get flustered by anything anyway."

"What do you mean?" Kel asked.

"I was standing right there when the call first came in from Interpol. She seemed more annoyed that the call had interrupted our conversation than concerned about why someone from Interpol was calling," Amy said. "All she wanted was to talk about wedding colors and diamond rings." Amy looked from Kel to Brent as a new understanding of the situation dawned on her. She shook her head, annoyed that she hadn't considered all of the possibilities earlier. "The boyfriend."

"What?" Brent asked, clearly recognizing that light in his wife's eyes. "What are you talking about?"

Amy sat up a little straighter. "Gina's so cavalier about what's going on in the office that she might be the leak without even knowing it. She may be passing information to her boyfriend without realizing how critical it is."

"Didn't she say her boyfriend is a pilot?" Quinn asked. "If he's out of town a lot, he could be using his job as a cover story."

"And since he calls her every night, she wouldn't have had the information to pass on to him in time for Akil's men to know the raid was about to happen," Amy added.

"Do we have a name for this guy?" Kel asked.

Amy shook her head. "No, and she doesn't have a picture of him at work anywhere that I could see."

Kel motioned to Quinn. "Pull up all of the photos we have on Ramir's associates. Let's see if we can get this guy identified."

Amy's eyebrows lifted. "Kel, it's two in the morning."

"It will take an hour or two to get the photos together," Kel told her. "We can wait until five or six before we go have a chat with the secretary."

"In that case, I'm going to take a nap."

"Get one while you can," Kel agreed. "After we talk to Gina, we're going to close up shop here." He then motioned to Brent. "I want you to check on our transport to the *Truman*. I want it here by oh-seven-hundred. It's time we get into position to see what's going on inside the fortress."

"I hope Seth and Vanessa are okay," Amy said quietly.

"Don't worry." Kel's voice was tight. "We don't leave anyone behind."

19

Seth stood out on the balcony listening to the voices overhead. He didn't need to see the faces of the three men speaking to sense the tension between them. He could hear it. Their voices were low, but he could hear them clearly from where he stood on the thick balcony railing right below where Akil was currently standing. He recognized Halim's voice as well, and there was one other man present whom he couldn't identify.

"Why were the weapons still there?" Akil demanded. "I told you to have them moved yesterday."

"Sir, I'm sorry, but I told you that we had a problem with one of the planes," the unidentified man said. "They were getting ready to load it up when the cops got there."

"And what happened to your source?" Akil asked now, apparently speaking to Halim.

"The information came in late." Halim's voice was tense.

"I can't afford these kinds of mistakes, especially now that Morenta is here." Fury vibrated through Akil's voice.

"We can still go forward," Halim said now, although Seth sensed that he was maintaining a healthy distance between himself and Akil.

Halim continued to speak. "The detonators have already been delivered, we have enough explosives hidden in Arizona to strike, and most of the antiaircraft guns have already been shipped."

"What exactly did we lose?"

The other man started rattling off a list of weapons, most of them automatic weapons, along with a few specialty items including grenade launchers and two antiaircraft guns.

Seth's head whipped around when he heard the balcony door open. He let out a relieved sigh when he saw it was Vanessa. Silently he held one finger to his lips and then pointed to the balcony above them.

She nodded, quietly closing the door behind her.

Akil's voice lowered so that Seth could barely hear him. "The strikes have to be timed perfectly for this to work. We only have three days to work out the details with Morenta." He paused for effect. "Believe me, none of us want to deal with him if anything goes wrong."

"Nothing will go wrong," Halim said, repeating the same words he had spoken the night before. This time though, Seth thought he could hear doubt in his voice.

Seth didn't step back onto his balcony until after he was sure the three men had gone back inside. He then squatted down and eased himself quietly back onto the balcony next to Vanessa.

"What happened?" Vanessa asked quietly in case anyone was on the balcony above or below them.

"I'm guessing there was a raid at La Playa," Seth told her.

"Do you think it was your squad?"

He shrugged. "If it was at La Playa, I'm sure the Saint Squad was involved somehow."

Vanessa looked at him quizzically. "Why are you called the 'Saint Squad'?"

"You know. Like Latter-day Saints." For the first time in days, Seth let himself relax with a genuine smile.

Vanessa's eyebrows shot up and she gaped at him. "Don't tell me you're working with a bunch of Mormons."

Seth felt an odd little flutter of nerves in his stomach as he considered how Vanessa might react to the truth. His grin faded as he took a deep breath and forced himself to look directly at her. "All of us in the squad are LDS."

Vanessa's mouth dropped open. Then closed. Then opened again. "You're *Mormon?*"

Seth nodded, the insecurities creeping back in. Would she have married him so many years ago if he had been Mormon, or had the real reason been that she didn't love him the way he loved her? "Yeah. Four years now."

Her mouth dropped open once more. She shook her head and asked incredulously, "Why didn't you ever tell me?"

"I tried." Seth leaned back against the balcony railing. He needed to put some distance between them before he did something stupid. Something like kissing her when she would know it wasn't just for show.

"I came back to see you, but I heard you had gotten married."

"Seth, I'm so sorry. That was just a story I had going around to explain why I disappeared the first time I went undercover."

"Now I know." Seth gave what he hoped was a casual shrug.

He started to reach for the door, but Vanessa grabbed his arm. "We have to talk about what happened between us."

"What is there to talk about?" Seth managed, the anger and hurt welling up in him even as he tried to fight it. He kept his voice low, but he still spoke with intensity. "You dated me for six years. *Six years.* We talked about getting married, we talked about our future. Not once did you ever tell me that marrying me was out of the question."

"I tried to explain that it was because of my religion." Vanessa's whisper was equally passionate. "You're Mormon now. Surely you understand how important a temple marriage is."

"But you were Mormon the whole time we dated. How could you have let us get to that point?" Seth asked. Something squeezed at his heart as he forced himself to continue. "You knew I wanted to marry you."

Tears glistened in Vanessa's eyes. Her voice was barely louder than a whisper when she admitted, "I never thought I was going to say no." She stared up at him for a long moment. Her voice was soft as she continued. "Seth, I never meant to hurt you. Until you asked the question, I never realized how important it was for me to have a temple marriage."

"And I stupidly assumed that it wasn't a big deal." Seth didn't want to see the vulnerability on her face. Despite the years that had passed, the hurt of their last day together still left a deep ache that had never completely faded. Even now that she was trying to explain, he realized he wasn't ready to forgive her. "Besides, you never gave me the chance to change."

"You're right, but be honest," Vanessa insisted, swiping at a tear that spilled over. "Would you have gotten baptized so that you could marry me?"

"I don't know." Seth shrugged. "Maybe."

"Would you have done it for me or because you believed in the gospel?"

"What difference does that make?" he asked, even though he knew the answer.

"It would have made all the difference." Slowly, Vanessa reached up and touched his cheek. She blinked back the tears and stared for a moment. Then she dropped her hand and stepped back. "Good night, Seth."

Seth watched her slip back inside, his heart aching as he tried to identify the swirl of emotions running through him. Would he have gotten baptized so that Vanessa would marry him? He had loved her enough that he would have seriously considered it. Would he have taken the time to really understand what baptism meant? Probably not.

As he stared out into the night, he asked himself another question. Now that religion was no longer an obstacle, was it possible for him and Vanessa to move past the hurt and pain and once again find the love they had shared so long ago? And could they possibly build a future together?

A two-man patrol came into view, and Seth let out a sigh. Who was he kidding? It didn't matter if he could look past the hurt or if she still loved him. Vanessa worked undercover, and he was a Navy SEAL. Even if they did manage to get out of the fortress alive, he couldn't be sure he would ever see her again.

The familiar ache spread through his chest, and he wondered if he could survive losing Vanessa twice in one lifetime.

20

"Amy?" Gina tied the belt to her robe as she stood in the open doorway to her apartment, her eyes still struggling to adjust to the early morning light. "What are you doing here?"

"Sorry to wake you up, Gina, but I need to talk to you."

She shook her head, still half asleep, as her eyes shifted to focus on Brent. "Who are you?"

"Amy's husband," Brent said simply. "Can we come in? It's really important."

"Yeah, sure." Gina moved away from the door, leaving Brent and Amy to close it behind them. She headed for the tiny kitchen and started rummaging around for a clean cup. "Can I get you something to drink?"

"No, thanks." Amy followed her to the kitchen. "Gina, I need to know if you have a photo of your boyfriend."

"Roberto?" Gina thought for a minute and then shook her head. "No, I don't. He doesn't like having his picture taken."

"You said he calls every night even when he's out of town, right?"

"Yeah, he's really good about that." Gina gave her a sleepy smile.

"Do you ever talk about work?"

"No, he doesn't like to talk about his work."

Amy shook her head, wondering if Gina could really be this clueless or if she was still half asleep. "Not his work, your work."

"Oh." Gina poured herself a glass of orange juice and then moved over to the mound of clothes that was hiding her couch. She shoved a pile of her laundry aside and sat down. "I guess we talk about my work sometimes. I mean, he always asks how my day was and if anything interesting happened."

"And what do you tell him?"

"Just basic stuff." Gina shrugged. "You know, the crazy things Carl has me doing and what our latest projects are."

"Gina, you know that everything that goes on in the office is classified."

Gina looked at her, a bit bewildered. "I'm only a secretary. I don't deal with the classified stuff."

"You've got to be kidding me," Brent muttered under his breath.

"What?" Gina sat up a little straighter, finally appearing completely awake. "You still haven't told me why you're here, or why you're asking about Roberto."

With a shake of her head, Amy emptied the manila envelope she held, sliding a dozen photos out of it. "Can you tell me if any of these men are Roberto?"

Gina shifted to take the photos, flipping through the first six quickly. She then looked at the photo in her hand, and her eyes lifted to Amy's. "Why do you have a picture of my boyfriend?"

Brent moved quickly to see which photo she had identified. Ignoring Gina, he spoke to Amy. "It's Roberto Havar. He's one of Ramir's pilots."

"What are you talking about? He flies for Air Caribe."

"No, Gina. He doesn't," Amy told her firmly. "He's a pilot for an arms dealer, and he's been using you for information."

Gina's face paled, but still she shook her head. "I don't believe you."

"You don't have to believe me, but you can't talk to him again," Amy told her, aware that Brent had moved outside to make the phone call to Carl Dowdy.

Tears welled up in Gina's eyes, and she shook her head again. "You're wrong about Roberto. I know you are."

"I'm sorry, Gina," Amy said softly. "But I'm not wrong."

* * *

"Where are the infrared satellite photos of the fortress?" Kel demanded the minute he walked into the boardroom his squad had claimed as soon as they arrived aboard. After turning Gina over to Carl Dowdy for questioning, they had flown out to the *USS Harry S. Truman* and were now hoping to find their missing man.

Kel had been stuck in debriefings during his first hour on board, but now he was clearly ready to get his team into action.

"We're still waiting on them," Amy told him.

Amy was grateful that looks couldn't kill when Kel turned to glare at her and asked, "What?"

"I'm just the messenger." Amy held her hands up in surrender. "Intel said they should be here in fifteen minutes." She looked at Kel once more and stood up. "Why don't I go wait for them up in communications? Maybe they'll work a bit quicker if I'm looking over their shoulders."

She moved past Brent and heard him mutter, "Especially if they think Kel might come up himself."

Suppressing a grin, Amy left the room and made her way through the maze of hallways to the comm room. She approached Lieutenant Dana Carillo, hoping for some good news. "Please tell me you have the infrareds. If I go back without them, you may have to start planning our funerals."

Dana's eyebrows rose, and the corners of her mouth lifted in the beginnings of a smile. "I gather the commander is getting impatient."

"Now, that's an understatement." Amy nodded. She had worked with Dana before, and they had developed a friendship the last time they had been on an assignment together. "Do you know when they're coming in?"

"Actually, they just got here. I had a feeling you might be heading up here, so I printed them off." Dana retrieved the printout off the printer tray and lifted it up. She stared at the top page a moment and then looked up at Amy. "They aren't thinking of going in here, are they?"

"I don't know. Why?"

"Look at this." Dana pointed to a cluster of red dots in three different areas on the photo. "With the multilevel structure, it's hard to tell exactly how many people this is picking up, but it looks like we're talking about a couple of hundred."

"Are you serious?" Amy's stomach clenched as her concern about this mission tripled. She hadn't been with the Saint Squad when they had first considered going after Fahid Ramir at the fortress, but she was familiar with the mission where they had ultimately captured him and his family. She also knew all about the young boy who had been killed as a demonstration of what happened when Fahid didn't get what he wanted. By all accounts, Akil was just as ruthless as his brother, and neither of them compared to Morenta, the man he was rumored to be working with. Amy thought of Seth and wondered whether he and Vanessa would really be able to keep up the charade that they belonged among these monsters.

She stared down at the photos for a moment before looking back at Dana.

Dana met her stare, her expression somber. "I know your guys are good, but getting in there might take a miracle."

Amy tried to fight against the fear that bubbled up inside her as she considered that it wasn't only Seth who was in danger. She knew that Brent and the rest of the Saint Squad had every intention of going in and bringing Seth and Vanessa home—no matter the odds. She took a deep breath as she took the photo from Dana, reminding herself that these men were among the best in the SEAL teams. "If anyone can come up with a miracle, it's the Saint Squad."

"I sure hope so."

* * *

"I'm starting to feel like a prisoner here," Vanessa said, fisting her hands on her hips. She was still frustrated by the situation with Seth from the night before, and transferring that frustration to Akil had been effortless when she had been informed that she was no longer permitted to eat in the dining room.

Instead of accepting her uncle's latest directive, she had insisted on going up to the penthouse to meet with him face-to-face. She tried not to think of the violence she had seen shimmering from him during their last confrontation, instead focusing on the need to uncover his plans.

"Lina, until Morenta leaves the compound, it isn't safe for you to be wandering through the house."

"Let me get this straight. You insisted that I stay here, even though you knew Morenta was coming, only so you could lock me in my room?" Vanessa's voice was indignant. "Why did you bring me here in the first place? I could have stayed at La Playa and been perfectly safe."

Akil's voice was tight. "La Playa was raided by the police yesterday."

"What?" Vanessa managed to look surprised. "Is that why you brought me here?"

He shook his head. "I brought you here because this is the safest place for you." He motioned for her to sit down. "I didn't expect to see Morenta here. We were supposed to meet in Colombia, but he insisted on coming here instead."

"Are you sure you trust him enough to do business with him?"

Again, Akil shook his head. He reached out and touched Vanessa's hand. "He is a necessary evil in my business, but that part will be over soon."

"Tell me what you're planning so I can help."

"It is safer if you do not know," Akil insisted. "Morenta will be leaving soon. Please indulge me and stay in your room until then. I do not want you seen by him and his men. Seth can go to the kitchen and get you whatever you need."

Vanessa let out a sigh. "When will he leave?"

"The day after tomorrow," Akil told her. "Once he is gone, we can discuss the future."

Vanessa looked at him quizzically, wondering if he would provide enough information for her to piece together his plans. Realizing that she wasn't going to get anything else out of him at the moment, she nodded and stood. "I hope you know what you are doing."

"Trust me." Akil granted her a small smile. "I know exactly what I'm doing."

21

Seth stood in the kitchen next to the dining room door as he waited for the meal that he would take upstairs to Vanessa. Several of Morenta's men were eating lunch in the dining room as they spoke in Spanish about their upcoming travels. Although Spanish was not one of the languages that Seth was completely fluent in, he understood it well enough. Unfortunately, the voices were often hushed and he was only able to pick out a few words.

Several mentions of Arizona confused him, and he tried to figure out what kind of target a terrorist would go for there. Then he heard the word *electricidad*. Electricity. A previous conversation with Vanessa flashed through his mind. He had asked her what these men were trying to accomplish. One of those possibilities was that they were trying to somehow weaken the borders between the U.S. and Mexico.

Could these men be planning some kind of attack on the power plants in Arizona? An attack that would weaken their defenses and allow the drug trade easier access?

Seth considered what he had seen on the sneak-and-peek missions over the past few weeks. The training facilities he had infiltrated had not included the shooting ranges he might have expected. Instead, the people residing there seemed to be working on something more elusive than guns, something that required planning and patience.

While weapons were certainly plentiful at each location Seth had visited, he and his teammates had also identified materials that could be used in making explosives. Seth heard someone step up behind him, and he had to use every ounce of willpower to keep from turning around.

"Hear anything interesting?" Halim asked softly, his voice carrying a hint of accusation as well as some genuine curiosity.

Seth turned to look at Halim and gave a casual shrug. "I was just wishing that I could speak Spanish," Seth admitted. He had been caught spying on Morenta's men, and he knew denying it would only raise suspicions. He considered what Vanessa had told him the night before and opted to be as truthful as he could without giving away his identity. "I don't know about you, but I don't trust these guys. I'll feel a lot better when they're gone."

Halim looked a bit surprised by his answer. After a brief moment, he let his gaze turn back to the men in the dining room. "You aren't the only one."

Tension rippled through the room when the door opened and Morenta entered with his bodyguards. Several of his men hastily finished up their meal and left the room, and others lowered their eyes to their plates as though afraid to be caught looking at their boss. Morenta didn't acknowledge anyone in the room as he crossed to the table that had clearly been reserved for him.

His dark eyes were hard and cold as they swept the room, and he waited briefly to be served. Seth could almost feel the evil emanating from the man and was grateful he wasn't in Morenta's line of sight. Turning back to look at Halim, Seth spoke quietly. "I hope Akil knows what he's doing."

"He does," Halim assured him. "But I suggest you make sure we keep Lina out of sight. It's best not to take any chances."

Seth nodded, a little surprised by Halim's obvious concern for Vanessa. In that moment, he looked like a normal man, one who cared deeply for those close to him. Seth reminded himself that Halim also had a dark side, one that could turn to murder with the least bit of provocation. When one of the cooks approached with Vanessa's food, Seth stepped toward the door. He glanced over at Halim once more and motioned to the dining room. "Watch your back."

Halim nodded, and Seth could feel his eyes on him as he left the room.

* * *

"I don't like the looks of this," Amy said to the four men who were currently studying the various satellite photos.

Quinn ignored Amy's concerns and tapped a finger on the photo of the airstrip at the fortress. "Do you think this is the same plane that was at Morenta's villa in Cali?"

"It's a good possibility." Kel nodded. "If the plane went to Cali to pick Morenta up, it would explain why there are so many people at the fortress right now."

"And it would also indicate that Morenta and Akil Ramir are planning something together," Tristan commented.

"Now that's scary," Amy said.

Kel gave a brief nod. "The rest of SEAL Team Eight arrives in the morning."

"When do you want to go in?"

"We can brief the rest of the team tomorrow after they arrive and go in tomorrow night."

"Kel, that's crazy." Amy spoke up again.

Kel turned to look at her. "I'm not leaving Seth and Vanessa in there."

"I agree, but we have to be logical," Amy told him. "According to what Vanessa told Seth, we still have another week until whatever they're planning goes down. Doesn't it make sense to give Seth and Vanessa a bit more time to figure out what's going on?"

"Akil didn't confide in Vanessa about his plans before. There's no way he's going to include her now."

"We can't be sure of that." Amy folded her arms across her chest. "She's hardly seen Akil over the past year that she's been undercover. Now that they're staying in the same place, she might have a better chance of figuring out what he's planning."

"Amy, face it. That's not going to happen," Kel disagreed. "Our best chance is to strike while everyone is at the fortress."

"In Nicaragua," Amy stated sarcastically. "We can't pull an all-out strike there, and you know it. And there's no way the Nicaraguan government is going to help us out, especially if they find out that Morenta is there."

"Then what do you suggest?"

"I don't know, but maybe it's time we spent some time praying about our options, because this is bigger than anything we've ever faced before." Amy turned and unlatched the hatch that led into the hall. "I'm going to go see if we have updated photos."

Kel watched her go and then turned to look at Brent. "You know, your wife can be a real pain sometimes."

"I know," Brent conceded. "The annoying thing is that she's usually right."

* * *

Vanessa stood up the minute Seth entered the room with their breakfast. She looked down at the floor for a moment before lifting her eyes to meet his. Her voice was unusually timid when she said, "I thought we could eat out on the balcony."

Seth simply nodded and followed her through the door. He had avoided talking to her that morning before he left to go down to the kitchen. He didn't know it was possible for the hurt of the past to come back full force, but he had spent the night mourning the reality that he and Vanessa would never have a future together. It was as though the past wounds had reopened, and a new layer of pain had been added to them.

His heart literally ached as he moved past her and set the tray on the white wicker table. He waited for her to take a seat before he sat beside her.

"What did you find out?" Vanessa asked, keeping her voice low.

Keep it business, Seth told himself. He picked up a baguette and broke it in half before finally lifting his eyes to meet hers. He took a deep breath and let it back out. "From what I've been able to piece together, it looks like one part of the plan is to take out at least one power plant. I've heard Arizona mentioned a couple of times, and Morenta's men have been talking about electricity."

"A couple of years ago there was a threat against the nuclear power plant outside of Phoenix. Do you think that could be the target?"

"Maybe." Seth paused as he buttered his bread. He then lifted his eyes to meet hers once more. "With Morenta involved, I think there's more than one target."

"I can't figure out what they're planning to do with the helicopters," Vanessa told him. "There's no way they would be able to fly into U.S. airspace without being intercepted, but everything I've heard makes me think that the attack will take place on U.S. soil."

Seth leaned forward and rested his elbows on his knees. He nodded in the direction of the airfield where the attack helicopters were parked. "Obviously you were right about them getting a hold of some Z-10s."

Vanessa nodded. "Yeah, I remember worrying about it because they carry the LR3 missiles. I'm sure you know those missiles can take down a target a good hundred miles out with decent accuracy."

Some of the tension from the night before eased out of him as Seth shook his head and let out a soft laugh.

"What?"

"I was just thinking how strange it is to be having this conversation with you. Most women don't have a clue what a Z-10 is, much less know its capabilities."

"Yeah, well I'm still trying to adjust to the fact that you could climb up the side of a building if you wanted to." Vanessa gave him a pointed look. "It's like you're Superman."

"Superman leaps tall buildings." Seth's eye lit with humor. "Spiderman is the one who climbs them."

Vanessa rolled her eyes and grinned. "Spiderman then."

Seth nodded at the ground below, where one of the patrols was crossing into their line of sight. "Just don't tell those guys you think I'm a superhero. They're suspicious enough of me as it is."

"With good reason."

"How did you learn so much about the Z-10s? That information isn't exactly readily available, even for field agents in the CIA."

"Believe it or not, my main specialties are weapons and aircraft," Vanessa told him. "In fact, the Agency even tried to teach me how to fly."

"What do you mean 'tried to'?"

"I did pretty well with the flying part. It was the landing I never managed to figure out."

"That part is kind of important." Seth gave in to the urge to grin.

The rumble of a helicopter engine sounded, and Seth watched for the helicopter on the pad beside the fortress to come into view as it did every morning. As he watched it fly over the trees, he looked back at Vanessa, possibilities flooding his mind. "What kind of security does that nuclear power plant in Arizona have?"

"It's pretty tight, especially since it's the largest in the country. Not only is the security tight on the ground, but the plant is under restricted air space, and there's an Air Force base nearby that is on standing orders to intercept."

"But it's a small base, isn't it?"

"Yeah, why?"

"I was just thinking," Seth began as he stood up and paced to the railing. Turning back to look at her, he continued, "A few years ago there was a controversy about a power station that was built in southern Arizona near the California border."

"I don't remember that."

"There was a debate over where to build it because most of the land in the southern part of the state is federally protected. A big chunk belongs to an Indian reservation, and then there's some military-owned land and national parks," Seth told her. "Apparently, they managed to get it built despite many people's concerns that it was too close to the Mexican border."

"How close?"

"Sixty, maybe seventy miles."

"Which is definitely in range of the missiles on the Z-10s."

"Yeah." Seth nodded. "They wouldn't have to cross into U.S. airspace. They could fire from Mexico."

"For what purpose?"

"That power plant doesn't serve the public. It serves the military." Seth paused for a moment. "Including the Marine bases in Yuma and Fort Huachuca."

"Fort Huachuca—as in the military base that monitors communications for terrorist activity?"

"Exactly." Seth nodded. "If that power plant were hit, the Arizona border would be completely vulnerable."

"That power plant probably also powers the new surveillance grids along the border."

Seth stared at her. "That may be exactly what's driving this whole thing. If Morenta thinks the new security is going to shut down his drug routes into the U.S., he may be trying to knock it out before it becomes operational."

"And for whatever reason, Akil has been drafted into helping him."

"It's a perfect match in that respect." Seth shook his head as everything began falling into place. "Morenta has the money to back Akil's goals of putting together a major terrorist strike, and he also eliminates a major obstacle that could stand in the way of his business."

"So if they pull this off, Morenta's drug trade continues, business as usual."

"And Akil Ramir makes world headlines by creating a nuclear disaster," Seth added. "The fallout alone could affect the entire western United States."

"We only have another week before this is going to happen," Vanessa reminded him. "How are we going to get the word out?"

"Morenta leaves the day after tomorrow," Seth told her. "As soon as he's gone, we'll see if we can pick up any more information, and then we'll get out of here."

"Do you really think we can get out of here alive?"

His eyes darkened, but he nodded. "I'll get you out of here."

22

Seth woke to a constant knocking on his door. He sat up, instantly awake, but as he listened for a moment, he realized the sound wasn't coming from the door that led to the living area, but rather the French door that led out onto the patio.

He pulled on a pair of camouflage pants and a plain T-shirt before opening the door to find Vanessa outside on the balcony. The sky was still dark, the blackness of the night just beginning to turn deep blue in the east.

Remembering the listening devices in his room, he stepped outside and listened to make sure no one was on the balcony above them before he asked, "What's going on? It's four in the morning."

"Four-fifteen, actually," Vanessa told him, looking surprised that he guessed the time so closely without the aid of a watch. "I'm sorry to wake you, but I thought you should see this." She lifted a hand and pointed at the airfield.

A supply truck was parked near one of the airplanes, and at least a dozen men were moving its contents onto an airplane.

"Do you think those are the antiaircraft guns I heard Halim talking about?"

"It's a good guess." Seth nodded. "The crates are about the right size."

"You know, I've been thinking," Vanessa started, her voice low. "If they're concerned about having antiaircraft guns in place, they're expecting some kind of retaliation."

"Either that, or they want them as a precaution to protect the helicopters."

"But if they're expecting retaliation, the power plant you were telling me about might only be the first target," Vanessa continued. "Think about it. What would happen if they were successful in taking out that power station?"

"I already told you. The military bases in that area of the country and probably the new electronic border defenses would be without power."

"And wouldn't the fighter planes at the Marine base be called in to respond?"

"Yeah, I'm sure they would," Seth agreed. "They would have emergency generators to power the flight tower and all of the essential areas on base."

"What about the planes at the Air Force base?" Vanessa asked. "Would they be dispatched too?"

"Probably." Seth's eyes narrowed. "What are you thinking?"

"I'm thinking that these helicopters are capable of flying in under our radar. If Fort Huachuca isn't fully operational, they aren't as likely to pick up the radio communication of these terrorists, and with our fighters deployed, there's a good chance they're going to try to sneak one of these Z-10s in to go for that nuclear power plant." Silence hung between them as they considered this possibility.

"If they succeeded, it would be disastrous," Seth said soberly.

"How secure is the core at the nuclear power plant?" Vanessa asked, quickly adding, "What would happen if the plant was hit by one of the LR3 missiles?"

"Remember Chernobyl?" Seth asked. "This has the potential of being twice as bad."

Vanessa nodded slowly and added, "Besides the initial explosion, we'd be dealing with a massive radiation leak, and the fallout would likely affect the entire western United States if not the whole country."

Seth's lips pressed into a hard line. "We need to find out if your theory is right."

Vanessa nodded somberly. "I know."

"We also need to get a message out to my squad."

"How are you going to do that?" Vanessa looked at him as though he had lost his mind. "We're practically being held prisoner here in our rooms, and you know they have to be tracking all communications in and out of this place."

Seth looked at her, clearly amused. "I wasn't planning on using a phone."

"Then what?"
"Trust me."

* * *

Seth had been watching the pattern of movement all day. The two-man patrols, the guards on the balcony on the roof, and those on the seventh floor. He had offered countless silent prayers asking for guidance as he contemplated his options. Finally, he was confident he could do what he needed to.

Darkness had fallen, and Seth was now dressed in the same clothes he had been wearing when he first arrived—black pants and a black shirt—only now he was barefoot. Whoever was monitoring the surveillance cameras in the living area would have seen him and Vanessa retire to their separate bedrooms more than two hours earlier. Now he moved through the door onto the balcony and started his watch.

The guard on the balcony below went through his usual ritual. He paced from one side of the balcony to the other before setting his weapon down and pulling out a cigarette. Seth took that as his cue to begin his descent. He found his first handhold and started down the side of the building. Dropping to the eighth floor was a simple feat, especially since the occupants of the eighth floor were nowhere to be seen.

Then began the more complicated part of the journey: slipping down past the seventh-floor balcony without being seen by the guard. Quietly, steadily, Seth climbed lower. He let the night surround him, his movements nearly silent.

Almost an hour passed before Seth's feet finally touched the ground. He stood still for several long moments, identifying the location of the motion detectors before beginning to pick his way through the electronic security devices. He dropped to the ground, using the darkness as cover when he heard one of the patrols heading in his direction. They circled around the helicopter and then moved off across the expanse of lawn.

Seth flexed his tense muscles, thinking wryly that Spiderman probably didn't get so stiff after spending an hour stuck on a wall. As the guards moved away from him, Seth began moving forward again. His intended destination was the Z-10 helicopter on the pad beside the fortress. Although he would have preferred trying to transmit a message on an aircraft he was more familiar with, he doubted he could make it to the airfield and back in the amount of time he had without being spotted. Instead, he continued working his way toward the lone helicopter.

After crossing the last few yards, he ducked beneath the Z-10 and checked the exterior for alarms. He found one and was quickly able to deactivate it. He then slipped into the cockpit, ducking down so that he wouldn't be visible to anyone outside. Deciphering the communications equipment took a few minutes longer than Seth had anticipated, but he was finally able to make his years of experience working with various systems pay off.

Piggybacking a signal so that it wouldn't be picked up by Akil and his men was going to be tricky, but he was determined to do it. Nearly an hour later, Seth had coded two simple messages that would begin transmitting as soon as the helicopter's engines were started. The first said simply, *Target AZ power plants*. The second message contained three more essential items. A date, a time, and a place.

* * *

"What's their target?" Quinn asked with his usual impatience. Although Kel still wanted to go in after Seth as soon as possible, the higher-ups weren't convinced that such a risky mission was in anyone's best interest. Now the squad was faced with the dilemma of proving that Seth and Vanessa were really being held at the fortress and that the intelligence they were gathering was critical—no easy task, considering that they had been out of contact for days now.

"With the intel Vanessa gave us through Seth while she was at La Playa, we should be able to narrow this down," Amy insisted.

Kel nodded, but his expression was grim. "Amy, get me everything you can on these surveillance grids along the border." He then motioned to Tristan. "And I want you to see if you can get a lead on those helicopters. Someone has to know something about them."

"I'll run an analysis on the movement in and out of Morenta's villa. Maybe we can track the target that way," Brent said.

Kel nodded, his expression serious. "Pull whatever strings you have to. Seth's already been under too long. It's time to bring him home."

* * *

The surveillance grids were a deep, dark mystery as far as Amy was concerned. She had tried uncovering information by working through her contacts in naval intelligence without any success. A friend at the FBI didn't know anything about the grids either, and the message she had left for her contact at the CIA had yet to be returned.

She knew that the Drug Enforcement Agency probably had a clue, but she didn't have any solid contacts there or in the Department of Immigration. Instead of trying to finagle sensitive information out of people she didn't know, she had finally resorted to asking the communications center on board to patch through a secure call to Senator James Whitmore, her father.

"Hi, Dad," Amy said as soon as his voice came over the line.

"Amy?" His voice was both delighted and confused. "I didn't realize you were back home."

"I'm not." Amy hesitated a moment. "Look, I hate to ask, but I need a huge favor."

"It always worries me when you start a conversation with the words 'I need a favor,'" Jim told her with humor in his voice. "What do you need?"

"I need everything you've got on the new surveillance grids along the Mexican border," Amy told him.

Jim's voice went from friendly to stunned. "How do you know about that? That information is strictly need-to-know."

"And I need to know," Amy insisted. "Dad, you know I would never ask if it wasn't important, but I have to find out if the grid is already operational and where it's being operated from."

He was quiet for a moment. Then he asked, "Is this a subway problem?"

Amy knew he was referring to the first time he had met the Saint Squad. They had been in the middle of a terrorist threat, one in which the intended target had been the Washington, DC, subway system. "Yeah, I think so."

"I'll see what I can find out," Jim told her. "But remember. This information stays need-to-know."

"I understand," Amy assured him. After hanging up with her dad, she started to leave the comm room but was stopped by a commander.

"I think you'd better see this." He held up a single piece of paper.

"What is it?" Amy reached out her hand. She read over the two lines and looked back up at him, confused. "Where did this come from?"

"It was a coded message we picked up this morning." He turned and pointed to a computer screen. "We never saw an aircraft come onto our radar, but we're sure that's where it came from. It was moving right along the coast of Nicaragua."

Amy's smile was instant, and her eyes lit up with excitement. "This is exactly what I was looking for."

23

"What in the world were you trying to pull?" Vanessa fisted her hands on her hips and fought to keep her voice low. She had gotten up in the middle of the night to see if there was any new activity on the ground. Assuming Seth was in his room, she had nearly had a heart attack when she'd turned just in time to see him climb over the railing onto the balcony.

When he appeared so suddenly, she'd assumed he had climbed up to the penthouse again. It wasn't until they were eating lunch and he saw one of the helicopters land on the helicopter pad that he told her about the message he'd sent the night before. The realization that he could have gotten himself killed without her even knowing what he was up to pushed her already strained nerves into overdrive. "You could have been killed!"

Seth blew out a breath and sat down in one of the wicker chairs on the balcony. He eased his weight down gradually as though he was worried that the chair wouldn't be able to support his weight. After settling into his seat, he ran a hand over his face before looking up at Vanessa. "You know, the only real danger was that I just about had a heart attack when I saw you standing here."

Vanessa's eyebrows lifted. "I thought you were trained to expect the unexpected."

"Honey, you could write the book about doing the unexpected," Seth muttered with a shake of his head. "I don't know what you're so upset about. I told you I was going to send a message."

She stared at him in disbelief. She had known this man once, almost as well as she knew herself. Now she was faced with the reality of just how much he had changed over the past six years. Logically she knew what a SEAL was trained to do. Seeing Seth in action, however, was completely surreal. "Seth, you climbed down nine stories, past who knows how many armed guards. Surely you realize how dangerous that was."

"Now, there's the pot calling the kettle black." Seth pushed himself out of his seat, his voice taking on an edge as he stepped toward her. "You know, the only good thing about not knowing what you've been up to since I saw you last is the fact that I didn't have to worry about where you've been this year."

"I can take care of myself," she whispered defiantly.

"I've seen that," Seth admitted. He took another step, his eyes darkening as he rested his hands on her shoulders. His voice softened as he added, "But it wouldn't have stopped me from worrying."

Vanessa's heart picked up speed as she tried to decipher Seth's expression. He had looked invincible when he'd climbed back onto the balcony, and he had been unshakable when he'd told her what he had accomplished during the night. Now she saw something she hadn't seen in years, a look of vulnerability. She had done that to him, she realized suddenly. Somehow she was able to make this man who was larger than life become a mere mortal once more. He started to lean down as though he was going to kiss her and then stopped as though he suddenly realized what he was doing.

Unwilling to let the moment pass, Vanessa leaned forward and slid a hand around the back of his neck. Reaching up, she pressed her lips to his. The kiss was brief, and she felt the muscles in his neck tense under her hand as he pulled away from her. Then he looked at her with uncertainty. "What am I going to do about you? Every time I think I have you figured out, you go and do something unexpected."

Vanessa kept her eyes on his, searching for any hint of how he felt about her now. She knew that even if he did still care about her, he didn't trust her, at least not on a personal level. "I know you may not believe this, but I never stopped loving you."

Seth's head jerked back, and he looked down at her as though he wasn't sure he had heard her right. Vanessa could almost see his mind processing her words in the way his features softened as the truth seeped through him. Then he leaned forward, and their lips met once more. Unlike the brief kiss Vanessa had given him, this kiss overwhelmed her.

Vanessa let herself get lost in the kiss. Memories tumbled over one another. The first day Seth dropped her off at her house and met her father, the way he fought back the tears at his uncle's funeral, and the laughter he held back when he had boosted her through her dorm room window when they had been out past curfew. Even the way Seth always tasted of Gatorade and sweat after every track meet. He changed the angle of the kiss, and she felt herself sigh. Now he tasted of freedom.

When he finally drew back, he looked dazed. His voice was low, barely a whisper. "I've missed you so much."

"I missed you too." She touched her hand to his cheek, hope surging through her, hope that Seth still loved her. She blinked back the sudden well of tears. "Do you think you can ever forgive me?"

Seth's eyes darkened once more, but he didn't answer. Instead he simply drew her into his arms and held on.

* * *

"It has to be from Seth," Amy said excitedly as she handed the communications report to Kel.

"Of course it's from Seth." Quinn shifted so he could read the message over Kel's shoulder.

Kel turned and stared at him for a full two seconds. And Quinn took a step back.

Returning his attention to the paper before him, Kel read the message out loud. "Target Arizona power plants." He looked at Amy for a moment and then spoke to the room in general. "It looks like they know what's going on."

"Is there any more?"

"April 12, oh-two-hundred, fortress."

"April 12th is the day after tomorrow," Brent noted. "That should give us time to get the rescue mission approved."

Before Kel could respond, the telephone rang. Amy picked it up to find her father on the other end.

"I'm not sure if this is what you're looking for, but the surveillance grids go online on April 15th," Jim Whitmore told his daughter.

"As in five days from now?" Amy asked, a new sense of trepidation shooting through her. "Do you know where the monitoring station is?"

"Yeah. It's in Sierra Vista, Arizona."

"Isn't that where Fort Huachuca is located?"

"It sure is." Jim paused a minute, and Amy could hear him rustling through some papers. "Information regarding personnel working on the project is classified, but if you need any more information, you can call Hank Rodriguez. He's in charge of the border patrol down there."

"If this information is need-to-know, why would the border patrol know that this system is coming online?" Amy asked, suddenly feeling like something was out of place.

"Only Hank and his assistant, Gordon McAllister, know about it. They were brought in since they have the most information about the weaknesses along the Arizona border," Jim told her. His voice took on a serious tone when he asked, "Should I even ask what you're working on right now?"

"Probably not, but if you wanted to have the military run a training operation down there, maybe before the 15th, it might be a good idea," Amy suggested.

"With Apaches," Kel interrupted her conversation, apparently approving of her suggestion.

"Kel really likes it when the Apache helicopters are involved."

"I see," Jim said solemnly. "Well, I guess it's about time we find a squad that needs some extra time on training exercises."

"Thanks, Dad."

"Amy, you stay safe," Jim told her, his voice filled with concern. "That goes for the rest of your squad too."

"We will," Amy promised. "I'll talk to you later."

As soon as she hung up, she turned to see everyone staring at her. She knew she probably didn't need to repeat the information her father had given her, but she relayed it anyway.

"With the operational date of the surveillance grid coinciding with when we think the terrorist strike is going to take place, we have to assume the two are related," Brent commented.

"Brent and Quinn, I want you to start working on the mission plan to go in after Seth," Kel said, then nodded at Tristan. "Go see if the rest of SEAL Team Eight has arrived. Tell them the mission briefing is at oh-eight-hundred tomorrow. I'm going to go brief the captain."

"What about me?" Amy asked as Kel moved for the door.

"Give Ellison over at CIA a call. Let him know that we've identified the potential targets."

Amy nodded and reached for the phone once more. Ignoring the activity of the rest of the squad, she placed the call and managed to reach Ellison on the first try. She relayed the first part of Seth's message and was surprised when she met some resistance.

"Your information doesn't make any sense," Ellison insisted. "The reactors at the nuclear plant in Arizona are designed to withstand the kind of attack you're talking about. Even a direct hit from a missile isn't going to break through all of the layers of reinforced concrete."

"All I know is that the message received identified power plants in Arizona as the target," Amy told him. "I think we need to proceed as though the nuclear plant is one of the power plants being targeted."

"You said power *plants.* Plural," Ellison said as though suddenly catching up with her. "So you think that there is more than one target."

"That's exactly what we think," Amy agreed. "I don't know where Fort Huachuca gets its power, but I would definitely look at giving that plant extra security as well."

"What else do you know?" Ellison asked now.

"We think that this strike is going to happen on or before April 15th."

Ellison's voice became solemn. "I see."

"I thought you might," Amy told him. "I'm sure you are aware that all of this is need-to-know. There's no way to be sure if we've plugged up all of the leaks."

"I can't believe that Ramir has more than one source."

"Perhaps not, but our source thought there could be," Amy reminded him. "And it pays to be cautious."

"Believe me, this experience has given me a new appreciation for the term 'need-to-know.'"

24

Seth spent all afternoon watching, waiting, and remembering. Vanessa's words played over and over in his mind, and he wished he had the luxury of reveling in those memories and taking time with Vanessa to make new ones. Instead, he had banished her to the interior of her suite for the rest of the day to make sure she wasn't seen by Morenta as he prepared to leave. He also needed some distance from her so he could concentrate on what he had to do to get her out of the fortress safely.

He didn't know if he could afford the feelings she was stirring up in him. Logically he couldn't imagine how he and Vanessa could possibly build a future together, but logic wasn't winning over his dreams of being with her after they escaped from this prison. He knew that he was starting to believe in miracles because he knew it was going to take a miracle to get out of the fortress safely. He would need another miracle to find a way to keep Vanessa in his life permanently this time.

Letting out a sigh, he tried to shift his thoughts back to work. He studied the movement of the guards on the ground, worried that there wasn't much preparation taking place on the airfield. As he tried to analyze what the lack of activity meant, he struggled against the thoughts of Vanessa that were invading his mind once more.

He was finally realizing that he hadn't been the only one who was hurt when she refused his offer of marriage. Could it really be that Vanessa had also been unable to move past that moment that had shattered their plans together?

She had asked him to forgive her, and Seth was now realizing that it was no longer necessary. Understanding why she had made her decision and the fact that she hadn't intended to deceive him about their future together had erascd whatever grudge he had been holding. He was also faced with the reality that the biggest obstacles between them now were the men outside holding guns.

When darkness began to fall, Seth finally gave up his post on the balcony. Not only had he not seen Morenta leave, but he also hadn't seen any indication that he was going to. The airfield had been uncommonly quiet throughout the entire day.

He walked into the living area where Vanessa was sitting on the couch, impatiently flipping through the same magazine she'd been holding when he had last seen her. He fought back a grin. "Must be a good magazine."

Vanessa gave him a tormented look. "I am going crazy being cooped up in here. Hasn't Morenta left yet?"

"Not yet." Seth shook his head. "I'll go down and get us some dinner and see if I can figure out what's going on."

He pushed the button for the elevator and was surprised when the doors slid open to reveal Halim standing inside.

"I was about to come look for you," Seth told him. He moved back so Halim could step off of the elevator. Seth glanced over at Vanessa. "We thought Morenta was leaving today."

"So did I." Halim's voice was tense. He stared at Vanessa for a moment before looking back at Seth, animosity showing on his face.

As though marking his territory, Seth sat down next to Vanessa and motioned to the seat across from him. The muscle in Halim's jaw twitched, but he lowered himself into the chair.

Seth asked, "What happened?"

"His paranoia is surfacing again." Halim shook his head. "He is convinced that one of his men is spying on him."

"How much longer do we have to deal with him?"

"It looks like he will be staying until tomorrow."

"I'll be glad to see him go." Vanessa spoke up now. "I can't wait to get out of this room."

Halim stood, looking from Vanessa to Seth. "I'll have some dinner sent up."

"You know, considering that these elevators aren't locked off, don't you think it's about time you gave me my weapons back?" Seth suggested. "Morenta has a reputation for being unstable. I'd like to be ready for him if he decides to pay us a visit."

Halim clenched his teeth and seemed to consider whether he should trust the man who had shown up so unexpectedly. Finally he said, "I'll talk to Akil."

Seth nodded and watched him disappear into the elevator.

As soon as the doors closed, Vanessa let out a heavy sigh. "I can't believe he hasn't left yet."

"Just a little longer," Seth assured her. He just hoped he was telling her the truth.

* * *

"Are you sure this is going to work?" Tristan asked skeptically. "The last time we planned on going into the fortress, they didn't have a bunch of attack helicopters parked there."

"Yeah, but last time we were trying to take someone out by force," Kel reminded him. "This time we're picking up people who actually want to come with us. Big difference."

"I still don't like the approach here." Tristan pointed at the beach where they would insert.

"We don't have a whole lot of options." Brent shifted so that he had a better view of the satellite photo on the table in front of them. He tapped a finger on the photo, considering Tristan's reservation about inserting on the open beach. "Although it might be better if we angled in on this side."

"I say we take out those Z-10s while we're there too," Quinn commented now. "Why try to figure out where they're going to be next week? We can get rid of that part of the threat when we go in and get Seth."

"I agree with you, but we don't have any authority in Nicaragua." Kel shook his head in frustration. "The powers that be won't let us do anything but go in and retrieve our people."

"If they won't let us take out the helicopters, maybe we can track them instead, especially since we'll have everyone from SEAL Team Eight on board," Brent suggested. "We can hand that task over to one of the other squads."

"That's not a bad idea." Kel turned to Amy. "See what you can do to get us the equipment we need. Convince whoever needs to be convinced that we have to be able to track these choppers."

"I love how I always get handed the easy jobs." Amy shook her head and moved toward the door. "All you guys have to do is go shoot at people."

"Yeah, well don't go slugging anyone to get your way." Kel fought back a grin and jerked a thumb toward Quinn and Brent. "That's what we have these guys here for."

Amy laughed and shook her head again as she left the room. As soon as she was gone, Quinn looked over at Brent and Kel. "Do you think Amy will get permission?"

"You know, that's one of the great things about her dad being a U.S. senator." Brent grinned. "Half of the people on board are afraid to tell her no."

"And the other half know that she's on a first-name basis with the president," Tristan added, only half exaggerating.

Kel gave a curt nod. "She'll get us what we need one way or another. We need to proceed as though tagging the Z-10s will be part of the mission. We only have a few more hours until our final mission briefing."

"I sure hope Seth is ready for us."

"Don't we all."

* * *

"What's the story?" Seth spoke quietly as he slipped into the seat beside Halim in the dining room. Once again, he had waited and watched patiently all morning for any sign of Morenta leaving and so far hadn't seen any. A handful of his men had apparently finished their lunch and were now headed for the elevator.

Halim watched the men file out of the room before answering Seth. "Akil is supposed to have dinner with Morenta to finalize their plans one last time before he leaves."

Seth blew out a breath. "He's going to be here all day?"

"I'm afraid so."

"Lina is going stir-crazy. I've got to find some way to get her out of our suite for a while."

Halim immediately shook his head. "No. She cannot be seen."

"Do you at least know what time he's is supposed to be leaving?"

Now frustration sounded in Halim's voice. "How would I know? I thought he was leaving yesterday morning."

Seth nodded sympathetically. "I don't envy your job right now. I wouldn't want to deal with Morenta or any of his men."

"You won't have to." Halim stood and pulled a handgun out of his waistband. For a moment he held it pointed at Seth.

Seth kept his eyes on Halim, refusing to look at the weapon he held. If Halim chose to take his life right now, the chances of Vanessa getting out of the fortress alive were slim. He also knew that if he made a defensive move, he might as well admit that he wasn't who he claimed to be.

Thirty long seconds ticked by before Halim finally turned the weapon and offered the butt of the gun to Seth along with a reluctant thread of trust. "Akil agreed that you should be ready in case something unexpected happens."

"Tell him thank you." Seth gave him a brief nod. He watched Halim leave the room and then blew out a long breath. In approximately twelve hours his team would be arriving, and at this point, he couldn't be sure if he would even be able to get Vanessa out of her suite. He was running out of time, and he knew it.

* * *

Vanessa could feel the waves of tension coming from Seth. Outwardly he looked completely relaxed sitting on the balcony, but she knew better. Something was definitely bothering him, and it wasn't simply the stress of being stuck in the fortress.

Even though she knew Seth wanted her to stay out of sight, she stepped to the side of the doors leading from the living area to the balcony. Through the sheer curtains, she could see the airfield and the lack of activity there. She pulled open the door and slipped out onto the balcony.

Seth turned to face her, his face filled with concern. "What are you doing out here?"

Vanessa sat down in a chair and nodded at the airfield. "No one is even out there, and when I'm sitting down no one can see me anyway."

Seth scanned the airfield and the ground below before reluctantly nodding in agreement.

"Tell me what's going on." Vanessa looked out at the water. "Why hasn't Morenta left yet?"

"He's supposed to be meeting with Akil one last time tonight."

"Then tomorrow hopefully I can find out what's really going on."

"We aren't going to be here tomorrow."

"What?" Vanessa sat up straighter in her chair. She stared at him a moment and then her eyes narrowed. "Tell me what's going on."

Seth let out a sigh. "I messed up." He shook his head and took the seat beside her. "When I sent the message to my team, I thought I gave us enough time between when Morenta would leave and when I wanted them to come in and get us." Seth's eyes met hers, and he shook his head again. "I didn't anticipate Morenta staying the extra day."

"Seth, you had no way of knowing he would delay his departure." Vanessa reached over and squeezed his hand. "When are they coming?"

"Oh-two-hundred," Seth told her. "I had planned for us to go out onto the beach and then simply disappear when my squad showed up. The guards change over at about two, and I was sure we could slip out the front door as they were changing over. I didn't expect that you would still be under house arrest though."

"So you're worried about getting me out," Vanessa concluded.

Seth nodded. He stared out at the water for a moment before turning back to her. "I know this may sound weird, but would you mind if we prayed about this?"

Vanessa gave him a surprised look.

"My squad prays at the start of every day and before every mission," Seth explained. He didn't seem the least bit embarrassed as he added, "I think we could use the Lord's help in figuring our way out through this mission."

Vanessa just stared, and then slowly a smile crossed her face. "I think that's a really good idea."

Seth slid his chair closer and reached for her hand. Then he offered a prayer unlike anything she could have ever expected. It wasn't his words so much as the emotion behind them. He asked the Lord for guidance and to watch over and protect them and those who would come into harm's way in the coming hours.

Warmth spread through her as she considered the many miracles that had already taken place for Seth to have found the gospel in his life and for him to be praying with her right now. Seeing him exercise his faith so sincerely touched her, enhancing the love she had felt for him when they had dated so many years ago as well as the years they had been apart.

When Seth closed the prayer, she was quiet for a moment. She then lifted her eyes to meet his as flashes of inspiration flooded her mind. She managed a little smile and asked, "There aren't any cameras in the elevators, right?"

"That's right." Seth nodded, looking at her a bit puzzled. "In fact, that's the biggest weakness in the security here. Unfortunately for us, the elevators are in the center of the building, and there are cameras at every landing."

"What time does the kitchen close down?"

"Between ten and eleven. Why?"

"If you don't think we can slip out the front door, maybe we could get out through the kitchen on the second floor." Vanessa considered. "After all, the lights will be off after the kitchen closes down, so the only monitors we should have trouble with are the ones in the lobby."

"The windows on the second floor have alarms on them," Seth told her, but his features softened, and Vanessa could tell he'd gotten some inspiration of his own.

"What?"

"The weight room."

"What about it?"

"It's on the fourth floor, and those windows don't have alarms. We might be able to leave that way," Seth suggested. "The elevator opens right up into the weight room area, and I only noticed two surveillance cameras in there."

"Seth, I hate to burst your bubble, but I'm not exactly Spiderman—or Spiderwoman. You can climb down the side of the building, but I haven't exactly learned that skill yet."

"You're about to," Seth told her.

"You can't be serious." Vanessa eyed him suspiciously.

"The one advantage of these renovations is that the east wing is right under the window in the gym," Seth explained. "We'll drop down onto the roof, cut over to the back side of the building, and climb down that way. Then we just have to cut over to the jungle and work our way back to the beach."

"Seth, you're still talking about having me climb down two stories," Vanessa reminded him.

"Don't worry. I'll help you through it," Seth said as though daring her to back away from the challenge. Then he nodded toward the living area. "But first we need to work on blinding some of the surveillance cameras."

"How are we going to do that?" Vanessa asked. "It's not like we've got the equipment or access to tap into their system."

"No, but I can disable one of the cameras in the weight room and make it look like a malfunction. That area is probably of low enough priority that no one will bother to check it out as long as the other one is working. Even if they do, hopefully they won't have a replacement camera here on site," Seth told her. "That should create enough of a blind spot for us to slip through the far window."

"What about the cameras up here?"

"I think we'd better do some laundry."

"Laundry?"

"Yeah." Seth nodded. "Believe it or not, it works every time."

25

It would have been too easy had Akil and Morenta chosen to eat dinner on the penthouse balcony. Instead they were at the table right inside the doors that led to the penthouse balcony. The closed doors.

A short time earlier, Seth had made one final trip down to the kitchen to pick up some dinner for him and Vanessa even though food was the last thing on his mind. He had lingered long enough to find out where this final meeting was going to take place before returning to his room and escorting Vanessa out onto the balcony where they could eat and talk in private.

While Seth was downstairs, Vanessa had taken care of her laundry, so to speak. The room was literally littered with the shirts and skirts that she had worn since her arrival, each piece hanging strategically to create blind spots for the men monitoring the surveillance cameras in the suite.

Seth had tested those blind spots the minute he arrived back in their suite. He had blocked the elevator doors long enough to disable the chime that announced when the elevator arrived, figuring that if anyone saw the elevator doors, they would come question him before they were finished with their dinner.

Now that nearly an hour had passed since Seth arrived back with their food and they hadn't had any unexpected visitors, he was hopeful that their escape plan might actually work. At the moment, he and Vanessa were out on the balcony, knowing that the conversation they had been waiting to hear was about to begin in the suite above them. Seth pushed the last of his dinner around his plate and glanced up at the ceiling. "As soon as it gets a bit darker, I'm going to climb up and see what's going on."

Vanessa's eyebrows lifted. "Morenta is totally paranoid. He probably has bodyguards by the balcony doors."

"I'll be careful," Seth told her. "I at least want to get another good look at Morenta. It's not like many people get that opportunity."

"I guess it would have been too simple for me to fall for a guy who wants to see regular celebrities. No, I fall for someone who wants to spy on a mass murderer." Vanessa pushed back her plate and leaned on the table. "I'm going to be really ticked if you go get yourself killed so close to when we're planning to get out of here."

Seth chuckled as he leaned back in his chair. "Duly noted."

Vanessa stood and stepped closer to him, suddenly serious. She rested her hands on his shoulders, and Seth couldn't help but look up into her eyes. "I don't want to lose you again."

Seth stared up at her as she leaned closer and touched her lips to his. For an instant he was lost. This was what he wanted, these sweet, simple moments with Vanessa. The shared dinners and conversation, her sweet kisses, and even the arguments. He wanted to simply be with her. Always. His heart squeezed in his chest as reality crept in that neither of them had the kind of career that would give them those opportunities.

When she pulled away, all he could do was stare at her.

"I mean it," she continued, her eyes serious. "I don't want to lose you."

"I don't want to lose you either," Seth managed, "but I can't afford any distractions right now either."

Vanessa nodded slowly and stepped back. Suddenly brusque, she glanced upward before looking back at him. "Do you really think that you'll be able to see anything if you climb up to the penthouse?"

"There's only one way to find out."

* * *

Vanessa had been right about Morenta's paranoia. Seth had climbed high enough to peek over the side of the railing of the penthouse balcony, but all he could see were bodies. Large bodies.

Rather than the private meal that Seth had anticipated Akil and Morenta having, there appeared to be at least half a dozen men sitting around the dinner table that had been set up near the balcony doors, and another dozen or so men were mulling about the room. Seth figured that the four stationed near the exits, the two by the elevator, and two more by the balcony doors were bodyguards for Morenta.

Morenta might have been considered paranoid, but Seth considered him cautious. Not many people recognized a balcony as easy access, but the SEAL teams knew it was exactly that. One of the bodyguards shifted, and Seth ducked below the solid railing of the balcony to keep from being spotted. Keeping himself pressed into the shadows, he waited a minute before cautiously peeking over the edge once more.

Seth had climbed up shortly after nine o'clock to spy on this late dinner, and now he was getting antsy that the hour had grown so late. His stiff muscles told him he had been there for hours, but he took a quick peek at his watch anyway and was frustrated to see that it was nearing midnight. He shifted his gaze once more to the penthouse suite.

Because of the two broad-shouldered men standing in front of the French doors, he could only catch glimpses of the people at the table. He saw someone clearing plates away from the table as the men continued to talk. He then saw Morenta motion to one of his men. The man offered the oversized briefcase he held to Akil. A moment later two sets of keys dropped into Morenta's open hand.

The moment Morenta closed his fingers around the keys, his eyes flashed with an odd combination of satisfaction and anticipation. Underlying both was an unnerving threat of violence.

Morenta gave Akil a hard stare and then a subtle nod. Then everyone pushed back from the table, and Morenta's men headed for the elevator. For the first time since his silent arrival, Seth was able to see clearly into the penthouse. Akil had apparently handed the briefcase off to Halim because Halim was now standing in the background holding it as Morenta stepped forward and shook hands with Akil.

Akil's face paled slightly when Morenta leaned closer and appeared to whisper something to him. Then Akil gave him a curt nod.

Seth didn't know what had been said, but he guessed that Morenta had issued his standard threat, the same threat that caused so many people to avoid doing business with him. The old, *if anything goes wrong, you and your family will pay for it.*

Aware that he wasn't likely to gain any new information, Seth began the descent to his own balcony, where Vanessa was waiting impatiently.

"Well?"

"I couldn't hear anything, but I did see an exchange. It looked like money for vehicles."

"What kind of vehicles?"

"Judging by the size of the briefcase and the fact that I only saw Akil hand over two sets of keys, I'd say we're talking about a couple of the helicopters over there."

"Morenta with Z-10s?" Vanessa's eyes widened. "None of this makes any sense. Every time I think we're starting to figure out what's going on, we find a new piece of information that changes everything."

"I guess it's possible that Morenta's men are going to strike rather than Akil's," Seth suggested.

"But all of my information indicates that it was Akil running those training camps for the past few weeks," Vanessa reminded him. "Why would he go to all of that effort if his men weren't going to be involved?"

"You're right. None of this is making any sense," Seth said quietly. He glanced out at the airfield, where there still wasn't any indication of Morenta preparing to leave. "But we can't worry about that now. It's time for us to get out of here."

"What time do we leave?"

"Fifteen minutes," Seth told her. "Right now, we're going to go inside and let the security guys hear us say good night. Then at twelve-thirty, we're going to meet at the elevator and go downstairs."

A surge of adrenaline rushed through her. "I sure hope this works."

"We'll get out of here," Seth assured her once more. He took her hand and reached for the door handle. "Come on. Showtime."

Vanessa stared up at him and nodded. "Okay."

They both walked into the living area just as the elevator doors slid open. Halim stepped out, a gun in hand. Seth didn't have to look twice to know that the weapon was one of his own.

"Akil is letting me have my spare?" Seth asked, somewhat surprised when Halim simply handed the weapon to him.

"With good reason." Halim nodded. He looked at Vanessa somewhat apologetically. "Morenta knows that Lina is here."

"What?" Seth's surprise was genuine. "How?"

"I don't know." Halim gave a shrug. "We think he paid someone off to find out who was staying here." He looked around the room at the laundry drying everywhere. He motioned to one of the shirts hanging over the edge of a chair. "What is all of this?"

"Laundry."

"Why didn't you have the servants take care of it?"

"Boredom set in," Vanessa said dryly. Then she waved a hand and got back to the more important subject. "How would Morenta know about me?"

"We gave him the eighth floor suite, the one right below yours. He must have figured that whoever was staying on the ninth floor was important to Akil," Halim told her. He then turned and addressed Seth. "Akil has decided to send Lina to her father's villa in France until his business dealings with Morenta are complete."

"When?" Vanessa asked before Seth had the chance to.

"I'm not sure yet. We are still working out the details."

"Give me a plane, and I will fly her out of here tonight," Seth suggested strongly. He went over the timeline in his head. If he could get in the air by one-thirty, he could get a message out in time to have his team abort the rescue mission. "We need to get her out of sight where Morenta can't get to her."

"You can fly?" Halim asked suspiciously.

"I was a pilot for Fahid among other things," Seth informed him. "At times like these, it pays to have people you can trust who can take care of the aircraft."

"We still don't know when Morenta is leaving," Halim told them. "Akil will certainly want to wait until he and his men are gone before we move Lina."

"If we wait, how can we be sure he won't decide to take Lina with him for insurance?" Seth pushed. He knew that if Akil was willing to let Seth have both of his weapons, he would likely increase his security both in the building and on the grounds.

"Akil has increased the number of guards at the airfield. He also is making sure that Morenta has some of our men available to escort him to the plane when he is ready to leave."

"You know how risky this is," Seth stated, his eyes serious.

Halim looked at Vanessa for a long moment before turning his eyes back to Seth. "I trust that you can keep her safe."

"I'll do everything I can," Seth said sincerely. He then added, "I will plan on seeing you in the morning so we can make arrangements to move Lina."

Halim nodded. He then turned and stepped back into the elevator.

As soon as he was gone, Seth turned to Vanessa. He leaned down and kissed her softly. "Try and get some sleep, okay?" He then leaned closer and whispered, "Fifteen minutes."

Vanessa nodded. "Good night."

26

Vanessa changed into dark clothes and the previously white tennis shoes that Seth had darkened with shoe polish. Then she waited for the minutes to pass by. She trusted Seth, but she didn't know how he was going to manage to get her past all of the security. Sure he had slipped out and sent a message out to his squad, but he hadn't been dealing with any extra baggage at the time—namely her.

Her heart was racing when the time finally came to leave her room. She had deliberately left her door ajar, just wide enough so that she could slip out without moving it. Following the path that Seth had outlined for her earlier, she padded through the dark room.

She reached the blind spot by the elevator and stood anxiously waiting. In the darkness, she couldn't see Seth moving toward her, but she trusted that he was there. She listened for any sound, for any sign that he was coming, but there was none.

When the doors of the elevator began to open, she froze. How could she explain why she was standing here in the dark? What if it was Morenta or one of his men? She started to back away, but then she saw him. Seth was standing in the living room on the other side of the elevator holding a single finger up to his mouth.

He motioned for her to duck down, and she responded immediately. Then, the elevator doors slid open, and a man stepped into the room carrying an AK-47 assault rifle. Vanessa didn't see Seth move, but suddenly the weapon was on the ground and a muffled groan sounded. A split second later Seth's elbow came up with enough force to render the man unconscious. He then quietly lowered him to the floor.

Seth kicked the assault rifle toward Vanessa and proceeded to search the man. He paused long enough to remove the man's cell phone from his pocket and then pull a pistol out of a shoulder holster. He glanced back at Vanessa for a moment and then turned back to the man and unbuckled his holster. Still holding the cell phone, Seth handed Vanessa the handgun and the holster. She tried not to think about the way her hands were shaking when she took it. She watched Seth grab the assault weapon and slip the strap over his shoulder. With Vanessa still staring at him wide-eyed, he ushered her into the elevator.

Her heart pounding, she took a deep breath and slowly let it out. Her hands still shaking, she engaged the gun's safety, put the weapon in the holster, and then strapped it over her shoulder. When she looked up at Seth, he once again lifted a finger to his lips, but this time he gave her a nod of encouragement. She continued to stare at him, still stunned at how quickly he had pulled the man out of the elevator. Logically she understood the kind of training he had gone through to become a SEAL, but seeing his training in action had boosted Seth up to the top of her list of superheroes.

As they neared the fourth floor, Seth stepped to the front of the elevator and motioned for Vanessa to step behind him. The lights were all off when the elevator doors slid open. Together they moved to the wall closest to them and edged alongside it to the window. Even though Vanessa knew Seth had already checked the window for alarms earlier that day, she watched him examine it again before sliding it open.

He then turned back to her and spoke, his voice low. "I'm going to climb down first. As soon as I reach the bottom, ease yourself out the window and let yourself drop down. I'll catch you."

"You'll catch me?"

"Trust me," Seth insisted. "You have to trust me."

Vanessa was still shaking with adrenaline, but she nodded.

A moment later, Seth was out the window and pressed against the side of the building as he steadily lowered himself down onto the roof below him. When he looked up and motioned for her to follow, Vanessa climbed out so that she was sitting on the window ledge. She knew that once she dropped down with Seth, there would be no turning back. Of course, with an unconscious man in her suite, she had probably already passed the point of no return.

Gripping the windowsill with her hands, Vanessa eased the lower part of her body over the side, scraping her stomach on the ledge. Ignoring the pain, she pushed back farther until her whole body was dangling from the window ledge. She started to twist to the side so that she could look down at Seth, but before she could, she felt his hands grip her legs.

She took one deep breath and then, trusting Seth to help her, she let go. Two seconds later her feet were firmly on the roof beside Seth. She looked up at him, wondering how he could make it seem so easy.

Seth was staring at her, but he didn't speak. Instead he gave her shoulder an encouraging squeeze and pointed to the back of the building. He kept his body pressed against the side of the building, and Vanessa followed suit. When they reached the side, Vanessa looked down and then shook her head as she looked back at Seth. There was no way she could climb down the twenty feet to the ground.

Seth lifted his eyebrows and leaned close. "Would it help if I dared you?"

Annoyance flashed in Vanessa's eyes. Seth knew she had never been able to turn down a challenge, and he was using it against her now. She shook her head in frustration, but when she spoke, she asked simply, "How do I do this?"

"First take off your shoes and give them to me," Seth instructed her. As soon as she handed them to him, he tied the laces through his belt loop. "Now, you're going to start by easing yourself over the side. Then you find a good foothold. We're going to lower ourselves a few inches at a time."

Vanessa let out the breath she had been holding. "Okay."

Seth lowered himself down and found his first foothold. He then waited as Vanessa followed suit. She struggled, fighting against gravity and her own fears as each time she tried to ease her weight down her foot slipped.

Leaning closer to her, Seth whispered once more, "Relax. I know you can do this." He reached over and helped guide her foot to where a brick protruded out from the wall slightly. To her surprise, he shifted his body so that he was behind her instead of beside her.

"You're going to fall," Vanessa whispered, worried at the way he had to shift his body away from the wall as he tried to shield her.

"No one's going to fall," Seth whispered back, the warmth of his breath tickling her ear. "Move your right hand down. Run your fingers along the wall until you find something to hold onto."

Vanessa closed her eyes. She had to do this. She could feel the solid wall of muscle behind her and the leather of her gun holster digging into her skin. The thought of what might happen if she and Seth didn't get out raced through her mind. She took a calming breath, uttered a silent prayer, and slowly followed Seth's instructions.

When she couldn't find a finger hold, she let Seth guide her hand and then gripped the rough spot in the wall tightly. "Okay, now what?"

"Just a few inches at a time," Seth reminded her. He helped her shift down by a few more inches and then adjusted his position to match hers. Their progress was painstakingly slow, but gradually they made their way downward.

When suddenly the heat from Seth's body was no longer pressed against her, Vanessa froze and gripped the wall tighter.

"It's okay," Seth said in a low voice as his hands came around her waist. "I've got you."

Vanessa let her body relax, and she looked down to see that she was within four feet of the ground. Seth quickly lowered her down and pulled her next to the building. Vanessa leaned her head against the side of the building, her fingers and toes aching. She wasn't going to think about what Seth had helped her accomplish yet. She knew they still had a long way to go.

Beside her, Seth untied her shoes from his belt loop and handed them to her. He nodded at them, a silent signal for her to put them on. While she pulled the first shoe on, Seth shifted the automatic weapon he held, pointing it out into the darkness.

He looked like he was about to go to battle, and Vanessa was struck with the very real fact that they were in the middle of a war, one they were going to have to fight their way out of. When he turned back to her, he tapped his watch. She looked down at her own watch, her eyes widening. They had less than twenty minutes until his squad was supposed to arrive, and they still had to cross the open yard.

Seth took one step forward and then held up a hand, signaling her to stop. He pushed himself back against the wall once more and nodded for Vanessa to do the same. Together they faded into the blackness of the shadows. A moment later she understood why. Footsteps were coming toward them.

The two-man patrol came into sight, crossing from the airfield to the beach and then circling wide around the building. Only once did one of the guards glance directly at the spot where Vanessa and Seth were standing, but he never moved close enough to see into the shadows.

Minutes ticked by, and Vanessa could feel Seth's growing impatience. The patrol had robbed them of ten precious minutes, and the moment the guards moved around the corner out of sight, Seth tapped her shoulder and together they moved forward.

In the distance, the engine of an airplane came to life. Vanessa guessed that Morenta was finally going to leave. She only hoped that the activity on the airfield would keep the guards busy for the next few minutes.

Vanessa followed closely behind Seth, watching as he probed the ground in front of him before putting his weight down. She had thought that he would move faster through the open field. When he pointed out a booby trap, she understood why he was moving so cautiously.

They were halfway through the open yard when they heard the shouts from up above them echoing through the stillness of the night.

27

Seth took two seconds to look up, to see that the lights in the ninth-floor suite were now illuminated, and to see the guards who were scrambling to find them. He calculated the distance they still had to cover and the time they still had until his squad arrived. The Saint Squad would be on time. He was sure of it. But would they understand if he was late? And more importantly, could they afford for him to be late?

With the activity on the airfield, Seth doubted it.

He had hoped to continue working toward the jungle and then circle back to the beach, but he knew there wasn't time. He motioned for Vanessa to drop to the ground, pleased that she did so without question. Using the cover of darkness, they crawled forward and headed straight for the beach.

Seth could still hear shouts in the distance as well as the engine of an airplane on the airfield. *Make that two,* he corrected, as he heard another engine start up. His internal clock told him that if they could keep their pace, they would be able to arrive at the beach on time, maybe a minute late.

They were only twenty feet from where the grass gave way to sand when Seth heard the whirring of helicopter rotors. His heart kicked into overdrive as he considered the implications of that sound. The Z-10 he had sent the message from was equipped with heat-sensing radar. The moment it lifted above them, the pilot would know they were there, unless they could get into the ocean quickly so that their body heat would be camouflaged by the cold water.

Seth grabbed Vanessa's arm, dragging her along as he sped up his pace and tried to ignore the sound of an airplane taking off. Less than two minutes and his team would appear. He knew they must be inserting at this very moment. He also knew that if they were coming in underwater, they wouldn't hear the helicopter. They wouldn't know of the danger.

Suddenly, the sound of gunfire erupted, and the helicopter became the last of Seth's worries. His first thought was that somehow one of his squad members had been spotted. Then he realized that one of Akil's patrols was running toward him and Vanessa. Apparently the gunfire had only been a warning, but Seth had little doubt that those bullets would hit their target the next time.

Gripping the assault rifle, Seth glanced over at Vanessa and spoke over the chaos. He couldn't think of his feelings for her or what he would do if they didn't get out of here alive. He had to focus on the specifics of this mission and let his training take over.

"When I tell you, run for the water." He could see the panic in her eyes, but there wasn't time to explain. He had to trust that his squad would be there. He had to trust them to get her to safety even if he couldn't follow.

Seth shifted slightly, angled his weapon, and yelled, "Go!"

In that instant, Seth opened fire on the guards as Vanessa jumped to her feet and sprinted across the last section of yard. Seth's shots were accurate, and both guards dropped to the ground. Seth then turned and ran after Vanessa, listening for the footsteps and commotion that were sure to be headed his way.

He heard the helicopter lift off, drowning out the sound of the approaching guards. He glanced back in time to see three guards round the corner. Seth turned to shoot, determined to protect Vanessa. But before he could pull the trigger, shots rang out; however, this time the bullets weren't coming toward Seth and Vanessa. They sounded from the jungle and sparked toward the guards.

Seth felt new hope surge through him. His squad was here to take them home. He couldn't see them, but he had no doubt that the men covering him from behind the nearby palm tress were the other members of his squad. In front of him, Vanessa reached the sand and stumbled forward. Seth reached down and pulled her up by her arm, practically dragging her toward the water.

Suddenly Kel and Brent were by his side, HK-47s in their hands as they fired rapidly to ward off the dozen mercenaries on the ground as well as the snipers up on the roof of the fortress.

"We've got Zodiacs behind those trees," Kel told Seth. "Get her out of here. We'll cover you."

"Got it." Seth kept his hand firmly on Vanessa's arm and pulled her down the beach toward the safety of the trees. He could hear the helicopter moving overhead and saw the sparks of one of his teammates' gunfire shifting toward the new target. Then he heard the unmistakable sound of the Z-10's gunfire.

The scene could have been straight out of a war movie, bullets coming down from the aircraft, marking the beach as they searched for their targets. Only this wasn't a movie. Those were his friends on the beach behind him, and it wasn't some movie star he was holding on to. This was the first and only woman he had ever loved.

"Come on!" Seth heard Quinn shout from the trees.

Seth and Vanessa sprinted the last few yards and dove for cover in the trees. The sound of bullets striking bark rattled above them. Seth turned back to see Kel and Brent still on the beach, but only one of them was standing. Even from this distance Seth could tell that it was Brent who leaned down to pull Kel up out of the water.

"Give them some cover fire!" Seth shouted, not taking the time to consider how severely injured their commanding officer might be. He pushed Vanessa's head down and turned to fire at the men who were quickly closing in on Brent and Kel. In the distance he could hear the helicopter circling to come through for another pass.

No longer were there just a dozen men heading toward them, but rather fifty. Beside him, Vanessa had pulled her gun free and was lying on the ground firing off shots. Miraculously, Brent and Kel cleared the treeline without being hit by any of the crossfire.

"Get to the boats now!" Brent ordered. He still had one arm wrapped around Kel and the other holding his HK-47.

"How bad is he hit?" Seth asked, moving to help with Kel even as he motioned for Vanessa to follow Tristan, who had taken point.

Even though Seth had been talking to Brent, Kel answered, his voice pained and clipped. "Don't worry about me. Let's go."

Seth looked down and saw the trickle of blood running down Kel's leg as he and Brent moved forward and Quinn took position behind them. The helicopter buzzed overhead, strafing the jungle with gunfire. They all dropped for cover, forced to wait until the helicopter moved to circle once again before they could start forward.

"We need to call in for some support," Seth told Brent, his gaze still on Vanessa as she continued to follow Tristan.

"Already did. They'll come in as soon as we're in the water."

The next three minutes seemed to last forever. The helicopter shot off another round above them, causing them to take cover once more. Quinn's weapon sprayed off several rounds each time Akil's men got too close. Finally, when Seth wondered if they were ever going to make it, they emerged into a little clearing where two Zodiac boats were waiting.

Tristan jumped into one and reached over to help Brent and Seth pull the now semi-conscious Kel in behind him.

"Vanessa, get in that one." Seth nodded to the other boat as Quinn shot off another round and came into view. A moment later, they cast off, Quinn and Seth pulling one boat out past the surf, and Tristan and Brent pulling the other.

Shouts and gunfire followed them the moment they were clear of the surf and pulled themselves into the boats. Seth didn't have to look to know that Akil's men had finally figured out where they had disappeared to and had decided to take their frustration out on them.

"Stay down!" Seth ordered Vanessa before turning to Quinn. "Where's our backup?" Then a missile whizzed through the sky, and the helicopter exploded into a fiery ball falling out of the sky.

"Does that answer your question?" Quinn asked dryly.

28

"How are you doing?" Seth laid his hand over Vanessa's, and she looked up at him from her hospital bed.

"I'm okay. How's the commander?" Vanessa asked. As soon as they had arrived onboard the *USS Harry S. Truman,* they had been taken to sick bay to be checked out, but Vanessa hadn't heard anything about Kel's condition except that he had been medivacked to the United States.

"He'll live." Seth's eyes were somber, and he gave her hand a squeeze. "Doc said the bullet lodged in his thigh. He's scheduled for surgery this afternoon at Bethesda Naval Hospital. We probably won't get word about how bad it is until later tonight."

Vanessa stared up at him, touched and a little surprised to see how deeply Seth seemed to be sharing Kel's pain. "You're worried that this could end his career, aren't you?"

Seth jerked a shoulder and avoided her eyes, instead looking at the bandage on Vanessa's shoulder. "What did Doc say about you?"

"It's nothing. Two stitches is all," Vanessa told him. She vaguely remembered the sharp pain in her arm when she had dropped to the ground when the helicopter had opened fire on them, but she hadn't even realized she was bleeding until she had gotten to the infirmary and the nurse had seen the tear in her sleeve. She'd assumed that she had caught herself on something when she dove to the ground, but after looking at the hole in her shirt, she and the doctor both came to the same conclusion. She had been very lucky. It had been a bullet that grazed her skin.

"You scared me."

"I still can't believe we made it out of there." Vanessa trembled as she looked up at him. "I've never been so scared in my life."

"Me neither," Seth said softly. He gave her hand a squeeze and nodded toward the door. "You try to get some sleep. I'll come back and get you when it's time for your debriefing."

"Shouldn't that be happening now? We have no idea what Akil and Morenta are going to do now that we've disappeared, especially after that firefight took place at the fortress. For all we know, they might move up their plans."

Seth shook his head. "If anything, it will probably set them back while they regroup," he told her. "I've already given the captain our basic information. We'll both go through the more in-depth interviews in a few hours."

Vanessa stifled a yawn. "In that case, shouldn't you get some sleep too?"

"Don't worry about me." Seth forced a smile. "I'll see you in a little while."

* * *

"How's Vanessa doing?" Brent asked as soon as Seth walked into their boardroom.

"A couple of stitches, but she's okay," Seth told him. He glanced around to see Amy sitting at one of the three computer stations on one side of the room. Tristan was standing in the center of the room, looking through a stack of satellite photos.

"A message came down a few minutes ago. That CIA guy, Ellison, is supposed to be arriving in a few hours for another set of debriefings."

"All right." Seth turned back to Brent and asked, "Any more news about Kel?"

"Not yet." Brent shook his head.

Seth dropped into a chair and ran a hand over his face. "I'm sorry, Brent. I should have taken Akil Ramir out instead of going with him."

"Why didn't you?" Brent asked now, curiosity in his voice rather than accusation.

"I was afraid that his plans would go forward whether he was alive or not," Seth told him before admitting his deeper fear. "I was also worried Vanessa would be hit. Halim already had his gun drawn when he came into the boathouse."

"Both of which were good reasons to go undercover instead," Brent stated matter-of-factly.

Seth shook his head, not convinced. "I never should have had you come in after us. I could have kept sending messages out instead."

"Yeah, but for how long?" Brent asked. He shook his head and continued. "Seth, this isn't your fault. If we hadn't gotten you out when we did, there's no way to be sure you could have given us all of the information you gathered. Not to mention that you were never prepped to go undercover at the fortress in the first place."

"Still, this never should have happened."

Amy pushed back from her computer station and crossed the room to face the two men. She folded her arms across her chest and stared at Seth. "Are you finished beating yourself up yet?"

Seth turned to look at her and recognized the defiant look in her eyes. He knew Amy well enough to know how to avoid a confrontation with her, but he stepped into the line of fire anyway. "Amy, it's my fault that Kel was shot," Seth told her. "There was a reason we didn't go in after Fahid Ramir at the fortress three years ago. The risks were too high."

"And Kel knew the risks. Now it's time to get over it," Amy stated. "Besides, this is one of the risks you all took when you signed up to be SEALs."

"Yeah, but you know that we tend to avoid missions where we're sure to have people shooting at us."

"Did you pray before you sent that message out?"

"What?"

"You heard me," Amy insisted. "When you sent out the message giving us the time to be at the extraction point—did you pray before you sent it?"

"Yeah." Seth shook his head, bewildered. "What does that have to do with anything?"

"We prayed before they left to meet you too," Amy told him. "And we trusted the Lord to watch over everyone during this mission, even knowing the risks."

Her posture changed from confrontational to understanding. She laid a hand on Seth's arm and continued. "Kel put his life in the Lord's hands, and this is what happened. For some reason, this is a challenge he has to go through. One way or another though, he's going to be all right."

"I hope so," Tristan muttered under his breath.

"And you." Amy wagged a finger at Tristan, sounding much more like his mother than a coworker.

"What? I didn't do anything."

"No, but you're going to." Amy pointed at the door. "Go find a phone and call your wife. Chances are the news will leak out about a sailor getting injured. You don't want Riley to think it's you."

"Why would she think that the injured sailor is me?"

"Men." Amy sighed heavily. "Just trust me on this."

Quinn walked into the boardroom and effectively interrupted Amy's lecture. "I think we caught a break."

"What?" Seth asked anxiously.

"We got something from that cell phone you lifted off the man in your room. They confirmed that he was one of Morenta's men," Quinn told him, riffling through the file he held. "Intel tracked all of the calls for the phone numbers that were in his address book. We definitely found some interesting conversations."

"What did you find out?"

Quinn finally found the paper he was looking for and handed it to Seth. "Look at this one."

Brent moved closer so he could read it as well. The descriptive line on the top of the page annotated that it was a dialogue between two men.

Voice 1: You said your security was infallible. I lost three men last night.

Voice 2: What happened last night had nothing to do with my security and everything to do with you. Who were those men?

Voice 1: I could ask you the same thing.

Voice 2: Tell me where Lina is.

Voice 1: Ahhh. You think I sent some of my men in so that I would have some extra insurance.

Voice 2: The thought crossed my mind. One of your men was found unconscious in her room.

Voice 1: A minor casualty in a much larger picture. It is time for us to look to the future. Get your people in place. I want everything to stay on schedule.

Voice 2: Return my niece to me, or nothing will happen. On schedule or otherwise.

Voice 1: Perhaps you don't understand. We will go forward with the plan or you can be certain you will never see your niece again. I will talk to you again in three days after you finish your work.

Seth read through the text twice before looking up at the rest of his squad and handing the paper back to Quinn, who then passed it to Amy. "This had to be Akil and Morenta talking."

"Morenta actually took credit for taking Lina," Brent said with a shake of his head. "You've got to love the nerve of this guy."

"You know what this means?" Amy asked after reading through the text as well. "Ramir doesn't have a clue that the SEALs were at the fortress last night. Other than the men he lost during your skirmish, he is likely to go forward on schedule."

"Yeah, but Morenta knows we were there. He might not know it was U.S. Navy SEALs, but he has to know that someone else came in and took Lina," Brent reminded her.

"Morenta may not care who was at the fortress last night," Seth said now. "He's ruthless enough to push past anything that gets in his way. If he wants this border surveillance system destroyed, I don't think he's going to let on that he knows there may be some unexpected obstacles, especially if he's having Ramir do the dirty work."

"And letting Ramir think that he has Lina not only hides the fact that there may be some opposition to their plans—it also gives him some added influence to get the job done," Tristan surmised.

"Exactly," Brent agreed.

"We've got to figure out where they're planning to attack from," Seth said, stating the obvious.

Brent nodded. "And soon."

29

Vanessa stepped into the conference room on the ship and looked around. A television in the corner was on, but no one seemed to be watching it, and several people were scattered around the room. To her surprise, Seth wasn't one of them. She had expected him to get her for this debriefing, but instead a civilian named Amy had come to escort her here. Amy motioned to the long table situated in the middle of the room. "Go ahead and sit down. The rest of my squad should be here shortly."

"Thanks," Vanessa said as Amy moved to the head of the table, where an officer was speaking with an enlisted man. She thought that both of them had been among those who had rescued her from Akil Ramir, but she couldn't be sure. Even after all of the training she had gone through, she was having trouble distinguishing exactly what had happened in the early morning hours, especially after the first shots were fired.

As Vanessa reached for a chair, a man in civilian clothes stood and offered a hand. "Vanessa, I'm Rick Ellison. CIA."

She shook his hand, trying to remember where she had heard his name before. "You're the one who sent Seth in to find me."

"That's right." Rick waited for her to sit down and then took the seat beside her. "I don't know if you are aware, but we did find a leak at the field office in Santo Domingo."

"No, I hadn't heard." Vanessa shook her head. "That's good news."

Before Rick could say anything else, Seth walked in with another man in uniform. Seth's eyes met hers briefly before he and the other man sat down across the table from her and Rick Ellison.

"Let's get started," the man at the head of the table said. He stood long enough to flip off the television, effectively silencing the broadcast about a trial in Phoenix for a drug smuggler. He then introduced himself as Lieutenant Brent Miller before proceeding to introduce everyone at the table, including Seth, his teammates, and their intelligence officer, Amy Miller.

As soon as the introductions were made, Amy asked Brent, "Where do we stand on locating the Z-10s?"

"The other SEAL squad did succeed in placing locators on two of the Z-10s at the fortress. They weren't able to tag the third one because of the activity during our escape," Brent informed them. "The other Z-10 was shot during the encounter."

"There were other SEALs there last night?" Vanessa looked at them wide-eyed.

Brent nodded. "A two-man team went in through the jungle to infiltrate the airfield. One of our main objectives was to be able to track these helicopters so that we could determine where Ramir is planning to strike from."

"Where are the helicopters now?" Ellison asked.

"They're both still at the fortress," Brent Miller informed him.

"I'll need the frequency of the tracking devices so that the CIA can keep tabs on these helicopters as well," Ellison said as he jotted down some notes.

"Negative," Brent said, his voice commanding. "This information is need-to-know."

Ellison looked up, clearly surprised that he was being denied access. "But now that the mole has been identified, surely we need to give the intelligence community the means to battle this potential terrorist threat."

Seth spoke now. "You only identified one mole. Our impression was that Halim had more than one source."

"Your impression," Ellison repeated. "You don't have any facts to support this theory. It's hard enough to believe that Ramir managed to trick one woman into leaking information. Having a second source is highly unlikely."

"The mole you identified was a woman?" Vanessa asked. "When Halim spoke to me about his sources, he definitely indicated that one was a man who could be trusted. He never spoke of a woman."

"Halim might have been referring to Roberto, the woman's boyfriend. Besides, how can we be sure he trusted you?"

"He didn't trust me," Vanessa said bluntly. "But he believed I was Lina Ramir, and he didn't have a reason to lie to me."

"I agree with Vanessa," Seth said now. "I overheard Halim and Akil talking, and they talked about their sources—plural."

"With the intensive background searches and routine polygraphs we do at the CIA, I really have a hard time believing that two people got past the system."

"Halim never said the mole was CIA," Vanessa told him. "For all we know, it's someone working at Fort Huachuca. It could even be some senator's aide on Capital Hill."

"That's true," Amy agreed. "I can try to get a list of everyone who has access to this information."

"We need more than the names on a piece of paper." Vanessa's eyebrows lifted. "This strike is supposed to happen within a couple of days."

Seth nodded in agreement. "Vanessa's right. We need to get out to Fort Huachuca and meet the people involved."

The door opened, and the executive officer walked in. "Excuse me, Lieutenant, but we have a problem."

"What's wrong?" Brent took the piece of paper that was handed to him. He quickly skimmed through it, his mouth tightening into a hard line as he looked back up at Ellison. "How many people in your agency know about this impending terrorist threat?"

"Only a handful," Ellison told him. "Why?"

"Those helicopters aren't at the fortress anymore."

"But you just said—"

"The tracking devices are still at the fortress, but the last set of satellite photos revealed that the helicopters are no longer there."

"What?"

"It seems that someone tipped Ramir off that we tagged them."

"I don't know how that could have happened." Ellison shook his head in disbelief. "I didn't know anything about the SEALs planning to track the helicopters until just now."

"If someone didn't tip him off, how else could Ramir have known to look for the tracking devices?"

"I hate to say it, but it's possible Halim was just being paranoid." Vanessa shook her head. "After that firefight last night, it's likely he had the helicopters checked out before they lifted off."

Quinn spoke now. "It doesn't matter how they found the trackers."

"But it does matter if Ramir knows that we're on to him," Ellison insisted.

"Maybe it was Morenta who located the trackers," Seth said, considering. "He obviously knows that someone was at the fortress last night, and we think that he bought two of the helicopters from Ramir."

"That's true," Vanessa agreed. "And since it appears that Morenta wants their plans to move forward no matter what, we know he wouldn't tell Akil if he did find them."

"And if Ramir is the one who found them?" Ellison asked.

"Morenta would probably take credit for it, just like he took credit for kidnapping Lina," Seth told him.

Impatiently Quinn spoke once more. "Regardless of who found them, we need to figure out where the Z-10s are now."

"He's right," Brent agreed. "Tristan, get us some transportation to Arizona."

Tristan gave a brief nod and pushed back from the table. As he left the room, Ellison stood up. "I can't stress enough that I need constant updates on what you find."

"In that case, I suggest you set up an office for Amy at CIA headquarters. She can act as our liaison," Brent told him. If he noticed the surprised look on Amy's face, he didn't show it. "If our information is correct, whatever Ramir is planning is going down the day after tomorrow. We need every satellite image specialist you've got looking for those Z-10s. Finding those helicopters is our best chance to stop this strike before it starts."

"Fine." Ellison nodded. "There's a military transport scheduled to take me and Vanessa back to Virginia in an hour. I'm sure there's an extra seat for Amy."

Vanessa turned to face Ellison. "I'm going with them."

"What? What do you mean you're going with them?" Ellison shook his head. "I came here to escort you back so you could bring everyone in our agency up to speed on the situation."

"Right now I'll be more valuable trying to stop Akil," Vanessa told him. "And the best place to do that is by going out to Arizona with the Saint Squad." She turned to look at Brent for confirmation of her decision. He gave her a subtle nod, but when she looked at Seth, she could tell he clearly didn't agree with her decision.

Brent stood up, effectively ending the meeting. "Everyone go get your gear together. Plan on leaving in one hour."

Vanessa stayed where she was, unsure of what to do next. She didn't have any belongings to gather, nor did she have any quarters assigned to her. She watched the room empty as Amy pulled Brent aside and Seth approached her.

Vanessa didn't have to wait for Seth to say the words. She already knew from the expression on his face that he didn't want her to come to Arizona. "Seth, I'm coming."

"I don't want you there," Seth insisted. "This strike is expected to happen within forty-eight hours. I don't want you anywhere near the target area."

"So you want me to sit around and worry about you instead." Vanessa crossed her arms across her chest. "Sorry. Not going to happen."

"There's no reason for you to come."

"Yes, there is," Vanessa insisted. "I've spent the past year watching Ramir's associates come and go through La Playa. I have a better chance of spotting a plant than anyone, and you know it. Besides, if Amy is going back with Ellison, your squad will already have someone working the CIA angle of things."

"The fact that Brent is sending Amy to Langley proves that this situation is too high risk." Seth nodded to where Amy was clearly questioning Brent's decision.

"I don't get what Amy going to headquarters has to do with anything."

"Amy is Brent's wife. He must be really worried if he's willing to risk Amy's wrath to keep her out of the action."

"We're all worried." Vanessa lowered her voice. "But we didn't risk leaving the fortress to back down now. We can win this battle, but you have to trust me to help." She put her hand on his arm and added, "Seth, this is my job too."

Seth let out a sigh—the one that Vanessa recognized as his "I don't agree with you, but I know I'm going to lose this argument" sigh. Resigned, he motioned to the door. "Come on. You can wait in our boardroom while I get my gear together."

30

"What do we have so far?" Brent asked the moment he boarded the military airplane that would take them to Fort Huachuca.

Quinn looked up from one of the aisle seats. "It looks like Morenta is back in Colombia, but we have no idea if Ramir is still at his fortress."

Seth stowed his gear, shoving it into place a bit harder than necessary. He still couldn't believe that Vanessa was coming with them into what might very well turn into a war zone within the next forty-eight hours. He took a steadying breath and looked over at Brent. "I think Ramir's still there. That's where he feels the safest."

"Regardless of where he is, we still don't have anything conclusive on where those Z-10s are parked," Tristan said as he continued to flip through the stack of satellite photos he held.

"I have to believe those antiaircraft guns were headed for Mexico," Vanessa said, looking down at her own set of photos. She had taken the window seat behind Tristan as though inviting Seth to sit beside her, but her focus was clearly on finding the Z-10s. "And it would make sense; the antiaircraft guns would be needed to protect the helicopters' new home base."

"Yeah, but these guys aren't going to leave everything out in the open for the satellites to see," Quinn commented.

"You never know." Vanessa sat up a little taller in her seat and tapped the photos she held. "They're going to assume that we don't know where to look with the satellites."

Tristan chimed in now. "If we aren't finding anything, we may need to get those satellites retasked to show us some other areas."

"Retasking satellites isn't exactly an easy feat," Brent reminded him.

"No, but if it will help us stop another 9/11-type of attack, we'll need to do it," Vanessa said. "Ellison will take care of that for us, but we can't be sure that the analysts will have time to find what we're looking for."

"Then how do we find the Z-10s?" Quinn asked.

"If we find the leak, we find a source," Vanessa replied.

"One of our spy planes is also supposed to do some flyovers to see if they can spot anything," Brent told them. "But I agree with Vanessa. The quickest way to find what we're looking for may be to find the leak. If it really is someone in Arizona, you can be sure they're going to be leaving town before the strike."

"If they haven't left already," Seth said as the plane's engines started up.

Seth sat down next to Vanessa and looked over at her. Her focus was still on the photos she held, her brow furrowed in concentration. His heart did one slow roll in his chest, and warmth washed over him. He was amazed that after carrying around the hurt Vanessa had caused him for so many years, somehow over the past few days he had let it go.

He still didn't know how they could possibly carve out a future together knowing the demands of their careers, but surely if their love could survive a six-year separation, just maybe they would be able to work something out—assuming they lived through this.

Determined to talk some sense into her about her decision to come to Arizona, Seth bided his time. He waited until they lifted off and he saw Quinn slip on the earphones of his iPod. Beside Quinn, Tristan leaned back in his seat to take a nap.

Seth waited a few more minutes before shifting to face Vanessa more fully. Then he said simply, "Twenty-four hours."

"What?" Vanessa looked up from the photos she had been studying, her eyebrows drawing together.

"I want you to promise me that after we give you twenty-four hours to meet the critical personnel in Arizona that you will take a transport back to Washington."

"Seth—"

"Vanessa, I'm worried about you." He laid his hand over hers. "And I'm afraid that my concern for you will distract me from what I need to do if this situation turns ugly."

"Seth, it isn't fair to ask me to leave," Vanessa said. She looked at Tristan and Quinn sitting in front of them and lowered her voice. "I finally have you back in my life, and now you want me to leave you behind and pray that you'll come out of it alive?"

Seth looked at her incredulously. "You would rather be there and pray that *both* of us come out of this alive?"

One shoulder lifted. "If something happens, I don't want to wonder if I could have made a difference." She shook her head now as though gathering her thoughts. "I've invested over a year of my life to make sure that Ramir doesn't succeed in attacking the United States, especially on our soil. I can't turn back now."

"If we can identify the mole, then will you leave?"

"I can't give you any guarantees." She gave his hand a squeeze. "But I'll consider it."

Seth let out a sigh. "You know, you always have been a pain."

"Yeah." Vanessa nodded and then grinned at him. "I thought you used to love that about me."

"That was before you started playing spy," Seth said dryly. "You'd better take a nap while you can. Once we get to Fort Huachuca we'll be running nonstop until this crisis is over."

* * *

The moment the door burst open and their escort shouted, "Uncleared!" to the room full of cubicles, the flurry of activity started. Vanessa understood that flurry of activity. She was perfectly aware that the dozen or so employees in the room were busily covering up all of their secret documents to make sure that she, Seth, and Brent didn't get a look at what they were up to.

She figured she didn't need to see what they were covering up. She needed to see their faces. Quickly, her eyes scanned the room. Then she took a more thorough look at the occupants.

The first cubicle was occupied by a young administrative type. She turned over two pieces of paper and then looked up with curiosity to see who had come to visit. Her eyes then stayed glued to the men, lingering on Seth a bit too long for Vanessa's taste.

The older woman at the next desk scooped a stack of papers into a file and looked up at them with impatience. Her body language said that she was on a deadline and that the unexpected visitors were going to put her behind schedule. The man beside her had the opposite reaction. He seemed completely unaffected by the interruption. Vanessa guessed that if anything, he welcomed the excuse to take a break.

One of the employees that occupied a cubicle on the far wall simply covered up his classified documents and then proceeded to go about his business. The man at the next cubicle stood, walked to the desk next to his, and began talking in hushed tones to the woman sitting there.

As Vanessa looked at the other members of this task force, she was somewhat annoyed that she didn't see any obvious problems. A man rushed out of the single hard-walled office in the area, his face flushed with annoyance.

"Who are you?" he demanded.

"You must be Drew Bauer." Brent extended his hand. "I'm Lieutenant Miller. This is Lieutenant Johnson and Vanessa Lauton. We need a few minutes of your time."

"I'm afraid I don't have a lot of time right now." He didn't ask why they were there. Rather he motioned to the young woman beside him. "If you want, you can make an appointment for next week."

"That will be too late." Brent's eyes met his and held. "We need to meet with you now."

The man let out a frustrated sigh and then looked at the escort with them. "Who told you to bring them in here?"

"Senator Whitmore."

Another sigh. "Give me a minute." He turned and walked into his office. A few minutes later he opened the door once more and motioned for them to come inside. "Exactly what do you need?"

"We need to find out who leaked the information about this surveillance system of yours."

"What?" Bauer looked at them, stunned. He sat down in the chair behind his streamlined desk and motioned for them to take a seat as well, even though there were only two chairs opposite of his desk. Vanessa and Brent both sat with Seth taking up position behind Vanessa. Bauer shook his head skeptically, and his voice was demanding as he continued. "What makes you think there's a leak? This information has been well controlled since this system was conceived."

"We've seen that, but the fact remains that at least one terrorist group is aware of both this system of yours and the date it is supposed to become operational."

"That's impossible." He shook his head. "Half of the people out in that room don't even know when we're going operational."

"We need to know which half," Brent told him. "Do you know who outside of your office would have this information?"

"Not many." He shook his head, then jotted down a list of names and handed it to Brent. "Besides five of us in my office, Hank Rodriguez with the border patrol would know, along with my commanding officer, Adam Garrison, and the Senate Intelligence Committee. I don't know if anyone else in the senate has this information or not."

"I doubt it, but we'll find out," Brent told him. "And I already have two of my men going to meet with Hank Rodriguez."

"What about your intelligence oversight committee?" Vanessa asked Bauer. "Surely someone at the CIA or Drug Enforcement Agency must have this information."

"General Garrison was very specific that he wanted the operational date strictly controlled." Bauer shook his head. "You can see why I'm having a hard time seeing how this information could have gotten out."

Vanessa considered for a moment. "Is anyone in your office on leave right now, or planning to take leave soon?"

"No. Even though only a few people know when we're becoming operational, everyone has been involved in the testing phase, so no one is allowed to take leave right now. The restriction on leave won't be lifted for another three weeks."

"It sounds like you've done everything right, but the fact remains that a leak exists somewhere," Brent said. "We'll need to talk to these employees."

Bauer stood up and pulled open the top drawer of a two-drawer safe. He picked up two files on his desk and put them into the drawer, closed it, and then spun the dial. "You can use my office, but I want to sit in on the interviews."

"That's fine." Brent nodded. "If you'll call the first person in, we'll get started."

31

Tristan approached the thin older man who had just walked out of the border patrol office in Tucson. He appeared to be about sixty and looked like he'd spent the better part of those sixty years outdoors. "Excuse me, but could you tell me where I can find Hank Rodriguez?"

"You found him. I'm Hank." He looked from Tristan to Quinn and then back to Tristan again. "What can I do for you?"

"I'm Tristan Crowther. This is Quinn Lambert. We need a few minutes of your time," Tristan said in his typical relaxed tone.

Hank looked over their uniforms and asked, "What are a couple of sailors doing in the middle of the desert?"

"We came across some information we need to talk to you about."

"I need to take a ride down to the checkpoint on I-19. You're welcome to tag along if you've got an hour to spare."

"That'll work." Tristan nodded, ignoring Quinn's impatience. They both knew that time was short, but they needed whatever information this man could give them. They followed Hank to a government car and proceeded to get in, with Tristan claiming the front seat.

Hank slid behind the wheel and pulled out of the parking lot. As soon as he pulled into traffic he glanced over at Tristan. "So what's on your mind?"

"How much do you know about the new surveillance system that's coming online here in Arizona?"

Hank didn't so much as flinch at the question. "I don't know what you're talking about."

"Would you know what we were talking about if I mentioned that Senator Whitmore sent us out to see you?"

"Jim Whitmore sent you, huh?" Hank seemed to consider this information for a moment. He shrugged a shoulder and gave a little nod.

"Then you know that all of this is pretty high-tech stuff. And as Jim says, it's strictly need-to-know."

"He gave us that line too, sir," Quinn chimed in from the back seat.

"Can you tell us who in your office falls into the 'need-to-know' category?"

"Just me and my deputy, Gordon McAllister."

"We'd like to talk to Mr. McAllister, too, then," Tristan told him.

"That'll be easy enough to do. He's the one running the checkpoint right now," Hank informed them. "Now, how about telling me what this is all about?"

"I assume you've heard of Morenta."

"Yeah. Everyone in my office knows about him." Hank nodded as he merged onto the highway. "Fact is, we think over half the drugs that cross our state line come through him."

"That would make sense since we think he may be planning a terrorist attack to prevent this new surveillance system from becoming operational."

"I don't know where you're getting your information, but Morenta isn't a terrorist," Hank told them, clearly not concerned. "He's interested in profit, plain and simple."

"And his profit is going to be dwindling quickly if his distribution lines are cut," Tristan reminded him.

"That's true, but I don't know how he would have learned about the surveillance system." Hank paused for a moment and seemed to reconsider. "But if he did know about it, that would make sense why we've been seeing more activity on our borders the past few weeks."

"What kind of activity?"

"We've had rumors of new camps of illegal immigrants springing up here in Arizona, but we're having a tough time tracking them down."

Quinn spoke now. "Is that why you have this checkpoint set up? Because of the rumors?"

Hank nodded. "We can find evidence of people crossing the border, but we can't track them down. It doesn't make sense that this many people can simply come into this country and vanish into thin air."

"How many people are we talking about?"

"From what we've seen, at least a hundred on foot in the past week alone. For that many to get through undetected, they had to have some help."

"What kind of help?"

"Someone had to be providing both transportation to get them past us as well as someplace for these people to stay when they arrived. The only good thing is that when we expanded our search further north, we scored a major drug bust when we found an airstrip northeast of Phoenix, where Morenta was flying in drugs." Hank glanced over at Tristan and shook his head once more. "But like I said, Morenta's only interested in profit. He's not a terrorist."

"We think he has some help with the terrorist side of things," Tristan admitted.

Hank glanced over at Tristan for a moment before turning his eyes back to the road. "You're serious."

"Yes, sir."

"What do you need me to do? Do you even know what the target is?"

"We've got some ideas," Quinn said cryptically.

Tristan skillfully redirected the conversation. "Tell us about your deputy."

"Gordon's a good man. He's been with this office for about three years now. Came over from the San Diego office."

"Does he have family around here?"

"He's married, but they don't have any kids yet." Hank pulled over to the shoulder as they approached the checkpoint. As soon as he put the car in park, he shifted to face Tristan. "I've got a lot of family around these parts. If there's something I can do to help you boys, you let me know."

"Thank you, sir." Tristan nodded. "For now, we'd like to meet your deputy."

"Wait here, and I'll send him over." Hank got out of the car and approached two uniformed border patrol agents. As Tristan and Quinn got out of the car, Hank spoke to one of the agents, who looked to be around thirty, and motioned to where Tristan and Quinn were standing.

The man approached them, a quizzical look on his face. "Can I help you?"

"That depends," Quinn responded, his eyes sizing up the man in front of him. "What can you tell us about Morenta?"

"You came all the way out here to ask about Morenta?" He looked from Quinn to Tristan. "Anyone at the office could have told you that he's responsible for running drugs across our borders. He's been a thorn in our side since long before I got here."

"What about Akil Ramir?" Tristan asked now. "What do you know about him?"

"Who?"

"Akil Ramir. Arms dealer."

Gordon shook his head. "Sorry. That one's new to me. If he's been smuggling guns into Arizona, he must be pretty good to have escaped our notice so far."

Tristan nodded and shook Gordon's hand. "Well, thank you for your time."

Looking a bit confused, he nodded. "No problem."

As soon as Gordon was out of earshot, Tristan turned to Quinn. "What do you think?"

"I don't know. Both of them were willing to talk to us, and neither one of them seemed to be hiding anything."

"I think we can cross Hank off of the list of suspects. If he's got that much family around here, I doubt he would be involved. Not to mention the fact that he's on a first-name basis with Senator Whitmore."

Quinn nodded in agreement. "Let's hope Brent and Seth are having more luck."

* * *

"Any luck with getting those satellites retasked?" Amy asked Rick Ellison when he walked into her temporary office.

"Yeah. It took some doing, but we've got the analysts concentrating on northern Mexico to see if we can find those helicopters," Ellison told her. "Have you heard anything from your team?"

"I've got the list of everyone we know of who had access to the operational date. Your finance people helped me research them, but we haven't found anything irregular. No large cash deposits, no unusual credit card activity. There isn't anything that would indicate that one of them is on Ramir's payroll."

"Then we need to expand our search to the other members of the surveillance task force. One of them might have managed to get the operational date even though they weren't supposed to."

"Already on it." Amy nodded. "Hopefully we'll have that analysis done within another hour or two."

"We only have another thirty-six hours, give or take."

"I know." Amy sighed wearily. "We're running out of time."

* * *

"We're running out of time." Quinn paced across the conference room the base commander had given them to meet in. Brent and Vanessa had both stopped to make phone calls on their way in, and Quinn's impatience to get started was growing more obvious as each minute passed. "If we haven't found the leak here, we're never going to find it in time. Besides, it's probably someone in Washington anyway."

"He's right. It's time we take a more defensive posture," Tristan agreed.

"I'm way ahead of you." Seth took the mission plan he had been working on and spread it out on the table. He still had to clear it through Brent and the higher-ups, but he hoped this plan would accomplish his two main goals: successfully defending the United States against the impending terrorist attack and getting Vanessa away from the danger zone.

Tristan leaned on the edge of the table and studied Seth's diagrams. "How long have you been working on this?"

"Since I found out Vanessa was coming with us to Arizona." Seth didn't give his teammates a chance to react to his admission; instead he pointed at the first diagram. "If we can get the base commander to agree to this live-fire exercise, all of our firepower can be in place before Ramir throws anything at us."

Tristan nodded in approval. "And we'll have the Air Force continue their exercises over at the Goldwater Air Force Range so we'll have air support ready."

"Yeah, but the Air Force range is on the west side of the state. If the strike comes from the east, the intercept time is going to be too high," Quinn said.

"We can park a few Apache helicopters here at Fort Huachuca," Seth suggested. Then his eyes narrowed, and he shifted his papers until he uncovered a map of the border towns. "We have to figure that those Z-10s are going to try to stay under our radar when they approach, right?"

"Yeah. I think that's a given," Tristan agreed. "What are you thinking?"

"If the missiles on our fighter planes can reasonably take out a target a hundred miles away, Ramir wouldn't want his helicopters to approach from the west. If they did get picked up by radar, we'd be able to take them out before they did any real damage." Seth picked up a pencil and drew a line that marked the area of Mexico that was within the hundred-mile radius of the Air Force range.

The corner of Tristan's mouth lifted, and he continued for Seth. "And even if we didn't know about the threat, Ramir couldn't be sure we wouldn't have some fighter helicopters sitting at Fort Huachuca. They can take out a target within fifty miles."

"Exactly." Seth nodded. Again he drew a line, this time marking off the area that was within fifty miles of the fort. He then tapped his finger where the two lines intersected. "If I was going to plan an attack, I'd want to put my base right around here. Just out of range, but close enough that I can get my shot off without having to travel very far."

The door opened and Brent walked in.

"Where's Vanessa?"

"She's still on the phone with her buddies at the CIA," Brent told him. "I talked to Amy a few minutes ago. Still nothing suspicious on any of the names we fed her, but she did talk to Kel's doctor. He came out of surgery okay."

"What's his prognosis?"

"Amy said they won't know for a while yet," Brent told them.

Vanessa opened the door and hesitated as she looked around the room at the men's grim expressions. "Is everything okay?"

"Yeah." Brent nodded. "What have you got for us?"

"The image analysts are doing everything they can, but there's too much area to cover. We might get lucky, but at this point, it isn't looking good."

"We think we narrowed it down." Seth tapped a finger on his map. He then proceeded to explain to Brent and Vanessa their analysis as well as his suggested mission plan.

"Seth, go meet with the base commander and see what you can do to get your plan implemented." Brent nodded his approval. "Vanessa, I want you to call CIA and have them narrow their search. I'll give Amy a call and have her coordinate with the Air Force. She said they've already diverted a few more fighters to the base in Phoenix in case Ramir goes after the nuclear power plant, but I'll feel better if we have a squadron of fighters in the air at any given time over at the Goldwater Range."

"What about us?" Tristan asked. "Do you want us to bring the border patrol in on this too?"

"It wouldn't hurt to have them beef up their patrols, especially along the border near the power plant." Brent nodded and turned to Quinn. "I want you to go see Bauer and find out if there's any way they can go operational early. Maybe we can use their new system to help us out."

"We'll need all the help we can get," Quinn muttered as the squad scattered to go about their assignments.

32

Vanessa sat alone in the conference room while the SEALs went about their assignments. She was looking through the latest batch of intel reports, none of which revealed what she needed to know. She flipped over another page, nerves humming through her. She hated this, the analysis and the waiting.

She had thought that once she was safely away from Akil Ramir and his organization, she would be able to relax. Now she knew how wrong she'd been. With the looming terrorist threat, it was killing her not to know what was happening inside Ramir's fortress.

The door opened, and she looked up to see Seth walk inside. His jaw was clenched, his expression serious.

"What's wrong?" Vanessa asked as he closed the door behind him.

Seth walked to the chair at the head of the table and leaned on the back of it. "Let's just say that the Army doesn't feel like playing nice with the Navy."

"The base commander didn't approve your plan?"

Seth shook his head. "He said that the intel we've gathered didn't warrant such a significant use of manpower, especially when it's almost a hundred degrees outside."

"Did he suggest any alternatives?"

"Nothing that will work effectively. Even my plan leaves more gaps than I'd like, but at least it would have put our people in the right places to intercept." He shook his head again. "Of course, that doesn't matter now. Bottom line is that Army generals don't like being told what to do by Navy lieutenants."

"Then maybe it's time to have one of your admirals have a chat with him," Vanessa suggested. "If we can't figure out where the Z-10s are attacking from, the chances of stopping those missiles before they strike are slim at best, and that's assuming we have all of our resources ready to intercept."

"I know." Seth crossed the room to her. "And I still want you to get out of the line of fire."

"And I'm still not going anywhere," Vanessa told him.

"Vanessa, please." Seth sat in the chair beside her and shifted so that he was facing her. His deep brown eyes were filled with concern as he reached for her hand. "My squad will likely be assigned to one of the fighter groups in this area. I don't want to leave and worry that you won't be here when I come back." He glanced up at the clock. "We likely only have about thirty hours left before this strike is going to happen."

He leaned forward and touched his lips to hers. "Please."

Vanessa felt herself softening. She knew she wouldn't be able to walk away until the project was complete, but she also knew that she was running out of possibilities to explore here in Arizona. "Tell you what. I'll make arrangements to leave when you do," Vanessa conceded. "I'm sure I can set up a transport back to Virginia for sometime tomorrow morning."

"Fair enough." Seth nodded. "Just promise you won't disappear on me again."

"I promise." Vanessa smiled and then leaned forward to kiss him once more.

The conference room door opened, and Seth immediately drew away and looked up.

"Whoops." Tristan looked at him apologetically even as he smothered a grin. He started to back out the door, but Quinn came in behind him and nudged him forward.

Quinn took one look at Seth and Vanessa and shook his head. "Another one bites the dust."

Brent followed them into the room and asked Seth, "What did the base commander say?"

"No go." Seth shook his head. He then explained the base commander's suggestions.

Brent shook his head, clearly frustrated. "What about the intel reports? Anything useful?"

"Nothing." Vanessa motioned to the map that Seth had marked up earlier. "The satellite photos should be coming in within an hour or two for this area. I just pray that the analysts find something soon."

Brent nodded in agreement before turning to Quinn and Tristan. "What about you two? What did you find out?"

Tristan spoke first. "Hank over at border patrol is sending all of his available people down this way. He said he'll ask for volunteers to pull some overtime so that he can give us extra support for the next forty-eight hours or so."

"Good. What about you?" Brent asked Quinn.

"Bauer said they might be able to push their schedule up by about twelve hours, but that's the best he can do. I guess someone from the power plant has to inspect the electrical hookups before they can flip the switch. The inspector is supposed to be arriving any minute."

"In that case, we might as well go grab some dinner," Brent told them. "Tomorrow morning, we'll join up with some of the Air Force boys and fly cover along the border. I know they've got a couple of F-15s for us to use, but I'm hoping we can also get another Apache helicopter."

"What about tonight?"

"Amy arranged for temporary quarters for us," Brent said and then turned to Vanessa. "As for you, I've got a seat on a transport plane that's leaving for Virginia in an hour."

Vanessa looked from Brent to Seth and back again. "Has he been talking to you?"

A knowing smile crossed Brent's face, but he shook his head. "This is simple logistics. We need you to be where the intel reports are being generated so that we aren't waiting on them getting sent. That's CIA headquarters."

"But Amy's already there."

"Yeah, but she doesn't have complete access to everything. You do," Brent told her. "There's nothing left to do here anyway. We're all going to grab some sack time, and then we'll be up in the air trying to find those Z-10s. You'll do us a lot more good tomorrow if you're already in Virginia when we go up."

"Will we have a direct communication link with you while you're in the air?"

"I'll tell Amy to set it up."

"All right." Vanessa looked from Brent to Seth. "You guys win. But you had all better come back safe."

"That's the plan," Tristan drawled.

Seth motioned to her. "Come on, Vanessa. I'll walk you out and we'll find someone to take you over to the airfield."

Vanessa nodded and followed him out into the hall. She fell into step beside him, surprised that he took her hand despite the people mulling about in the hallway. He didn't say anything until they approached the building lobby. Then he turned to face her.

"You know, as soon as this is all over, I'll be coming back to Virginia," Seth told her. "We still have a lot to talk about."

"I love you, Seth," Vanessa said, her voice lowering to a whisper. She saw the way his eyes widened when she said the words so easily. Then slowly his lips curved into a smile and she added, "Please be careful."

"I will." Seth leaned down and gave her a lingering kiss. "Now, let's see if we can find a ride for you over to the airfield."

He looked up to see a border patrol agent walking toward him. "Excuse me. Can you tell me where I can find Lieutenant Miller?"

"Yeah, he's in the conference room." Seth looked at him curiously. "I'm in his squad. Is there anything I can help you with?"

"I'm Hank Rodriguez. I'm here to give him an update on where I have my men stationed," Hank told him.

Seth introduced himself and Vanessa. Then he said, "I'll show you where Lieutenant Miller is. I just need to find someone to take Vanessa over to the airfield first."

"My assistant can drive her over there."

"Are you sure?"

"Yeah." Hank turned to look at Vanessa. "He's waiting right out front. You can't miss him. He's the one driving the border patrol car."

"Okay, thanks." Vanessa looked over at Seth, wishing for a few minutes alone before she left, but she didn't know how she could manage it. "Be careful, Seth."

"I will." He then surprised her by stepping closer and kissing her good-bye. The kiss was brief, but it was filled with promise. He then whispered in her ear, "By the way, I love you too."

Vanessa couldn't help the smile that crossed her face. Still smiling, she turned and walked outside, immediately spotting the border patrol car. She moved toward it, glancing over at the electrical junction box on the side of the building where the border patrol agent was talking to someone from the power plant.

Both men looked up at her, and her smile slowly faded as recognition dawned. Then everything moved in slow motion. Panic flashed in the familiar close-set eyes, and an instant later his gun was drawn. The other man barely had time to register what was happening before he was knocked unconscious with the butt of the previously concealed weapon.

Vanessa simply gaped at the man moving toward her, the man she had seen periodically at La Playa over the past year.

"Lina Ramir. Fancy meeting you here."

"What are you doing here?" Vanessa asked incredulously as she tried to shift back into the mindset of Lina Ramir. She looked at the power company logo on his shirt and was both stunned and annoyed that she had never considered someone like him to be the insider.

"I could ask you the same question," he said quietly, shoving the gun into her ribs as he took her by the arm and pushed her toward the border patrol car. "Or I could ask you who you really are, since no one with the last name Ramir would be in the United States right now unless they were behind bars."

"You're wrong about that since obviously I'm here." Vanessa tried to sound aloof, but she knew there was fear rippling through her voice. She then added, "There's no way you're going to get off of this military base without someone stopping you."

"You underestimate me." He pulled open the passenger side of the patrol car and motioned for her to slide all the way over to the driver's side. "Now, drive."

Vanessa glanced down at the gun and then closed her eyes. With a silent prayer running through her head, she reached for the key that was still in the ignition and started the car.

33

What began as a short briefing had turned into a strategy session with the Saint Squad and Hank Rodriguez. Knowing that they weren't getting the full support of the base commander, Hank had come up with some other ideas that they hoped could help them prepare for whatever Ramir had planned for them.

Seth glanced at his watch, calculating that Vanessa's flight should be leaving any minute.

"I still think we need more resources protecting the power plant down here," Brent said.

"I agree, but where are we going to get the added manpower?" Seth asked.

Brent's cell phone rang, interrupting their conversation. He answered it immediately. Concern filled his voice as he looked over at Seth and responded, "She isn't there yet?" He paused for a moment and then said, "I'll get back to you."

Brent hung up the phone, and his gaze focused on Seth and Hank. "That was the transport pilot. Vanessa never showed up. Who was supposed to drive her over?"

"Gordon McAllister," Hank told Brent. "I don't understand what would have taken them so long."

"Didn't McAllister know about the new surveillance grid?" Brent asked now.

"Yeah, but what does that have to do with anything?" Hank looked at him confused.

"We may have just found our leak the hard way," Brent told him as Seth's jaw clenched tightly and he pushed out of his seat.

Before Brent could give the order, Seth darted out of the conference room and sprinted through the hall and out the front door. Seth could hear the footsteps behind him as his team chased after him, but he could only think of Vanessa. Where was she? He didn't stop until he reached the curb where the patrol car had been. A white utility van was parked nearby, and Seth's eyes swept the area searching for any clue. Brent stepped beside him and together they started down the sidewalk. That was when they saw the shoe sticking out from behind the van.

Seth and Brent moved around the back of the van to see the man sprawled out on the ground between the back of the van and the side of the building. Brent looked past the rest of his team to where Hank was standing. "Is that McAllister?"

"Yeah." Hank rushed forward to check his injuries. "Call an ambulance. He's still alive."

"If McAllister doesn't have Vanessa, who does?" Brent asked, turning to look at Seth.

Seth's voice was filled with worry. "I don't know."

* * *

Vanessa gripped the steering wheel tighter as she approached the base exit. A young private was standing in the guard house watching the cars exit. Another was checking off those that entered. Vanessa slowed the car, her mind racing as nerves danced along her skin.

"Don't try anything funny," the man beside her said quietly. Vanessa remembered him as Tod Zimmerman; he had been a regular at La Playa, but she knew nothing about him except that he had been in Punta Cana several times over the past year, usually for only two to three days at a time.

Her mind whirled as she tried to remember the last time she had seen him. She felt sick as the memory came back to her with sudden clarity. Not only had she overheard Zimmerman talk to Halim about antiaircraft guns, but he had also been part of the conversation when Halim had discussed potential American casualties.

The gun Zimmerman held was still pointed in her direction, but his hand rested in his lap so that the guard would have to approach the car and look in the window to see it. Vanessa had little doubt that if the guard saw the gun, it would likely be the last thing he ever saw.

Her chest tightened as she considered her limited options. If she tried to signal the guard, he would likely die, and she might take a bullet as well. If she played along, she still might end up dead. Her CIA training had included instruction on what to do in hostage situations, but those were usually when someone else was being held hostage.

Vanessa took a deep breath as she slowed the vehicle further and the guard took another step into the street. Then the man gave a nod to them and stepped into the guard house to raise the gate.

"Let's go." Zimmerman said the moment the gate lifted.

Vanessa squeezed her eyes shut for a moment. Then taking a deep breath, she pushed on the gas pedal and left the safety of Fort Huachuca behind.

* * *

The conference room had transformed into a flurry of activity and barely organized chaos. Seth's first instinct had been to jump into a car and go after Vanessa and whoever had taken her, but Brent had stopped him before he'd managed to grab the closest vehicle. After ordering Seth to return to the conference room, Brent had reminded Seth that he had to at least know what direction Vanessa and her abductor were headed before he could track them down.

Seth paced from one end of the room to the other as he held his cell phone to his ear and waited for one of the guard stations to come on the line. Everyone was making calls, either trying to gather information on who had taken Vanessa and where, or lining up the equipment and personnel necessary to get her back.

When the guard came on the line and had nothing of consequence to report, Seth hung up and started dialing the next number on his list. Before he hit the TALK button, Brent shouted out to him.

"I've got something. The guard at one of the back gates remembers seeing a border patrol car leave about fifteen minutes ago." Brent spoke to everyone in the room, but his eyes were on Seth. "By his description, it sounds like Vanessa was the driver."

"Did he see who was with her?" Seth asked.

"He didn't get a good look at him, but he was sure it was a man." Brent shook his head. "The cops have a BOLO out on the patrol car, but so far no one has spotted it."

"Here's the info on that utility van from the power plant." Quinn held up a piece of paper he had jotted notes on. "The dispatcher said it's definitely one of theirs. They sent out a man named Brandon James to do an inspection today, but when I ran the name and social security number through the FBI, the guy didn't pop up. In fact, he doesn't exist."

"So he's using an alias." Brent shook his head. Sarcasm coated his voice as he muttered, "Perfect." He motioned to Quinn. "Get the utility company to e-mail us a photo. Also, see if they've got a cell phone number for him. We might be able to trace it."

Quinn nodded and picked up his phone.

Beside him, Tristan finished up his call and turned to face Brent. "I've got an Apache for us. It'll be fueled and ready to go in five minutes."

"Tristan, you have the most hours in the Apaches. Take it up and see if you can track down that patrol car."

Before Brent could assign a copilot, Seth spoke up. "I'm going too."

Brent stared at him for a moment, his eyes serious. Then he nodded. "I don't have to tell you that we're running out of time. We can't be sure when this strike is going to go down, so be ready."

"We will." Seth nodded and turned to Tristan. "Let's go."

* * *

"Where are we going?" Vanessa finally dared to ask as they continued to drive east. Her mind was racing, searching for some way out

"You'll see soon enough," Zimmerman told her. "It's not much farther."

"I hope not. We're almost out of gas." She glanced down, hoping the gas tank was really as empty as the gas gauge indicated. She didn't have a lot of options while she was behind the wheel of a car, but outside she might get a chance to fight back. Besides, anything that could stall them would give Seth and his friends more time to find her.

Her hopes for a delay disappeared when she looked up and saw the little Cessna parked on a makeshift runway. Dust was kicking up from the wind, but nothing else was visible except for the mountain range flanking both sides of the airfield.

Zimmerman kept the gun pointed at her and motioned toward the door. "Out of the car."

Vanessa moved slowly, reaching for the door handle and stepping onto the edge of the runway. Keeping her hands at her side, she turned to face Zimmerman as he scrambled out the other side of the car.

"Let's go."

"You aren't seriously expecting me to go with you." Disbelief hung in Vanessa's voice, and she grasped at the arrogance she had once shown as Lina Ramir.

He grabbed her arm and pulled her toward the plane. "It never hurts to have an insurance policy on board."

"It seems like I'm everyone's insurance lately," Vanessa muttered.

"What's that supposed to mean?" Zimmerman spared her a quick glance.

"First Morenta takes me from my home to make sure Uncle Akil doesn't back out of this plot they have going together. Then some Navy SEALs raid the place I was being held and I'm sent here to the United States. I had just about convinced them that they didn't have any right to hold me, and then you came along." Vanessa forced some annoyance into her voice. "Quite frankly, I'm pretty sick of being everyone's puppet."

"You won't have to worry about that much longer," Zimmerman said smugly.

"You do realize that my uncle will kill you if anything happens to me," Vanessa told him. "Then again, he might not get the chance. My fiancé might get to you first."

"Death threats won't work on me." His voice was filled with venom as he pulled open the door. "Get on the plane, *Lina.*"

Vanessa's eyes widened when he pushed her inside and she saw what was stored where the back seat should have been. She looked back at him, unable to hide the fear in her eyes.

"Like I said, death threats won't work on me."

34

"Border patrol and the local police have set up roadblocks, but there's still no sign of them," an Army lieutenant told Tristan and Seth as they crossed the tarmac to where a fuel truck was pulling away from an Apache helicopter.

Seth felt the knot in his stomach tighten. Where were they? And why hadn't he stayed with Vanessa until she was on that plane?

Beside him, Tristan spoke to the man escorting them. "They must be on back roads somewhere if they haven't been spotted."

"Since they went out the back gate, they might be on one of the dirt roads east of here. A lot of hunters go out that way during deer season."

"Thanks." Seth nodded. Adrenaline rushed through him as he climbed into the copilot's seat and slid his communications headset into place. Tristan strapped in beside him and started the engines.

Seth stared at the instrument panel in front of him, for a moment unable to function. He kept waiting for his instincts and training to take over, but he could feel himself going in slow motion. He uttered a silent prayer that somehow he could do his job, that he wouldn't fail now when the woman he loved was in peril.

The moment they were cleared for takeoff, Tristan looked over at Seth, his eyes filled with understanding. "We'll find her."

Seth nodded as he drew a deep breath. He cleared their takeoff with the air traffic controller, and seconds later they were in the air.

* * *

Vanessa could feel her mind going blank as she sat strapped into the copilot's seat in the small airplane. She knew she had to get out of here.

She had to get free. But how? Zimmerman had been in such a hurry to get to the airstrip, but now he didn't seem very anxious to leave. Could he be having second thoughts?

Mustering all of her courage, she spoke quietly. "You don't have to do this, you know."

Zimmerman angled his head to look at her, his eyes cold and intense. "I was chosen for this."

"You may have been chosen for this, but I wasn't," Vanessa said, her voice wavering.

"Perhaps you were, and you just didn't know it."

"You can't honestly believe that my uncle would want me to die alongside his suicide bomber."

"I doubt Akil Ramir would want his niece to die today, but I don't believe you're Lina Ramir," Zimmerman said smugly. "You were in a secure area of a U.S. military base, walking around without an escort. Obviously you aren't who Akil thinks you are."

Vanessa opened her mouth to dispute his observations, but he shifted, and the coldness and awareness in his eyes caused her to reconsider her words. "Even if you're right, what good does it do to take me with you? Who would I tell about your plans? We're in the middle of nowhere, and the car doesn't have enough gas to get me back to the base."

"That may be, but if any of your military friends figure out what I'm doing, a hostage may come in handy."

He glanced at his watch and then obsessively turned to check the road once more. She could only assume he was concerned someone would follow them, and she continued to pray for a miracle. If Zimmerman flew this plane into the nuclear power plant, the initial explosion would be nothing compared to the fallout if even one of the reactors failed. She shifted and took a good look at the explosives behind her. From what she could tell, even though the back of the plane was filled with C4, only a small portion of it was actually attached to a detonator.

As she studied the bomb, she could only guess that Zimmerman was going to detonate it, which would then cause the rest of the C4 to explode. Then she noticed it: a receiver that would allow the bomb to be detonated remotely. But why? When she had first seen the explosives in the back of the plane, she'd assumed that Zimmerman was going to detonate this flying bomb by crashing it into his target. Now she wondered if Zimmerman was really the one in control or if it was someone else.

A beeping sound rang out from his watch, and Zimmerman reached forward to start the airplane. Moments later they were airborne, and Vanessa took a deep breath as reality sank in. It didn't matter who was in control of the explosives behind her. No one was coming after her. No one would even know she was missing until it was too late. Too late for her, and too late for Seth.

Her chest tightened at the thought that Seth would be a victim too—if not from the initial blast, then from radiation poisoning after the attack. She squeezed her eyes closed against that thought and fought against the panic and hopelessness. Somehow she had to find a way out of this mess. Even if she wasn't going to survive the day, she might be able to make sure that Seth could see tomorrow.

* * *

"Something still doesn't feel right about all of this." Quinn paced across the room before looking back at Brent and Hank.

"I know," Brent agreed. He leaned on the table in front of him, staring at the files scattered there. "I don't understand why Ramir was running all of those training camps. If he was planning an air strike, he could have done it all at his fortress."

"A few of the camps looked like they were training in communications and explosives, but that still leaves at least two more that were mostly made up of the mercenary types," Quinn said. Then he stopped pacing and turned to face Hank. "You said you had a big drug bust outside of Phoenix last week."

"That's right."

"How did you know it was Morenta's men you busted?"

"They all had the same tattoo on their hand. The one Morenta's nephew has," Hank told him. At their blank expressions, he added, "We apprehended Morenta's nephew in a bust last year."

"Where's he being held?" Brent asked.

"His trial started last week in Phoenix."

"Morenta's nephew is in Phoenix?" Quinn asked as all of them considered the spin this new information put on their assumptions.

"Maybe that's the connection we've been looking for." Brent shuffled the files in front of him and flipped one open. "Morenta must be paying Ramir to help him break his nephew out of prison. That might also explain why Morenta was paying for Z-10s. He must be using one to transport his nephew out of the country."

Quinn nodded in agreement. "And in exchange, Morenta is helping fund Ramir's terrorist attack."

"If that's the case, there's no way the nuclear power plant could be the target," Brent said with a shake of his head. "Morenta wouldn't go to all of this trouble only to have his nephew die from radiation poisoning."

Hank nodded in agreement. "Not to mention that the nuclear power plant has so much reinforcement, even a direct missile hit wouldn't cause a radiation leak."

"Then what's the target?" Quinn asked.

"Logically, it would be something that would cover up most of the evidence of a jailbreak." Brent looked at Hank. "What other sites are considered to be high risk?"

"There are only two high-threat terrorist targets in Arizona. One is the nuclear power plant. The other is Hoover Dam."

"The dam?" Brent asked, rapidly trying to adjust his thoughts to this unconsidered new possibility. "What would happen if someone took it out?"

Hank's voice was somber now. "If that dam were to fail, it could flood half of the populated areas in the state."

"That's just the kind of target Ramir would go for," Quinn said. "And if Morenta's nephew was flown out after the jailbreak, no one would ever know he survived. One of those Z-10s could sneak in undetected to pick him up once the power plant was down."

"It likely won't even be a jailbreak. I saw on the news that Morenta's nephew is due in court again today," Hank told them. "If it were me, I'd try to break him out of the courtroom. It'd be a whole lot easier than getting into the prison."

Brent pointed at Hank. "Call the courthouse and see if you can convince them to shut everything down today." He then nodded at Quinn. "I want the base commander on the phone. Get the word to Seth and Tristan that the dam may be a target. And get us a ride to Phoenix."

Quinn nodded. "I'm on it."

* * *

"The analysts finally found something," Rick Ellison told Amy as he walked into her temporary office. He handed her a satellite photo and pointed to the left corner. "That is definitely a nest of antiaircraft guns."

"Did they find any of the helicopters?"

"Not that I know of, but we're going to have live feed from the satellite in about three minutes. Come on." Ellison motioned to the door. "Let's go see what we can find out."

Amy nodded and quickly followed him out the door and down the hall. She then showed her ID to the guard at the door and listened to Ellison explain that she was cleared to go inside.

She stepped into the room with muted lights. On one wall, the current satellite feed was projected onto a large screen. An analyst was sitting in front of the computer on the side of the room manipulating the image.

"What have we got so far?" Ellison asked.

"It's coming into range now," the analyst told him. He used the mouse to zoom in on the area where the antiaircraft guns had been spotted. "Here's where that photo was taken."

Amy looked at the image, unable to identify anything. Beside her, Ellison asked, "Can you zoom in?"

"Yeah." He hit several keys, and the image enlarged until they were looking at two people standing beside some mean-looking antiaircraft guns. "Looks like this is the place."

"What else is in the area?" Ellison asked.

The analyst shifted the image, looking first to the left, then the right. Then he scanned to the south and found what they were looking for. "Here we go. Z-10 attack helicopters."

"Where's a phone?" Amy asked. "I've got to let the Saint Squad know that we found them."

"Right there." Ellison pointed to a phone that was mounted to the wall.

"Where exactly is this?" Amy asked, nodding toward the screen.

"Here are the map coordinates." The analyst opened a second image that overlaid the image with the map of the area.

Amy picked up the phone and dialed. Brent answered on the first ring, and Amy didn't bother with a greeting. "Brent, you guys were right. We found a new nest of antiaircraft guns thirty miles southwest of Hermosillo."

"Are the helicopters there?" Brent asked, his voice unusually tense.

"Yeah. We're watching the live satellite feed right now," Amy told him anxiously. Her eyes widened when she saw the first helicopter go into motion. She turned to look at the analyst, covering the mouthpiece of the phone with her hand. "Is that what it looks like?"

"Yeah, it just lifted off. The rotors of the other one are in motion too."

"There should be three," Amy told him. "Where's the other one?"

The analyst shook his head. "We only have two helicopters at this location."

Amy spoke into the phone again, trying not to consider the ramifications of the helicopters lifting off a day before they expected them to. "Brent, we've got a visual on two attack helicopters. One just lifted off, and the other is preparing to. The third one is missing."

"We'll find it," Brent told her. "Call the command center out here and keep feeding your information to them. We're going to need it."

"I will," Amy told him.

"One more thing," Brent said before she could hang up. "Vanessa's missing."

"What?"

"We think she was abducted by someone who was working at the power plant," Brent told her. "Tristan and Seth are going up in one of the Apaches to find her. I'll have them expand their search to include looking for the missing Z-10."

"What about you and Quinn?"

"We're heading out with Hank Rodriguez. He thinks he figured out what all of those training camps were all about," Brent said. "The command center can keep you up to date."

"Be safe," Amy said even as the dial tone came over the line. She quickly dialed the number to the western command center, trying not to think about what the next few minutes might bring.

* * *

"We've contacted all of the local airports. No new aircraft will take off until further notice, and all small aircraft have been instructed to land immediately," General Garrison, the base commander, told Brent as they all stood in the radar room of Fort Huachuca. The general's willingness to cooperate had improved dramatically after receiving the latest intelligence reports.

"What about commercial airlines?"

The air-traffic controller answered, "Outgoing flights are still in the air. They will all clear our borders within twenty minutes. Incoming flights are being diverted."

"Good." Brent nodded his approval. "Do you see anything suspicious still in the air?"

"Hard to say right now since the small crafts are still scrambling to land. We'll have a better picture in a few minutes," the air-traffic controller informed him. "We have two fighter squadrons in the air searching for the missing bogie, and our Apaches are standing by."

A corporal sitting across the room hung up his phone and spoke now. "General, we may have a problem," he began. "The courthouse is refusing to evacuate."

Quinn's answer was immediate. "Call in a bomb scare."

"Excuse me?"

"You heard him." Brent nodded in agreement. "A lot of innocent civilians are going to get caught in the crossfire if we're right. If we call in a bomb threat, we'll have professionals on scene instead of a bunch of bystanders."

"Do it," General Garrison ordered.

"Yes, sir." Wide-eyed, the young corporal picked up the phone once more.

"I've got some helicopters standing by to take you and two of my squadrons to Phoenix. The local authorities have already been contacted."

"Thank you, sir," Brent said. "I'll leave it up to you whether to inform the locals that our bomb threat isn't real."

"It won't hurt for them to treat it like the real thing for a little while."

Brent nodded, the corners of his mouth lifting in a smile. "Agreed."

35

"Down there," Seth said to Tristan as he pointed at the border patrol car below them.

"It looks abandoned," Tristan replied.

"Take us down so I can check it out." As a precaution, Seth reached for his MP5 submachine gun and took a defensive position as Tristan lowered them to the ground.

The dust swirled up around them as the Apache landed thirty yards from the car. Seth pushed the door open and moved to the car. His search was methodical and quick. Front seat, back seats, and then the trunk. He then turned and ran back to the helicopter. "Nothing."

"This strip is only big enough for a small aircraft. Maybe the tower can track it."

Seth nodded, having thought the same thing. "Desert Sky, this is Scout One. We found the missing patrol car next to a small airstrip. Please advise on any small aircraft sightings in the area in the past twenty minutes."

"Scout One, we have upgraded to code red. All aircraft in the area have been ordered to land immediately," the voice informed him. "We have two that have not responded. One is east of Flagstaff, and the other is fifty miles north of your position."

"That's got to be them," Seth said, adrenaline pumping. "Receiving coordinates. We are proceeding to intercept."

The air-traffic controller responded, "Be advised, we have two attack helicopters heading our way. Apache squadron has been sent to intercept, but we have a bogie missing."

"Roger that," Tristan replied. "Do we have coordinates on the intruders?"

"Affirmative," the voice confirmed. "It appears they are targeting the new power plant."

"Understood," Tristan said.

Beside him, Seth located the radar contact he hoped was Vanessa and waited impatiently as Tristan chased after it.

* * *

"What's our situation?" Brent asked the local police chief the moment he and Quinn stepped off of the helicopter that had landed on the roof of the courthouse.

The older man looked up at Brent with a combination of wariness and curiosity. His tone was no-nonsense as he related the basic facts. "Arturo Morenta has been secured at the prison, and we have the National Guard surrounding the perimeter. The courthouse has been evacuated, and we've closed off the streets for a two-block radius." His eyes narrowed a bit as he added, "Now that we know the bomb scare wasn't real, we've sent our bomb squad home, but we still have a few patrols standing by."

"Sorry about the bomb threat. We ran into a little resistance from your guys at the courthouse," Brent told him.

"Are you going to tell me what's going on?"

"We're still trying to piece things together, but we suspect that there are a few dozen mercenaries hiding here in Phoenix who were planning to break Arturo Morenta out of the courthouse today."

The chief glanced skyward and then looked over at Brent. "With the amount of firepower I've seen overhead, there's got to be more to this than Morenta coming after his nephew."

Brent nodded, his expression serious. "We've got an impending terrorist attack. We think we have multiple targets, including at least one power plant and the Hoover Dam."

His face paled. "When?"

"Anytime now."

"Not likely if Morenta really wants to get his nephew back in one piece." The chief shook his head, a little color returning to his cheeks. "If they targeted the nuclear power plant, the fallout would likely kill him before he got out of the area."

"Actually, we think the nuclear plant is safe for that exact reason," Brent said. "Our guess is that an air strike is planned against a power plant near the border and will probably happen about the same time the mercenaries try to get Morenta's nephew out of here." Brent hesitated a moment before summing up the rest of their theory. "Then the terrorists would take out the dam, cover up any evidence of the breakout, and create as much havoc as we saw on 9/11."

"What can I do to help?"

"This is your town. Do you have any idea where the mercenaries might be hiding out, or how they would try to get into the courthouse?"

"There are some pretty rough neighborhoods around here, some of them with a lot of abandoned buildings. If it was me, I'd hide my troops out in one of them." The chief stared at him a moment before adding, "I hope you brought some extra manpower with you. We're not equipped for an all-out search in such a short amount of time."

"Some of our Army buddies came with us," Brent told him. "If you can narrow down where Morenta's men might be hiding, we'll put our infrared sensors to work. That should help us speed up the search."

"In that case, here's where I think you should look first." The chief described the most probable hiding places, most of which were located in the same section of town.

Moments later, Brent was headed back to the helicopter with Quinn. Together they hoped to put some of their special-forces equipment to work for them.

* * *

Amy listened to the updates from the command center as she watched the live satellite feed. The Z-10 helicopters were closing in on the Arizona border, heading straight for the new power plant. On the U.S. side of the border, a squadron of Apache helicopters was ready and waiting for orders to engage the inbound threat.

Even though the nuclear power plant was no longer considered to be a likely target, precautions were being taken there as well. A squadron of fighter planes was in the air outside Phoenix in the event that an enemy threat did occur there.

The activity of an actual mission always fascinated Amy—fascinated and scared her. The sharing of intelligence was so complicated. The radar operator combined his interpretations with the information viewed on the satellite feed to give the various pilots the locations of the impending threats. Tension hung thick in the air, and everyone performed their jobs in spite of it.

Despite the recent complications, Amy had analyzed the threats and was desperately hoping to check each one off as they were neutralized and as the various missions were completed. The first stage was stopping the two attack helicopters heading their way, thus protecting the new power plant in southern Arizona. Theoretically, the next step would fall on her husband's shoulders as he and Quinn tried to locate the mercenaries Morenta had sent in to get his nephew out of the country.

The other missions weren't as clear as Amy would have liked them to be, but she certainly knew the outcome she wanted. She hoped and prayed to hear any moment that Vanessa had been found safely and that whatever method was going to be used to damage the Hoover Dam would be stopped. She could only assume that the third attack helicopter was going to fulfill that part of Ramir's plans. The other possibility was that it would be used to help Morenta's nephew escape.

Even though the missing Z-10 hadn't been located yet, the military was well aware of the two Z-10s heading their way, despite the fact that they were still flying below radar. The satellite feed continued to display the images in front of her, images that were also being received by the western command center. Tension thickened as the enemy helicopters moved to within ten miles of the U.S. border before slowing.

"They're in missile range," one analyst stated with trepidation.

A moment later, Amy saw the flash on the screen and heard the analyst say the words that everyone had been braced for.

"Missiles inbound!"

The anxiety level in the room rose tenfold, clipped voices relaying information in short bursts, sometimes over one another.

"How many missiles?"

"Two. They're both heading for the power plant."

Someone switched on a speaker so that they could hear the chatter between the fighters and the command center.

One pilot's voice sounded calm despite the gravity of the situation. "Watchdog One, I have eastern missile. Firing!"

Amy watched one of the incoming missiles disappear from the satellite feed, followed by the second one.

Then came the order from the command center over the speaker. "Apache squadron, you have permission to engage."

"Apache One, engaging."

A split second later, missiles were heading across the Mexican border for the Z-10s. Both tried to evade, but one took a hit and looked like it was spinning out of control. The helicopter that managed to escape unscathed turned for its home base, where everyone knew the antiaircraft guns were waiting to counteract any retaliation. He made it within five miles of his safe haven before the Apache helicopter in pursuit fired once more. This time, he hit his target.

Cheers erupted in the room and sounded over the speakers, but Amy still felt the tension hanging. Somewhere out there, there was at least one more threat, and her husband was one of the men determined to get in its way.

* * *

Brent lay down on his stomach as he studied the abandoned warehouse across the street from his position on top of a nearby building. A couple of men were standing casually on the sidewalk, and two more were visible on the side. It was the picture he saw on his infrared that told him they'd found the right place. At least a hundred people were inside the building, most of them on the main floor.

If their assumptions were correct, the men inside planned to begin positioning for their attack on the courthouse within the next hour or two. Even though the warehouse was within walking distance of the courthouse, several large vans were parked along the street as though waiting to take Morenta's troops the few blocks to their destination. Brent guessed that those vans would also be used to help transport the mercenaries to high ground before the flood waters arrived.

Brent looked back at the local authorities who were now in place along with the military forces who were prepared to assist. When he was satisfied that everyone was in place, he spoke into his lip mike. "I'm in position."

"I'm all set down here," Quinn told him. "Do I have a go?"

"Affirmative."

Brent felt the roof beneath him rumble as the dumpster next to the warehouse erupted into flames and debris thanks to the small explosive Quinn had detonated there. The doors of the warehouse burst open, and the inhabitants rushed outside in confusion. Several of them dropped to the ground when a second explosion shook the ground, this time from an abandoned car on the other side of the building.

The local police moved in with precision, weapons drawn. The scuffle that ensued between the authorities and the mercenaries was almost anticlimactic. Not even one shot was fired as the men surrendered and a thorough search was made of the building they had been hiding in. Several minutes later, Brent received word from Quinn. "Area secured."

Brent stood up from his post and looked at the scene below. He had already received word that the threat against the power plant had been neutralized. Now that the mercenaries were in custody, only one threat remained. He could only hope that they could figure out how Ramir was planning to damage the Hoover Dam before it was too late. Otherwise the Valley of the Sun that was stretched out before him might end up underwater before the day was out.

36

Any minute now, Vanessa thought to herself. Zimmerman had been flying near the more populated areas of Arizona, first Tucson and then the outskirts of Phoenix. In a matter of minutes, she expected they would reach the open desert.

For more than an hour she had contemplated her options, running through every bit of training the CIA had given her. Now she was ready to act—as soon as she was sure that no one else would get hurt if her efforts failed.

The houses below them were becoming sparser, and she started her countdown. Thirty more seconds and then she would act. Even if she couldn't manage to take control of the little airplane, maybe she could force it down. *Thirty, twenty-nine, twenty-eight . . .*

She made it all the way to seventeen before Zimmerman turned the aircraft sharply to the north. Her eyes widened when she saw the Apache helicopter that had appeared in front of them.

Zimmerman swore under his breath and looked over at Vanessa. "Friends of yours?"

"Like I said, my boyfriend is as persistent as my uncle is."

"If that's your boyfriend out there, things are working out even better than I had planned."

"What do you mean?"

His lips curved up into an evil grin. "He isn't going to shoot me down with you on board."

"He isn't going to let you fly this plane into a power plant with me on board either."

"We aren't heading for the power plant."

"It doesn't really matter to me what you plan to crash into as long as you let me out of this plane first."

"I'll consider it." Zimmerman reached for the radio and handed it to her. "But first tell your boyfriend to give us some space. If he backs off, I'll land and let you go before I finish my mission."

Vanessa took the radio, studying Zimmerman's face for a long moment. He was good. His expression was serious, with no real clues of what he intended to do. But when he glanced over to the helicopter, Vanessa saw a flash of what she feared. He was only using her to obtain his objective. He was already a dead man in his mind, and there was no way he was going to land and let her go.

She took a deep breath and stared down at the radio for a moment, knowing what she had to do.

* * *

"Can you tell if she's in there?" Tristan asked, trying to reposition the helicopter so that Seth could see into the cockpit with the binoculars he held.

"It looks like her," Seth said as the radio started receiving.

When Vanessa's voice came over the radio, Seth looked over at Tristan, stunned.

"Seth, I'm supposed to tell you that if you back off, Zimmerman will land and let me go before he completes his mission." Vanessa continued in a calm voice, one edged with unspoken regret. "But you know what you need to do. We can't have another 9/11."

The radio went dead, and Seth's chest tightened as he inhaled sharply. He knew what she was saying. The plane in front of them was going to be used as a weapon, possibly to take out the Hoover Dam. She wanted him to shoot down her plane. Kill her and Zimmerman in order to stop the terrorist attack. One second ticked by and then another. He glanced at Tristan, knowing he couldn't do it.

"It's your call," Tristan reminded him.

He drew in a breath and blew it out as his mind raced. "She doesn't think this guy is serious about letting her go. We need to convince him that it's a good idea."

"What are you talking about?"

"If Zimmerman is using this plane as a weapon, he'll fight to stay in the air until he reaches his target."

"Yeah, I'm listening."

"Let's shoot a couple of rounds near them and see if we can get this guy to reconsider landing long enough to hand over Vanessa."

"It's a long shot."

"It's better than her idea."

"Good point," Tristan agreed as he veered left. "Bringing her around."

Seth opened communication with Vanessa's plane. "Zimmerman, we will escort you to the nearest airfield, where you'll hand over your passenger. If not, we'll open fire."

"You honestly want me to believe you're going to shoot down your girlfriend?"

"Ask her. She knows I will."

"No chance."

Seth took careful aim and called the bluff. "Firing!"

* * *

Vanessa screamed as bullets sparked in the air less than twenty feet from the plane. Beside her, Zimmerman muttered an oath as he abruptly changed direction away from the helicopter and the spray of gunfire.

Vanessa tried to catch her breath that was currently coming in gasps. Deep down she knew Seth was trying to help her; however, she also knew she was going to die if she didn't do something, and fast. *Think!* she commanded herself.

She looked over at Zimmerman, who wasn't paying any attention to her now. With a steadying breath, Vanessa shifted. She rested one hand on the latch of her seatbelt, silently praying for divine guidance. Then bullets sparked around them again.

Adrenaline rushed through her now as she sprang into action. In one fluid movement, Vanessa unlatched her seatbelt with her right hand and then immediately thrust her left elbow up, connecting with Zimmerman's throat. Her eyes widened in disbelief when the now-unconscious Zimmerman simply slumped forward, causing the plane to change directions once more.

For a split second, Vanessa didn't react, noticing only the throbbing in her elbow. Then reality struck. They were going to crash. She shoved Zimmerman back in his seat and reached forward to take over the controls. With some effort, she leveled out the plane and opened up communications once more. Her voice was shaky as she managed to say, "Thanks for the distraction."

Seth responded immediately. "What happened?"

"I can't believe that worked." Vanessa let out a nervous laugh. "I guess an elbow to the windpipe really can knock someone out."

"Good job, Vanessa," Seth said, relief sounding in his voice. "I'll get the coordinates for the nearest airport, and we'll escort you there."

"Seth, this plane is loaded with explosives," Vanessa told him, a new kind of panic rolling through her. "I told you before. I was taught how to *fly* a plane. I never learned how to *land*."

Despite her panic, she could almost picture Seth rubbing a hand over his face, trying to figure out what to do to save her. But there wasn't anything to be done. With the plane filled with explosives, she couldn't try to land near a populated area. And unfortunately, airports weren't exactly common in *un*populated locations.

She heard Seth's sigh over the radio, followed by his voice. "Check the plane for a parachute."

"Right, Seth. Like a suicide bomber would have a parachute on board." Vanessa's voice edged toward sarcasm, but beneath it was pure fear.

"Humor me and check anyway."

Vanessa uttered a prayer as she searched beneath both seats and then shifted around in her seat to search the back of the plane. The silence stretched for several seconds until she spoke once more. "Nothing."

"You're going to have to land the plane."

"Seth, I can't land." Vanessa's voice rose with panic.

Seth's voice was steady, reassuring. "You can. I'll talk you through it."

Vanessa shook her head even though there was no one to see her do it. "You aren't hearing me, Seth. If I try and fail, I'm going to leave a crater the size of the Grand Canyon."

"I'm not giving up on you," Seth insisted.

Before the argument could continue, Tristan broke in. "Vanessa, there's an old airstrip about thirty miles west of here. We'll have you try to land there."

"You won't have time to evacuate an airport and the surrounding neighborhoods before I run out of fuel. It could take hours."

"We're not going to an airport. This is the airstrip where those drug smugglers got caught last week. There aren't any houses or anything else for a good fifteen or twenty miles."

Vanessa considered what Tristan was saying, weighing her options. Finally logic broke through her panic. She didn't have a choice. She couldn't give up—she had to try. Her voice was shaky and uncertain when she spoke into the radio once more, but she knew she was saying the words Seth wanted to hear. "Okay, I'll try."

"Thatta girl," Tristan said as he changed their heading.

Then it was Seth speaking to her once more. "Okay, Vanessa, we're going to take a nice easy descent." He had her adjust her airspeed and altitude, keeping her completely focused on the mechanics of landing a small aircraft.

As the strip of pavement came into view, Vanessa felt another flash of panic. Even though Seth was speaking as though nothing could go wrong, she knew better. She also knew that she couldn't wait any longer to make sure Seth knew how she felt. She took a deep breath and interrupted him. "Hey, Seth. In case this doesn't work, I just want you to know that I really do love you."

"I love you too, but I'd rather hear you say that in person," Seth told her. "Don't think that an attempted terrorist attack is going to get you out of marrying me this time."

Vanessa couldn't help but smile. "Is that your idea of a proposal?"

"I'll give you a real one when we're both safely on the ground," Seth assured her. "Now, remember what I told you. Nice and steady."

Vanessa took in a sharp breath and let it out. "Okay. Here goes."

"You can do this," Seth reminded her, his voice reassuring as she approached the airstrip.

Out of the corner of her eye, she could see Tristan shift the helicopter to the north so they could have a better view of her approach. Then she heard Seth's voice again. "That's it. Keep your speed steady."

Vanessa tried to focus on his voice, on the constant flow of encouraging words. She knew that once she touched down, the hard part would be over. But what if she couldn't get through the hard part? Every previous failed attempt, every insecurity rushed through her as the ground approached.

She was too high on her approach. She knew she was too high. Still, she followed Seth's instructions, watching the ground blur in front of her. Then she felt the wheels touch down briefly, felt the plane bounce and lurch. And she pulled back on the stick to put the plane back in the air.

Her breath rushed out of her as the last little bit of runway disappeared out of her view.

"What happened?" Seth asked sharply.

"I couldn't do it." Vanessa's voice hitched, and she fought back the tears that threatened. She took one shaky breath and then another. "There wasn't enough runway."

"It's okay, Vanessa," Seth told her. "Circle around and we'll try it again."

Several minutes stretched out as Seth and Tristan guided her to try once more. No one spoke of her failed first attempt or what would happen if she came in too low.

"Okay, I can do this," Vanessa insisted, though she wasn't sure if she was talking to Seth or to herself.

As she approached once more, silence filled the air. She watched the ground approaching, feeling a little more confident that her position to the runway was greatly improved over her previous attempt. Her breathing was still ragged as she closed in on the runway, but she was determined to try this time. She had to if she wanted to see Seth again.

As she felt the panic bubbling up inside her once more, she heard Seth's soothing voice. "Come on, honey. You can do this."

The plane caught in the wind, tipping a bit to one side, and insecurity rushed through her again. Then she heard Seth's voice. This time, instead of assurances, she could hear impatience and challenge in his words. "Would it be easier if I dared you to land that plane?"

"That's not funny, Seth," Vanessa insisted, but the edge of irritation his words invoked helped push away the worst of the fear. "Okay. Let's try this again."

The wings straightened out, the plane dropped to within ten feet of the ground, and Vanessa drew in a sharp breath. The wheels bounced once, twice. And then she heard an alarm ringing over the radio.

37

The proximity alarm sounded in the Apache's cockpit, forcing Seth to tear his eyes from Vanessa's plane. He shifted his concentration to the instrument panel in front of him and immediately shouted, "Incoming!"

Tristan turned the helicopter abruptly as the missile came into view. He banked hard right a split second before the missile whizzed by and exploded on the ground below them.

"No!" The word erupted from Seth, and his eyes fixed on the flames spearing into the sky. He struggled to see if Vanessa's plane had been hit, but the smoke was too thick. Logically he knew that the missile might have missed the plane, but fear and shock paralyzed him as he assumed the worst.

Beside him, Tristan spoke in a clipped tone. "Come on, Seth. Work with me here. We're no good to her if we're dead."

Trying to fight the numb feeling that swamped him, Seth turned his attention back to the screen in front of him. He managed a deep breath and let it out in a rush. "New radar contact." He rattled off the location, a mere fifteen miles away. "I've got intermittent contact. It looks like the missing Z-10 is trying to stay under our radar."

Tristan gave a quick nod of agreement. "Preparing to intercept."

Seth glanced back at the smoke rising from the ground behind them before forcing himself to shift into combat mode.

* * *

Vanessa scrambled out of the plane and looked up. Her eyes burned from the smoke, but she could see the Z-10 overhead positioning itself against where she had last seen Seth's Apache. When the missile had hit the ground a short distance from the runway, her amazement that she had safely landed had been quickly overtaken by terror. Whoever was in that enemy helicopter was shooting at Seth, trying to steal away the future she had just begun to hope for.

She couldn't fathom that she had managed to get away from Zimmerman only to find Seth in immediate danger. She had to do something to help him, but what? Gunfire sounded above her as the two helicopters engaged. Vanessa stared into the sky, her mind racing, when she heard the voice coming over the airplane radio in Arabic. "Is the aircraft damaged? I repeat, can you take off?"

Vanessa ignored the voice as an idea began to form. She climbed back into the airplane and reached for the C4 that was attached to the detonator. With the bomb in her hands, she hurried to the side of the runway where a makeshift shed was located. She set the bomb down and studied the wiring.

If she could set some kind of timer, just maybe she could create a distraction to help Tristan and Seth. Drawing on all of her explosives training, she drew a deep breath as she bypassed the remote access. She then managed to set a timer. A moment later, she activated the detonator and then turned and sprinted away from the runway.

* * *

"This guy is good," Tristan conceded as he evaded another burst of gunfire. "Can you get a missile lock on him?"

"Negative. He keeps dropping off of our radar." Seth rested his finger on the trigger, waiting for the right moment. The smoke was clearing below them, but he didn't dare look down to see if Vanessa's plane had indeed landed safely. If he broke concentration, he and Tristan might not survive the next few seconds; however, if his worst fears were realized, he wasn't sure he wanted to.

Seth watched bullets spark from the enemy again. "Break left!"

Tristan responded, shifting up and left to avoid the incoming fire.

"Returning fire," Seth announced as he sent another spray of gunfire hurtling through the air. "I'm getting tired of this guy."

"What's the ETA on our backup?"

"Two more minutes."

"Might as well be an eternity," Tristan muttered.

An explosion rocked the ground beneath them. Seth and Tristan glanced briefly at one another as the Z-10 elevated to clear the explosion beneath them. A moment later, the radar lock beeped.

"Missile away!" Seth announced, seconds before the Z-10 exploded and broke into pieces.

Tristan backed away as the wreckage rained down to the ground. He then headed back to the airfield. Beyond a small structure that was fully engulfed in flames, the Cessna was parked on the runway.

"Take us down," Seth instructed, even though Tristan had already started to descend. The moment the helicopter settled onto the runway, Seth flung open the door and jumped to the ground. He hurried to the plane only to find the pilot unconscious. He didn't know what to think when Vanessa wasn't where he expected her to be. His heart raced as he looked around, seeing nothing but the fire in front of him.

He couldn't fathom that she had safely landed only to have fallen prey to a stray missile strike or whatever had caused this fire. She had to be okay. She just had to. The words repeated over in his mind, a kind of chant that turned into a pleading prayer.

Tristan stepped beside him and motioned to the fiery shed. "You don't think . . ."

Seth shook his head, but he wasn't sure what to think. He could smell wood burning and could see pieces of debris scattered all over the edge of the runway and onto the brown dirt that surrounded it. The smoke continued to assault his senses, burning his eyes and nose, but he couldn't turn away.

Then he saw it. A glimpse of movement.

Squinting, he took a tentative step forward. The smoke was so thick that he couldn't make out much of anything, but after a moment he saw the movement again, and this time he could see the vague form walking toward them. "Vanessa!"

He rushed into the smoke as she stumbled forward. Then she was in his arms. Seth scooped her off of her feet and moved away from the fire to where the air had cleared. He held her cradled in his arms, staring down at her, afraid to speak.

"You're okay," Vanessa managed, her cheeks streaked with soot and tears.

"Yeah, I'm okay." Seth nodded, his voice hoarse. He touched his lips to hers. "We're both going to be okay now."

38

The debriefings were over, the mission reports completed, and the word was in from the hospital about Kel. They were all hoping for good news, but they didn't get exactly what they wanted. The doctors had basically told them that Kel would be in recovery and physical therapy for the next several months. Only after he completed his treatment would the Navy decide whether he was fit to return to duty.

The whole squad was still struggling with this blow—and the fact that a replacement would be showing up any day to fill in for Kel. For now, Seth wasn't ready to worry about the new guy. He needed to put his own life in order. And that included tracking down Vanessa and spending some time with her. Alone.

He had already put in for a few days of leave so he could drive from Virginia Beach up to Northern Virginia to see Vanessa. She was temporarily working at CIA Headquarters in Langley until they decided where to send her next. His stomach clenched at the thought of the Agency reinserting her as Lina Ramir in Akil's organization. He knew it was a very real scenario, and a risky one, especially since she was the only person who had ever successfully infiltrated his organization.

Seth wasn't sure exactly how he was going to convince Vanessa to turn down an overseas assignment, but he prayed he could find the right words. He didn't know if he could stand to go another six years without her. He couldn't stand to go another six hours without her.

"Are you all set?" Brent asked from his seat beside Seth in the office they shared.

"Yeah." Seth nodded, scooping his cell phone off of his desk and slipping it into his pocket. "And you don't have to tell me to keep my phone turned on."

"Hey, guys." Amy stepped through the door, followed by Quinn and Tristan.

"What's up?" Brent asked.

"I just got the latest intel reports," Amy told him as everyone crowded into the office.

"And?" Brent asked.

"All of Ramir's training camps in the Caribbean have been shut down."

Quinn's dark eyebrows shot up. "Did Ramir shut them down, or did we do it for him?"

"Oh, we helped." Amy gave the team a cocky little grin.

"What about Ramir?" Seth asked, hoping that Vanessa would never have to go undercover again, at least not in Ramir's organization.

Amy's grin faded now. "He's still at his fortress in Nicaragua."

"I should have found a way to take him out when I had the chance." Seth shook his head, wondering what he could have done differently. He hated knowing that Vanessa might be the government's only weapon against Akil, and possibly the only way to prevent his next attack. "Who knows what he'll plan next."

Tristan spoke now. "Hey, at least you helped us figure out what he was planning this time before it was too late. We'll get him eventually."

"I hope so," Seth said.

"There is some good news out of all of this," Amy told them. "Even though Ramir is still out there, the reports indicate that he not only lost a lot of his manpower during our raids, but he's also hurting for money."

"Yeah, until Morenta decides to help him out again," Quinn commented irritably.

"I don't think that's going to happen anytime soon." The corner of Amy's mouth lifted once more. "Apparently the CIA identified and seized two of Morenta's offshore accounts. It's going to take a while before he'll be able to recover from the lost funds. Besides, Akil Ramir has shifted to the top of our most wanted list. The minute he leaves the fortress, he's likely to end up in prison right beside his brother."

Brent managed a little smile of his own. "Let's hope."

"I also heard from Kel's wife this morning," Amy added. "Apparently Kel is already up out of bed and has started physical therapy."

"Do we have any idea how long until he'll be back?"

Amy shook her head. "I thought maybe we could all go pay him a visit in the hospital this weekend and see how he's doing for ourselves."

"Sounds like a great idea." Brent nodded in agreement. Then he looked over at Seth and grinned. "After all, Seth is already heading up that way. I'm sure he won't mind if we tag along."

Seth immediately shook his head. He recognized the humor in Brent's voice, but he wasn't about to take any chances when it came to his plans for the weekend. "You can all go up and visit Kel. I'll make sure I stop by before I head back."

"Oh, come on, Seth," Brent pressed. "Don't you want to spend all of your leave with us?"

Seth chuckled and shook his head. "Not a chance." He stood up and grabbed his keys. Then he heard movement and turned toward the sound. And his jaw dropped open. Vanessa was standing in the doorway. "What are you doing here?"

"I'd think that would be obvious." Humor lit her eyes as she slowly smiled. "I came to see you."

"I mean, how did you get here—in my office?" Seth stepped out from behind his desk, now ignoring the other members of his squad who were watching in amusement. "This is a secure military base, and we're in a classified wing."

"Seth, I work for the CIA. Do you really think you boys have any secrets I don't know about?"

Now Brent stood and moved toward the door with a little smirk on his face. "I think we'll just leave you two alone for a few minutes."

As soon as Brent ushered the rest of the squad out of his office, despite some mumbled complaints by Quinn and Tristan, Vanessa reached out and closed the door. Then she looked back at Seth. "I know you were planning on coming and seeing me this weekend, but I finished early at headquarters, so I thought I would surprise you."

"You finished at headquarters? Does that mean you already have your new assignment?"

Vanessa nodded, and for the first time since she walked into the room, a touch of insecurity crept into her eyes.

"You aren't going back undercover as Lina Ramir, are you?" Seth demanded. He moved closer, grabbing both of her arms. "There's no way to be sure Akil will believe whatever story the Agency makes up about why you left, and no way to know whether he's still in contact with Morenta. If Morenta shows up, who knows which one of them will decide to kill you first."

"Seth, calm down," Vanessa interrupted. "I'm not going back under-cover. For now, the Agency is leaking the information that Lina Ramir is back in prison so that Akil won't keep looking for her."

"You're not going back undercover?" With his hands still gripping her arms, Seth leaned back and studied her face. "Then where are you going?"

"I wanted to talk to you about it, but it wasn't exactly a conversation I could have with you over the phone." Vanessa took a deep breath and slowly let it out. "I asked to be assigned to the Farm."

"As in the CIA's training facility here in Virginia?"

"It's actually a great opportunity." She managed a smile. "I thought I was going to be stuck at headquarters for the next year or two, but instead I get to be an instructor."

"You want to teach?"

"I do," she said, and Seth recognized the sincerity in her voice. "I know that my work undercover was useful, but it isn't the life I want. This new assignment will let me enjoy work again without all of the stress." She gave a nervous shrug. "But I do have to tell them by Wednesday if I want housing on the compound or not." She looked up at him sheepishly. "I wasn't sure what to tell them."

All Seth could do was stare. "Let me get this straight." He took a little step back so he could see her face more clearly. "You weren't sure what to tell them because you wanted to know what I think?"

"Well, yeah." Vanessa took a deep breath and straightened her shoul-ders. "I know when you talked about marrying me you weren't sure if I was going to live this long, but you haven't said anything else about it . . ."

"And you're wondering if I was serious," Seth finished for her, fighting back a grin. He released her and crossed the room to where his overnight bag was sitting by his desk. He unzipped it, fished around inside for a minute, and then pulled out a little black box. Standing up, he stepped closer once more and flipped open the lid. "Does this answer your question?"

She looked down at the simple diamond ring, the same one he had offered her so many years ago. "You kept my ring."

"Yeah, I kept it. I guess I couldn't bring myself to return it." Seth took the ring out of the box and held it up. "Please tell me you want it this time."

Vanessa managed a watery smile. "I always wanted it."

Seth took her hand and slid the ring into place. Then he pulled her hand up to his lips. "Perfect."

"Yes, it is," Vanessa said, her eyes meeting his.

He grinned now, and his eyes sparked with mischief. "So how much time do we have to give your parents to get plane tickets to come out here for the wedding?"

"I don't know . . ."

Before she could answer, Seth said, "Six weeks."

"What?"

"I think I've already waited for you long enough."

She laughed, pure joy radiating from her face. "I guess you could say that." She put her hands around his neck and pulled him down for a kiss. "I love you."

"I love you too, but there's one more thing I have to ask."

"What?"

Seth's eyes lit with humor. "Does your cousin Leonard have to come to the wedding?"

ABOUT THE AUTHOR

Originally from Arizona, Traci Hunter Abramson has spent the past two decades living in Virginia. After graduating from Brigham Young University, she worked for the Central Intelligence Agency for six years before choosing to stay at home with her children and indulge in her love of writing.

Traci also coaches the North Stafford High School swim team. She currently resides in Stafford, Virginia, with her husband, Jonathan, and their four children.